Dear Reader,

Things in Arkansas move a little slower than in the rest of the United States. Maybe it's because the beauty of the Ozarks invades the people who live here. We actually take time to get to know our neighbors. It's a perfect place to be a country vet. That's why I've been so happy here. At least, I was until Ali Cameron brought her workaholic self into my territory. The woman couldn't seem to grasp the concept of relaxation!

But, of course, I did what I could to make her see the error of her ways, even though I had no intention of falling for her. I'd already been through the wringer once where love was concerned, but she made me feel desire like never before! I knew her life was in New York and she had no plans to give it up, but somehow Ali discovered two loves here: Arkansas...and me. And though I never thought I'd say it, now my life is even better— all because she's in it.

All my best,

Adam Forrest

MARY LYNN BAXTER
Another Kind of Love

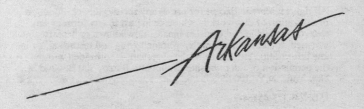

Published by Silhouette Books New York

America's Publisher of Contemporary Romance

SILHOUETTE BOOKS
300 East 42nd St., New York, N.Y. 10017

ANOTHER KIND OF LOVE

ISBN: 0-373-45154-7

Published Silhouette Books 1983, 1993

Printed in the U.S.A.

Chapter 1

Ali Cameron stood looking out over the muggy Manhattan skyline and angrily swiped at the tears that flooded her eyes. She *had* to get control of herself. But how? She had fought this silent battle at least a thousand times since the twofold tragedy struck her life three months before. No amount of self-administered psychology seemed to work.

As she gave way to the tears that now drenched her face, she realized her life suddenly had no meaning. *She* had nothing—not even her health. This sad fact tore anew at her insides with the same reaction as having her fingernails removed one by one without benefit of anesthetic. The pain was the same—brutal and piercing.

The sharp buzz of the desk's intercom jolted her out of her self-indulgent thoughts. She sniffed and grabbed a tissue from the corner of the desk before punching the button.

"Yes, Sara." Her voice came out much more sharply and clipped than she intended, but she had given firm instructions to her secretary that she was not to be disturbed unless it was an absolute emergency.

"I'm—I'm sorry, Miss Cameron, but your mother is on the line, insisting that she talk to you."

Ali chewed her lip in vexation. "Sara, please, tell her I'm not available. Tell her anything, I don't care. I—I can't, won't talk to her now."

Ali lowered her trembling body onto the comfortable desk chair and dropped her head into the palms of her hands. She could not go on like this. This continued agitation added to the seriousness of the bleeding ulcer that dominated her stomach and seemed to control her life— what she ate, how she slept, and the majority of her activities.

It was time she came to terms with her father's betrayal and the tragedy of his untimely death. She had no choice except to claw her way up from the depths of despair back to respectability and success. So what if her father had used her ruthlessly, dissecting her heart in the process? She could handle that. But, dear God, how it hurt. She had loved him dearly and still found it impossible to believe that without her knowledge he had sold the formula she had worked long and hard on to make Cameron Cosmetics number one in the cosmetics industry. No, at the moment it was all too much to cope with, because she had loved and trusted him above all else.

She gave herself a mental shake and again brushed the tears from her eyes. A tired sigh slipped through her lips and she willed her weary body to get up and move toward the coffee bar at the far end of her office. Pushing at the soft wispy fragments of hair that clung to her dampened cheeks, Ali lifted a small tea bag out of the box and dropped it into a cup. Unconsciously she reached for the pot of hot water that stayed ready for such emergencies as this and filled the cup to capacity. She could see her doctor's disapproving frown as she rolled the tea bag around in the cup and watched as it stained the water a reddish brown. But she needed this one cup of tea, she consoled herself.

With the cup of hot liquid in her hand, Ali made her way back to the long window at the north end of her plush office. She stared down at the bustling traffic of the inner city without seeing it. Not even the squeal of taxi brakes and the honking of horns nor the loud rumble of the buses that reigned over the streets penetrated her numbed senses.

Suddenly she knew what she had to do. She would take Dr. Todd's advice and get away from Cameron Cosmetics, her mother's domination, and the gut-wrenching responsibility of trying to save a drowning business from total collapse and the after-effects of her father's betrayal.

Dr. Todd's warning still rattled around clearly in her brain. "Ali Cameron," he said, "you *must* heed my advice and accept your friend's invitation to spend a few months on her dude ranch in Arkansas. It's your only alternative."

"But, Doctor," she had wailed, "how can I possibly go away and leave things in such a mess? You know the other stockholders are threatening to join forces and sell the company if I don't come up with an idea for a new project. And if that isn't enough, Mother is being her usual bitchy self. There's no way I can leave now or anytime in the near future."

"I beg to differ with you, my dear. It's no longer your decision. I'm ordering you to go, not only as your doctor but as your friend. Your mental health is out of my jurisdiction, but your physical health is sure as hell not! It's imperative that you do as I say unless you want to go un-

der the surgeon's knife and lose part of your stomach."
After letting that statement soak in, he added, "I know a
good doctor in Hot Springs who'll take good care of you."

A fleeting smile crept across Ali's lips as she remembered how she'd hung her head and acquiesced softly,
"Yes, Doctor."

That confrontation had taken place two weeks ago, and
she still hadn't made up her mind until this very minute to
take her doctor's advice and go to Arkansas. Her Uncle
Charles could manage the company's affairs for a few
months, until she was able to put the torn fragments of her
life back together.

In her thirty years she had never been this strung out
over anything, not even when her fiancé, Wes, was killed
in Vietnam. But she was strong-willed and determined. She
would cope. If only it weren't for the disillusionment and
the smothering loneliness that dogged her footsteps unmercifully, it would be so much easier, she thought. There
was no one she could turn to who could help her share this
tremendous burden.

A shudder ran down Ali's spine as her head lobbed like
a rag doll's against the glass. Maybe in Arkansas, helped
by her old and dear friend and the clear mountain air, she
would be able to heal her body along with her soul.

Even against the insurmountable odds her going would
incur, it was definitely worth a try. It had to work. It just
had to.

Adam Forrest glanced hastily down at the gold watch on
his wrist and rammed his half-ton pickup truck into park.
"Damn," he muttered under his breath. He was late.
Thirty minutes late to be exact, he thought with grim ill-
humor.

Cindy and Barry, but particularly Cindy, would be extremely unhappy when she learned he had kept their guest from the Big Apple waiting. But it was one of those things he couldn't help, he quickly assured himself. Old man Appleby's long-winded tale of his latest bout with arthritis lasted much longer than he had anticipated. And he hadn't the heart to cut him off in midstream. Maybe by taking the time to listen to the senile old man, he just might have earned a star in his crown, he mused, a humorless grin suddenly relaxing his tense mouth.

Uncoiling his tall frame from behind the wheel, Adam slammed the door behind him and made his way toward the small waiting room of the Fayetteville airport. His gait was measured to the beat of long, hurried strides. This chore was one he could have done without, he told himself as he bounded up the steps, taking them two at a time. But he had volunteered, so he had no one to blame but himself. He couldn't understand, though, why someone from the city of high finance would want to come slumming to the Arkansas hill country for rest and relaxation.

He was still shaking his head in bewilderment when he strode into the lounge area. Removing his Stetson, his eyes searched the room for a woman fitting Ali's description: tall, about five feet seven, brown hair with gold highlights. "You can't miss her," Cindy'd told him with a wink and an impish grin covering her face, "she's beautiful."

Now as his eyes continued to canvass the room, Adam saw no one fitting that description. In fact there were only two people in the room and they were both male. Where was she? Another expletive exploded through his lips as he stomped up to the ticket counter. Realizing he couldn't take his frustrations out on the young lady peddling the tickets, he relaxed his features and smiled openly and politely.

His white even teeth were a perfect backdrop for his dark tanned skin as he hunched his large frame across the counter and asked, "Pardon me, ma'am, by any chance did you notice a lady with uh—uh brownish-blond hair?" He paused and slid his hands down the side of his faded Levi's that molded his lean thighs to perfection. Damn! he thought. If he'd gone out of his way for nothing...

The young ticket agent eyed Adam closely for a moment, a knowing grin plastered across her lips, showing off her red gums like neon signs. She raised her hand and pointed over Adam's left shoulder, still grinning. "You mean that lady behind you, Mister?"

Adam swung around abruptly and stared into the most beautiful dark eyes he had ever seen. For one of the few times in his life, Adam was speechless. All he could do was stare at the woman who seemed to glide effortlessly toward him.

She was lovely. Her brown hair, more gold than brown, he quickly assessed, fell in luscious folds to her shoulders. Her wide-set brown eyes were perfectly placed, emphasizing the classic planes of her face. Instantly his gut instinct told him this woman was trouble spelled with capital letters. Was it because she reminded him of his ex-wife, Mary—big city born and bred stamped all over her? Or was it the sad, vulnerable look in her eyes that made her both desirable and dangerous? Adam couldn't tear his eyes away as he continued to appraise this beautiful creature from head to toe. She was dressed in what he knew to be a designer suit, tailored to fit her long, leggy look. The beige color of the two-piece outfit accentuated her slender waist and her shapely calves.

For the first time in years Adam felt his blood run hot at the sight of a woman. It raced at a blistering speed throughout his body, leaving him feeling contrite and suddenly unsure of himself. *Forrest, don't be an ass! Get hold of yourself.*

The uncertain tremor in her voice brought him back to reality. "Are—are you from the Peaceful Valley Dude Ranch?" she asked, her expression waiting, watchful. Then a smile tentatively broke through her burgundy-colored lips, never quite reaching her sad eyes.

Suddenly Adam had the urge to put his arms around this woman and reassure her that everything would be all right, that she wouldn't ever have to worry about anything again. Heaven help him! he thought. He *had* most assuredly lost his mind! The last thing he needed was to get involved with a woman, especially a woman who brought to mind in living, breathing color the horror of his past. Had experience taught him nothing?

Finally he forced himself to answer, pushing the words through tight, stiff lips. "Yes, I am." There was another lengthy pause. "I'm sorry to have kept you waiting, but I was unavoidably detained," he added by way of a buffer to counteract his abruptness. It wasn't normally in his nature to behave so churlishly, but this doe-eyed young woman had him running scared.

Ignoring his borderline rudeness, Ali said, "That's all right. I rather enjoyed the rest—though for a while I thought I might have been stood up." She smiled pleasantly, softening the accusation while hoping to elicit a response from this man other than his present ill-humor.

This was not the welcome she had envisioned. As a result uneasiness rumbled beneath the surface, threatening to overpower her outward calm. Why hadn't Cindy met her? Or if she couldn't, why not Barry? Anyone would have been better, she thought, than this abrupt stranger who made it quite clear he wished he had never laid eyes on her.

"Well, better late than never, I always say." His brief smile was faintly mocking. "I'm ready when you are."

More determined than ever not to let this hired hand, for surely that's what he was, crush her spirits, Ali extended her free hand.

"Before we go any further, don't you think we ought to introduce ourselves? I'm Ali Cameron."

Another mocking smile crossed his lips. "How do you do, Miss Cameron. I'm Adam Forrest."

Color stung her cheeks. His continued mockery was like a slap in the face. She longed to reach up and knock that false smile off his lips. She couldn't understand Barry hiring someone with a personality and manners as prickly as a porcupine. He *must* be good at his work, she thought as her hand made contact with his.

But the moment his flesh touched hers, an electric awareness replaced her hostility. A tingling sensation suddenly ran up her arm and then flooded throughout her body, leaving her weak and her face a darker hue in its wake. Quickly she withdrew her fingers from the callused folds of his and made the pretense of adjusting her shoulder bag.

Anything, she told herself, to give her time to get control of her emotions and eliminate the thick tension that bounced between them. Dear God, what had come over her? She drew a lung full of fresh air. She must indeed be in worse shape than she thought if she could react to a hired hand this way. She hated to admit it but the tingling sensation refused to subside even though they were no longer touching.

Adam's eyes narrowed. "Shall we go," he said simply, not bothering to hide his awareness of just how quickly she had withdrawn her hand. At least now, he thought, he wasn't the only one who was uncomfortable. But the old saying, misery loves company, offered him little comfort as he grabbed her luggage and pointed her in the direction of the parking lot.

Ali forced her expression to remain unchanged as she walked beside Adam toward a metallic-blue pickup truck that sat glistening proudly in the bright sunlight. Before she reached in her purse for her sunglasses to combat the harsh glare, she swung her gaze in his direction and saw another mocking grin. Damn him! she thought. For some unknown reason, he wanted to make her feel uncomfortable and defensive. Or was she the paranoid one, thinking everyone was still out to get her? It didn't matter, she told herself. She would take in stride whatever came her way. If riding in a truck with this Arkansas hillbilly was a test, then so be it. She would enjoy it to the hilt. Not one word of complaining would he hear out of her.

She had promised Dr. Todd she would use this trip as healing therapy. She was determined to look on the bright side of everything and everyone during the forthcoming months. Thoughts of New York, her family, and the company were all taboo. This was an absolute must in order for her to survive. And no frustrated cowboy was going to interfere and keep her from reaching that goal. The sooner she recuperated, the sooner she could return to New York and begin to rebuild the business along with her life.

Ali watched now as Adam Forrest slung her two pieces of lightweight luggage into the back of the pickup. She had decided at the last minute to travel light, packing mostly sun dresses, shorts, and jeans. Almost as an afterthought she had thrown in two casual dinner dresses. If she needed more clothes there were always the local shops, she had consoled herself. Now as she watched her possessions land with a thud in the bed of the truck, she was glad she hadn't packed anything that couldn't hold up to such gruelling treatment.

Adam then opened the door on the passenger's side and indicated that Ali should get in. After easing his large frame behind the wheel, taking care that his thigh did not brush hers, Adam placed the long tapered fingers of his left hand around the steering gear and with his right hand quickly turned the ignition key. Resting his arm on the back of the seat, he turned toward her. As if by accident their eyes met.

For a timeless moment Ali was hopelessly locked in the power of his blue-gray eyes. Her heart felt a sudden jolt as she sat motionless.

She wished he would stop looking at her like that. It was almost as if he could actually read the secrets of her soul and see the scars embedded in her heart. Ali dug her teeth into her lower lip to keep from trembling and tried to look away. But the pull of his eyes wouldn't let her. For some unaccountable reason she felt drawn to this rude, arrogant man. The breathless sensation in and around her chest had never happened to her before, at least not with such deep intensity.

What was there about him that made her feel disoriented, tense, off balance? He wasn't handsome, she thought critically, but he was attractive. His unruly crop of dark brown hair topped a wide forehead and thick eyebrows that set off the most unusual pair of slate-colored eyes she had ever seen. His well-defined lips were sensuous with lines of experience around them. She judged his age to be between thirty-five and forty. A jutting chin told her that here was a man who made the rules and expected others to follow them. His lean but wiry body added to the total package, making him dangerously disturbing.

Suddenly he jerked his head around, shattering the spell. He turned his attention solely to maneuvering the truck out of the airport parking lot. Before he made his complete about-face though, Ali had seen the abrupt darkening of his eyes, bringing to mind the brewing of a storm. Intuition told her he deeply resented anybody's intrusion into his life.

Resolving not to let this man intimidate her or get the better of her, she snapped her head back and drew herself upright. But some unknown force prodded her to tap his source of resentment. Why? She shrugged inwardly— maybe it was because he was different....

Keeping her voice cool but civil, she asked, "Have you worked for Cindy and Barry long?"

Adam jerked his eyes off the road and squinted them at her. "No, as a matter of fact, I haven't," he drawled lazily.

Was it her imagination or had she seen the corners of his beautifully sculpted lips twitch with the beginning of a smile?

Silence.

If at first you don't succeed, try again. Ali refused to let his mocking bluntness ward her off. "Do you like working on the ranch?"

Adam's concentration was centered on his driving. "Yes," he answered, this time with a crispness lacing his voice seemingly to discourage further conversation between them.

Ali's temper was registering on low simmer. "Mr. Forrest, are you always this rude or is it just something about *me* that sets your teeth on edge?"

Again Adam's eyes flew around to Ali's face. Immediately Ali took note of the vein that began to jump in his neck along with the grimness that scarred his mouth. Well, she had really done it, she told herself. He was absolutely livid. She was positive he would like nothing better than to stop the truck, dump her on the side of the road and forget she ever existed.

Adam sucked in his breath, searching for the words to put this brittle career woman in her place. How had he ever thought her vulnerable? There was no place for her here. She wasn't wanted or needed. *Whoa, Forrest. You're getting bent out of shape over nothing. After all, she's no concern of yours. Once you deliver her to the ranch, your responsibility ends.*

He couldn't understand what had gotten into him anyway. He had already reached the conclusion that it wasn't because she rekindled memories of Mary. It was something else—something much more potent. Mary had never stirred his senses to such an extent. Damn! Why did she have to be so easy on the eye? Beautiful hair that looked as thick and rich as honey, a long, graceful neck, and, God, what breasts. Their jutting roundness taunted him every time she moved her body. He'd even be willing to wager she wasn't wearing a bra.

A deep groan came from within him. It was uncanny, but this strange woman, sitting beside him as still and straight as an arrow and strung just as tightly as a bow, brought to mind all his long-buried frustrations he had been positive would never be unearthed again.

"Well?" Her soft but firm voice pricked his thoughts.

Adam sighed deeply. He had to hand it to her; she certainly had spunk. But he had no intention of satisfying her curiosity.

"Well, what?" He could be just as obtuse as she.

"Forget it," Ali countered bluntly, suddenly tiring of playing this juvenile game. She no longer cared what he thought of her. Nor did she care why he chose to be so overbearing and rude. For her own sake as well as his, she hoped she would be able to keep a wide berth between them once they reached the ranch. Nevertheless, it was hard for her to believe that Barry would have an employee who didn't seem to know how to behave politely. She was under the impression that hired hands were to be seen and not heard. Heavens! She sounded like a first-class snob; but *he* had earned those unkind thoughts and more, she told herself with renewed defiance. After all wasn't he trying his best to make her feel unwanted and unwelcome?

In spite of her determination to retreat behind a veil of self-pity, Ali couldn't seem to turn away from the look in those slate-colored eyes. It was deep and challenging.

"Oh, come now, Miss Cameron, surely you're not going to bow out now? Not when things are just becoming interesting," he goaded, making an attempt to curb his bold reaction to her behind another mocking smile.

Nonetheless, it was open warfare. He was challenging her. Ali knew it, and he knew that she knew it. She sensed the danger in pitting herself against this man, who was both exciting and alarming. Sparring with him would accomplish nothing. Didn't she have enough problems without adding another to her list? Instead, why not put him in his place and be done with it?

Forcing an unconcerned coolness into her voice, she said pointedly, "From now on, Mr. Forrest, you can keep your comments to yourself. The first thing I intend to do when we get to the ranch is report your high-handed behavior to your employer. I'm sure Barry, Mr. Medford to you, will no doubt be upset when he learns how you have conducted yourself in my presence."

Instead of the suitable rejoinder she had expected, Adam Forrest threw back his head and filled the close confines of the truck with a howl of laughter.

Ali stared at him aghast. She hadn't fooled herself into thinking her threat would draw an apology, but she certainly wasn't prepared for his laughter, which, if possible, made him more attractive. It was obvious from his reaction he had nothing to fear from Barry concerning his conduct. She shrugged. So much for her threatened promise, she thought grimly.

Taking advantage of the lengthening silence, Ali leaned her head back against the seat and closed her eyes. She had worked with men all her life—all types of men from all walks of life, but she couldn't remember ever letting one needle her so quickly or so thoroughly. What she needed now more than anything was a friend, not another enemy, but apparently she had made him the latter without knowing why or trying.

Suddenly she felt exhaustion seep through her bones, leaving her feeling drained and more lonely than ever. Maybe if she closed her eyes he would disappear....

"Miss Cameron, are you awake?"

Ali's befuddled senses picked up the well-modulated voice, yet she couldn't open her eyes. It seemed as if they were glued to her cheeks.

"Miss Cameron, we're almost at the ranch."

This time the voice was stronger, deeper. Her eyes fluttered open, and for a moment she groped for her bearings. Then she remembered; she was in Arkansas in the company of a stranger in a strange land. Blinking her eyes, she turned her gaze toward the window. She saw nothing familiar to her, nothing she could identify with. Homesick. Could she possibly be homesick? Her eyelids fell shut again while another deluge of self-pity washed over her.

"What's the matter, Miss Cameron? Wishing you were back in the city?" His voice was softly taunting.

Self-indulgence forgotten, Ali twisted around and glared at him. Her glance faltered against the steely look pouring from under the dark sweep of his lashes. What had she done to warrant such hostility from this stranger? she wondered. And *how* could she have thought him to be the least bit attractive? A frown marred her smooth brow as she ventured another look in his direction from under veiled lashes.

But there was no denying it. He was attractive. Again her eyes centered on his long, slender fingers wrapped confidently around the steering wheel. Why did they remind her of a surgeon's hands? Was it because they looked so strong and capable? Yet sensitive? For a moment she wondered what they would feel like caressing a woman's body? But not just any woman's body. Her body. *Stop it!* Even as she ridiculed herself, she continued her perusal of him. Judging from the strength of his thighs crowding his jeans, he had to make his living from working outdoors.

Suddenly as if aware of her unauthorized scrutiny, he moved, lifting a hand from the wheel to massage the muscles at the back of his neck. This action separated the hem of his T-shirt from the low waistband of his jeans, exposing a thin line of bronzed, muscled flesh. The sight of his skin had a sizzling effect on her. It opened her already heightened senses to everything else about him—the tangy scent of his cologne, the broadness of his chest and shoulders, and last but not least, it made her painfully aware of his nearness.

Realizing the troubled waters her thoughts were leading her into, Ali forced her attention away from him. But not before Adam had seen the confused shadow that drifted across her face, making her look forlorn and lost. For several seconds he fought a silent battle within himself. In the end his common sense won. He could not let himself become involved with this woman. Distance was the best and most effective weapon to counteract this looming threat. Anyway, he had Molly. She was more than capable of satisfying his needs. Wasn't she?

As the truck chewed up the remaining miles, Ali forced herself to notice her surroundings. She had read about the scenic beauty of the Ozark Mountains and now she was experiencing their beauty firsthand. It was like nothing she had ever seen. Tall hardwood trees covered the mountainside. The quiet serenity of their magnificence helped to soothe her uneasy mind and renewed her effort to enjoy her stay amidst this wooded tranquillity.

Excitement clutched at her insides as Adam swung the truck around a narrow curve only to find the picturesque beauty of the Peaceful Valley Dude Ranch sprawled out in front of her. It lay nestled at the foot of a huge mountain which dwarfed it, making the ranch appear much smaller than it actually was.

Forgetting her animosity toward her companion, Ali whirled around and flashed him a beautiful smile, adding a glow to her fragile features. "I'm so excited I can hardly stand it," she exclaimed. Her lissome body hovered on the edge of the padded seat awaiting their arrival with a girlish anticipation.

Adam found himself responding to her ardent enthusiasm. He couldn't take his eyes off the profile of her heart-shaped face as she sat deeply engrossed in the unfolding scene.

A smile gently tipped the corners of his mouth, relaxing the lines that had etched much deeper since taking on his passenger. "It's a wonderful place to live, all right," he acknowledged. "I can't think of another place on earth I'd rather be than here, breathing in the clean mountain air."

Ali spun back around to face him, shocked that something civil, if not amiable, had come out of his mouth. But when their eyes locked for a split second, she saw a shutter fall over his eyes. The smile disappeared.

Vowing not to let his attitude further taint her arrival, Ali turned her attention away from him.

Adam carefully steered the truck around another treacherous curve before he nosed the vehicle off to the right onto a narrow blacktopped road. The main part of the ranch was no longer in Ali's direct vision, but this was only temporary. Any minute now the sprawling ranch with all its lodges, barns, and stables would again come into view in all its splendor.

Over two years had passed since she had seen her college friend and roommate Cindy Medford, then Cindy Thomas. They had shared wonderful times together at a small, elite college in northern New England. Many a night found them sitting up way past midnight, gossiping instead of studying. They had exchanged their dreams for the future, each wanting and anticipating wonderful things. Cindy had wanted nothing more than to marry and have children, while she, Ali, had wanted to combine a career with a home and family. However, part of Ali's plans never materialized. Following the death of her fiancé, she had given up the idea of marriage and instead made the fascinating world of cosmetics her life.

It seemed as though much of Cindy's cherished dreams had come true. After graduating from college and following her parents to Arkansas, she had met and married the type of man about which she had so often fantasized. But Ali also knew that Cindy's life since college had not been all a fairy tale. She had lost her parents in a tragic accident, a brutal car-train collision. Now with Cindy's apparently successful marriage to Barry Medford and the purchase of the dude ranch a year ago, Ali hoped all was well with her.

Ali wished she might have been as lucky both with love and her career. The way she left things back in New York, she had a long way to go before the pieces of her life were in their proper place again.

The truck came to an abrupt halt, jarring her out of her deep introspection. Ali had barely placed her hand on the door handle, having definitely decided not to wait for *him* to come around and open the door for her, when she was greeted by an excited voice.

"Hi! It's about time you got here, Ali Cameron."

Ali literally stumbled from the cab of the truck straight into the arms of her friend. Cindy was laughing, crying, and talking all at the same time.

"Oh, Ali, it's so good to see you." Cindy's voice was just a decibel below an excited roar as she clutched Ali to her in a crushing bear hug.

Suddenly, Ali froze. "Cindy, *why* didn't you tell me?" she cried.

Chapter 2

Ali pushed her friend to arm's length and stared with shock at her protruding stomach.

Cindy's pale face turned beet-red. "I—I wanted to surprise you, that's why," she stammered nervously.

Ali was flabbergasted. "But—but Cindy, how could you have kept something so wonderful and exciting from me?" She shook her head as if to clear it. "How far along are you, for Heaven's sake?"

"About five months," Cindy replied. "But we'll talk more about that later. Right now, just tell me you're happy that I'm finally pregnant."

Ali grinned. "That goes without saying."

"I'm so glad to see you," Cindy laughed, grabbing Ali again and hugging her close.

Standing behind Cindy was her husband, Barry, a wide grin splayed across his angular face. Although Ali had never seen or met him, Cindy had sent her scads of pictures of them together over the years. She felt as though she knew him. He seemed perfect for Cindy. He was short, only a few inches taller than Cindy, but extremely muscular. His coarse leathery skin set off a mop of sandy hair, drawing attention to his deep-set eyes as he threw his wife an amused glance.

"Cindy, ease off a bit; let the girl get her breath," Barry said, his smile erupting into laughter.

Ali joined in the laughter as she disentangled herself from Cindy's strong arms. "Whew!" she exclaimed. "For a pregnant lady, you've got some grip, my friend! There must be a magic ingredient in your prenatal vitamins. But are you feeling okay?" Ali added, her eyes roving up and down Cindy's petite figure before coming to rest on her rounded upturned face.

The change in Cindy was marked. Her face had a pinched, unhealthy cast to it, Ali thought. But the same cap of bright red hair still clung to her head in soft, natural curls. Her pert nose remained splattered with numerous freckles—"angel kisses" was Cindy's pet name for them—and her large brown eyes were as expressive as ever, although now sunk far back into her head with none of their usual twinkling brilliance. Ali felt a twinge of uneasiness. Was it the baby? Or was it something else? There was a definite droop to Cindy's shoulders. And those nagging shadows Cindy sported underneath her eyes were a dead giveaway that all was not well. On the other hand, Cindy seemed happy, happy about the baby and happy with Barry. Ali sighed. Maybe she was imagining that things were worse than they actually were. She hoped that was the case.

"Ali, this is my better half, Barry."

Forced to pull her scattered thoughts together, Ali turned with a smile and held out her hand. "Hello, Barry," she said. "It's a pleasure to meet you at last and—congratulations."

An answering smile covered Barry's face as he leaned over and place a resounding kiss on Ali's cheek, followed by a growling chuckle that rumbled deep from within his chest. "I hope you'll pardon my familiarity, but I don't consider you a stranger." He paused and winked at his wife. "It's been 'Ali this' and 'Ali that' around this household for as long as I can remember."

"Oh, you big prevaricator," Cindy chimed in with a playful punch to her husband's midsection.

Barry raised his eyebrows in mock chastisement. "Take my word for it, it's true." He laughed. "Anyway, Ali Cameron," he added on a serious note, "we welcome you to our humble abode. Words can't express how glad we are to have you."

Ali felt tears stir behind her eyes. She forced her lips together to keep them from trembling. Their kindness acted as a salve to her wounded spirits. Turning away to blink back the tears, she opened her mouth and sucked in the fresh, clean mountain air. *I could get high on this stuff,* she thought as the blood tingled through her veins at a rapid rate. For once her problems didn't loom over her with smothering intensity. Yes, coming to Arkansas would indeed be a panacea for her shattered city nerves. A smile appeared and gentled her lips.

Then out of the corner of her eye, she saw Adam Forrest. His gaze swept over her with deliberate thoroughness. Her smile froze as her heart simultaneously flip-flopped against her rib cage. She willed herself to turn away. But she could not move. Her pupils remained pinned on their target. A lean hip, she noticed, was hooked on the front end of his pickup. His arms were folded in a lazy, relaxed manner across his broad chest. The glaring sunlight skipped over his dark head calling pertinent attention to the smattering of gray hairs nestled there.

Damn! He was a gorgeous hunk. But definitely not for you, Ali Cameron. The last thing you need is to get mixed up with an embittered ranch hand. You need someone who can make you laugh—surround you with sunshine.

As if he had read her thoughts, Adam uncoiled his frame from his position on the truck and with deliberate ease sauntered toward the three of them.

Coming to stand directly in front of Cindy, he dipped his head and peered into her face. He smiled—a beautiful heart-stopping smile. It lit his face from the top of his brow down to the prominent dimple in his chin.

Ali stood and watched in stunned amazement. She blinked, positive her eyes were playing tricks on her. This smiling creature in front of her simply could not be the same grim-faced man who had met her at the airport— who had mocked her relentlessly. From sheer willpower, Ali forced her gaping jaw to close. However, her limbs refused to budge.

"I guess I'd better be on my way," Adam was saying to Cindy and Barry, his voice a deep musical baritone. "I'll see y'all later." He leaned over and planted a swift kiss on Cindy's cheek.

This action jolted Ali from her stupor. She shook her head, seeing now, clearer than ever, she would have a hard time convincing her friends their ranch hand had done anything wrong! Talk about being able to turn on the charm! This man was a master at it. He was clearly a Dr. Jekyll-Mr. Hyde personality if ever there was one.

"Thanks, Adam," Barry said warmly as he pumped Adam's hand up and down, following this by a slap on the back.

Adam waved his hand. "Think nothing of it. Glad to help."

Without so much as a glance in Ali's direction, he swung on his heel and literally bolted to his truck. With a casual nod of his head he spun off in a cloud of dust with no backward glance.

Barry's voice drew Ali's gaze away from the retreating vehicle. "Shall we go in?"

Ali nodded vigorously, hoping to completely clear her addled brain. "Sounds like a winner to me," she responded, though her smile was weak and shaky.

Suddenly she felt tired, washed out. This had been a long, exhausting day and she was ready to sit down, prop her feet up, and visit with Cindy. Her friend had a lot of questions to answer for her. And she had equally as much to share with Cindy. A glass of tea would taste good to her dry mouth about now, she thought ruefully, but unfortunately it was off limits. Ulcers! What a nuisance!

A deep, frustrated sigh shook Ali's frame as she preceded Cindy and Barry into a large air-conditioned room. The cold air that slapped her in the face was welcome. It helped to revive her. This sudden attack of melancholy couldn't have been brought on by Adam Forrest's dismissal of her without even a nod in her direction, could it? To satisfy her own personal curiosity, however, she did intend to ask Cindy about this mysterious hired hand who seemed more like a friend to them than an employee.

"Well, what do you think of our humble abode?" Cindy quipped, mimicking her husband's terminology. "What you see is what there is." Her eyes were now clear and shining, all traces of the lingering shadows gone.

"Oh, Cindy, honey, it's adorable!"

And it was. A sense of peace settled over Ali as her eyes scanned the room, paying attention to every detail. It was all so different from her mother's pretentious home in Manhattan. So wonderfully different.

Her eyes caught a fleeting glimpse of a tiny kitchen graced by a brightly wallpapered breakfast nook and, beyond, two bedrooms before coming back to the family area. Although not a large room, it was nevertheless decorated in replica of Cindy's vivacious personality. A floral-printed couch dominated one side of the room. Two high-back chairs of green wicker with matching floral cushions were positioned on either side of the couch. Plants, pictures, an old-time Franklin stove, and a stereo system brought the remainder of the room to life.

"Are all the guest lodges this roomy and nice?" Ali asked as Barry unceremoniously dumped her luggage on the gold shag carpet in the bedroom separated from the family room by a short hall.

"Well, not quite," Cindy explained. "But don't get me wrong," she added, "the guest lodges are certainly no slouches. We've improved them a lot since we took over a year ago. There's still a lot we want to do, but—" She paused and lifted her slender shoulders in a shrug, "we've run into problems," she finished lamely.

Ali studied her friend closely for a moment. Cindy's eyes suddenly reflected that same dullness she had noticed when she first arrived, and her features were grim. Could her worry stem from financial problems? Ali wondered. Or something else? The baby? Ali was convinced Cindy was indeed hurting underneath her happy-go-lucky facade. She hoped that when she and Cindy talked, she would find out the answer without having to pry. Ali vowed not to add any additional strain to their lives, financial or otherwise.

"If you don't mind, honey," Barry laughed, sliding an arm around his wife and giving her a squeeze, "I'll just disappear and let you two jabber to your hearts' content."

Cutting a sly glance up at Barry, Cindy answered demurely, "Oh, come on, hon, don't run off. You know you're just dying to hear everything we have to say."

Barry rolled his eyes upward, groaning in mock despair. "No way!" he exclaimed, shaking his head. "I'm not ready for my ears to fall off yet." He grinned. "Two years is a hellava lot of territory to cover." Those last words were flung over his shoulder as he made a beeline for the door, slamming it behind him.

"Oh, Cindy," Ali cried, stepping across the hall into the bedroom and easing her tired body onto the side of the bed, "you're so lucky. He's absolutely perfect."

"Huh, there's nothing perfect about him," Cindy sniffed. But her eyes were glowing with pleasure at Ali's compliment. "You're right though, he is perfect," she added later with a wicked gin.

Ali, in a totally spontaneous gesture, stood up and threw her arms around Cindy and hugged her close for a moment. "Staying here with you is going to be my cure-all," Ali volunteered with a sudden break in her voice.

Cindy drew back and looked up at her. "The feeling is quite mutual, I might add." Her voice, too, was a trifle unsteady. Then she laughed. "Talk about gushy."

"You're right," Ali agreed, amusement hovering at the edge of her voice. "We'll save the serious stuff for later."

"Speaking of serious stuff, why don't I go get us something to eat and drink while you change your clothes." Cindy paused to brush an errant curl away from her face. "Don't put on anything fancy. Any old shorts and shirt will do. Remember you're slumming with country folk now."

With those aptly phrased words Cindy breezed out of the room, leaving Ali to her own devices.

Cindy pregnant—Ali still found it hard to believe. But she was happy for Cindy and Barry and excited, too, that she would be here when the baby was born. Ali rose and let her eyes roam around the room that was to be her home for the next few months. Though small and compact, it was tastefully decorated. Heavy oak furniture enhanced the muted yellow decor that ran throughout the room, gracing the walls and the ruffled bedspread with a tranquillity that was soothing. Open mini-blinds filtered through the sunlight creating dancing shadows on the walls.

Kicking off her high-heeled pumps, Ali walked to the window and looked out on the scene before her. The mountain in the foreground, dotted with thousands of hardwood trees, filled her vision. She was fascinated by the greenery and the feeling of freedom that surrounded her, so vastly different from the concrete close confines of New York City.

She drew away from the window, crossed the room, and closed the door. She wouldn't be at all surprised to see Barry's sturdy figure come strolling through the front door. She then lifted a piece of her luggage from the floor and plopped it down on the bed. The first outfit she came to was a pair of faded jeans and a sleeveless top. She changed into them with ease before digging into her overnight bag for a brush. After arranging her thick hair into a semblance of order, she left the room.

Cindy turned to look at her as she entered the kitchen. "Hi, you look great as usual." She grinned. "But why didn't you put on shorts? It's hot to me even if it is only the first of June."

Ali returned her smile with a shrug as she sat down at the table. "Actually, this outfit was the first thing I came to in my luggage. I didn't even bother to unpack anything else."

"Good," Cindy responded. "There's plenty of time to do that later." She smiled. "I'll help, of course."

Ali reached for one of the small finger sandwiches so deliciously displayed in the center of the table. "I'll take you up on that, of course," she grinned in between munching on her sandwich. "Mmmm, this is good. The food on the plane was disgusting as usual."

Cindy helped herself to a sandwich and sank down onto a chair across from Ali. "It's nothing but deviled ham mixed with pickle relish and salad dressing." She arched her eyebrows candidly. "Even if I do say so myself, it's good."

Ali laughed. "You haven't changed one iota." *Except that you look like hell,* she reflected silently. "So let's hear what you and Barry have been up to these last two years including an in-depth account of Junior here," she added, reaching over and giving Cindy's stomach a pat. "I'm still finding it hard to believe you're really and truly pregnant." *Now she'll tell me what's bothering her,* Ali thought. *I've opened the door—*

"You're not alone." Cindy averted her eyes. "Sometimes I myself *still* find it hard to believe." Her eyes darted back to Ali. "Let's talk about you first. I want a detailed account of all you've been through." She rushed on, "That is if you can bring yourself to talk about it."

Mixed emotions flickered across Ali's face, pain being the dominant one. Like Cindy, she wasn't ready to talk about her problems. It always left her feeling raw, exposed. "It's not that I don't want to tell you what happened," Ali finally admitted, tugging at her ear in nervous agitation. "It's just that it's all so damned depressing."

A sympathetic frown creased Cindy's forehead. Then she smiled suddenly. "Tell you what. Why don't we forget about baring our souls for a while longer and take a stroll around the ranch. There's so much to show you and several employees I want you to meet." Cindy got up and began covering the plate of sandwiches with waxed paper.

Ali drew a relieved breath as she reached for the bottle of 7-Up sitting next to her and poured it over her glass of ice. "I can't think of anything I'd rather do." She paused and sipped her drink. "Speaking of employees, what exactly does Adam Forrest do around here? Is he just a general handyman?" For reasons she refused to pursue, she found herself actually waiting for the answer with suspended breath.

Cindy stopped what she was doing and stared at Ali, an incredulous expression on her face. Then she burst into laughter.

"Adam Forrest? Work here?" she gasped, in between trying to control her mirth. "You've got to be kidding?"

"I *wasn't* kidding, but from the way you're reacting, I guess I should've been," Ali responded sarcastically.

The laughter disappeared instantly from Cindy's face like a slate wiped clean. "Why, Ali—Adam is not only a very successful veterinarian but a wealthy cattle rancher as well."

Chapter 3

Twice in one day, Ali reeled from shock. Her stomach acted accordingly; it lurched and churned with all the symptoms of having received a hard blow.

"Veterinarian? Rancher? *Him?*" Her words sounded foreign—shrill and hyper, not at all like her usual calm voice.

Cindy looked her straight in the eye but was hard pressed to keep her twitching lips from spreading into a full-fledged grin. "Yes, him," she countered. "And there's more—Adam is also our neighbor. He spends a lot of time here tending to our horses." Her eyes flashed mischievously. "He's almost like family."

"Oh, God," Ali muttered underneath her breath.

Cindy laughed openly now and shook her head. "Just wait until Adam finds out what you thought he was, and I quote: a handyman."

Ali's face turned beet red. She cleared her throat, trying desperately to swallow the lump that was steadily increasing in size. "I'm—I'm afraid he already knows. I—I made the mistake of telling him I was going to report his conduct to Barry."

A deafening silence fell over the room. Then Cindy's round eyes again sought Ali's face, stunned disbelief mirrored in them.

"Oh, no!" Cindy wailed at last, followed by sounds of musical laughter.

Ali gripped her hands together in her lap, thinking that she could cheerfully throttle her friend. But what good would it do? she asked herself. She was the one who had opened her mouth and inserted her foot, not Cindy. She was appalled by what she had done. She shook inwardly at the thought of having to face Adam Forrest again. No! She simply could not do it.

Seeing the distress signals flashing across Ali's face, Cindy wiped the laughter from hers and replaced it with a perplexed frown. She leaned across the table and patted Ali's hand. "Hey, what happened between you two? Whatever it was, it couldn't be *that* serious, surely?" She paused and took a sip of Ali's drink, which was sitting within arm's reach. "Knowing Adam like I do, I'm sure he thought it was funny." The beginning of another smile flirted with her lips. "So why are you getting so bent out of shape over such a small misunderstanding?"

Ali's soft mouth set into a frown and her chin popped up. "It's not that simple, I'm afraid," she retorted. "From the first moment I laid eyes upon *Dr.* Adam Forrest, the sparks flew. For some unknown reason, he took a strong dislike to me and made no effort to hide it."

Cindy raised her eyebrows. "Are you serious—Adam?"

"As serious as death and taxes," Ali responded grimly.

"Huh?" Cindy shook her head. "I still find it hard to believe that Adam would treat any woman like that, least of all you. Barry and I consider him to be our closest and dearest friend."

"Well, maybe he doesn't like women." Ali offered this assumption as a joke, but seeing the way Cindy's face sobered, she had apparently hit on something.

Cindy shifted uncomfortably. "Oh, he likes women all right," she declared, "but—"

"Just how much do you know about Adam Forrest?" Ali interrupted, unable to resist the question.

Cindy hesitated. "Well, if you're referring to his personal life, not much. He mentioned in passing right after we met him that he was married once and that his wife had left him. Of course we respected his privacy and didn't question him further." Her voice suddenly became guarded. "But I never got the impression he was bitter, especially since he's been seeing the same woman for the past few years. Her name is Molly Deavers," Cindy added by way of clarification.

"Who knows what dark secrets people harbor inside themselves," Ali remarked dryly, struggling to stifle the sudden feeling of discontent that flooded through her.

Another frown deepened the lines in Cindy's forehead. "He wasn't by any chance too forward, was he?" She paused as if groping for her next words. "You—you know what I mean."

Ali laughed sarcastically. "I know what you mean; but you can put your mind to rest on that score. He behaved just the opposite; he was rude and overbearing as hell." She intentionally failed to mention to Cindy the way her heart had fluttered in response to his blatant sexual attraction.

"Oh, Ali, I'm sorry about this." Cindy groaned. "Barry or I should have met your plane, but Adam was going into Fayetteville to get medical supplies, and he volunteered to pick you up." She took a deep breath. "I had no idea, of course, he'd be anything other than the perfect gentleman he always is around us. I'll talk to him...."

"No! Absolutely not," Ali responded, agitation clearly evident in her voice. "Let's just forget it, shall we?" She shrugged and threw Cindy a half smile. "After all, I don't have to be around him if I don't want to, and you do. Anyway, I may be imagining part of it. I've been paranoid as hell lately."

Cindy looked unconvinced. "I still think I should say something to Adam. If nothing else, at least to try and clear the air."

A panicky feeling rose up inside Ali. "No—no, please promise me you won't say a word to him. I'm sure, as I've already told you, I'm just paranoid."

"Well, from what I know of your situation, you've had enough to make you paranoid. Most people would have completely buckled under the load you've had to carry on your shoulders these past few months." Cindy paused to grimace. "No wonder you have a bleeding ulcer."

Ali tapped her long, tapered fingernails on the table. "If you don't mind, please, let's not talk about that culprit. I'm sure that as soon as I take my medicine on a regular basis plus soak up a ton of your glorious sunshine, I'll begin to feel better."

"What about a doctor? You *are* planning to see one while you're here?"

"Of course," Ali said. "My doctor gave me the name of a specialist in Hot Springs. One of these days, I'll take a jaunt over and pay him a visit."

Cindy smiled. "I'll see that you do, even if I have to prod you every step of the way. But needless to say, this wonderful mountain air will do more for you than all the doctors in the world." She spread her hands and laughed.

"You do realize that you've just gotten Dr. Cindy Medford's expert opinion."

Ali laughed in return. "Sounds good as any to me. In fact it's the best one I've had in months," she teased, feeling considerably more lighthearted and relieved to see that Cindy was showing signs of behaving like her old self.

Then suddenly Cindy's face sobered. "As long as we haven't made it outside yet, now is as good a time as any for you to tell me all that transpired in New York." Cindy completely ignored Ali's deepening frown and went on. "Your letters and the one phone call were rather vague. And don't give me that 'mind your own business' look, either," Cindy added, her eyes soft with loving concern.

Ali rose from the chair on wobbly legs and made her way to the kitchen window. She turned her back to Cindy and looked outside. The beauty and peacefulness of the scenery struck a sensitive chord within her. She wanted desperately to dodge her problems, to wave a magic wand and have the soothing mountain air swallow them up. But it was folly to think she could run from her past. It had to be faced. Cindy was right, she needed to share it. Maybe it would strengthen her, help her to find a ray of sunshine amid all the dark clouds.

Still she remained glued to the spot, loathe to break the spell. She watched as the patrons of the dude ranch strode around the grounds. In the distance she could see the swimming pool dotted with children and adults of all ages playing a game of water volleyball. Others were strolling between lodges as if they hadn't a care in the world. Adjacent to the noisy swimming pool area, she could see the stables, which housed the horses that carried the guests on the daily trail rides.

Her heart quickened its beat suddenly as she had visions of Adam Forrest's tall, lanky frame bending over and administering to one of the horses. The image of his broad chest with its whorls of dark hair at the base of his strong neck appeared before her eyes in vivid technicolor. And those deep, penetrating eyes that seemed to see clear through her....

A tiny live wire of excitement jolted her body. She sucked in her breath trying to get control of her crazy thoughts. What was wrong with her? How could she let herself think such disturbing thoughts about a man who couldn't have cared less if she disappeared from the face of the earth? A sense of confusion surrounded her like a smothering shawl. Could she be that lonely and desperate for a man's attention and touch?

"Ali—"

Cindy's quiet voice caused her to jerk like someone coming out of a trance. She turned around with a sigh, groping to clear her mind. "It's—it's not a pretty story," she said tonelessly.

"I'm sure it's not," Cindy responded, "but I want to hear it anyway."

"All right," Ali sighed, pushing aside the strangely hollow feeling inside her. "But only if you'll promise to tell me about the baby."

"It's a deal," Cindy replied.

"To make a long story short," Ali began, "my—my father traded the exotic face cream formula I had been perfecting for years in exchange for the cancellation of a debt against him. The party involved turned around and sold the formula to the highest bidder." Ali's heart began thumping loudly in her breast. "One month later Cameron's biggest competitor hit the market with it, making a big splash."

"Oh, Ali," Cindy cried.

Ali continued as if Cindy hadn't spoken. "I took one look at my father's face and knew he was involved. Don't ask me how I knew, but I did." She shrugged. "Maybe it was the way his face lost all its color when I came charging into the room like an enraged bull. Before I said a word, his face turned white as a sheet." Tears were now trickling down Ali's cheeks.

Cindy's hands tightened around her glass, whitening at her knuckles. "How could he have done that to you?" she hissed.

Ali smiled without humor. "Apparently it was easy. Or maybe he thought he could at least save the family business."

Cindy frowned. "I—I don't understand."

"The party to whom Dad owed the debt threatened to take Cameron Cosmetics if he couldn't raise the money. Somehow in his twisted mind he came up with divulging the formula to them instead." Bitterness underlined each word as the tears gushed unhampered from her eyes.

Cindy jumped up from the table and grabbed a tissue off the cabinet and handed it to Ali. "Shh, you've talked enough for now. At this rate, you'll make yourself sick."

"No—no, I won't. Please—let me finish." She paused and mopped the moisture from her eyes, giving Cindy a watery but grateful smile.

With a nod of her head Cindy returned to the table and sat down.

"Immediately I accused Dad of knowing more than he was admitting. One word led to another, and before I knew it, we were involved in a hellish verbal skirmish. Finally he admitted his part in the entire sordid episode." She paused to draw a deep, shuddering breath. "Two days later my uncle found him slumped over his desk. The doctor told us he'd had a massive heart attack and died instantly." Ali's voice was devoid of all emotion as she turned her attention again toward the window.

"I—I wish there was something I could say that would ease the pain," Cindy murmured softly. "But I'm afraid time is the only thing that can do that."

"Time and long hours of hard work," Ali echoed bitterly. "For years Phillip bled the company of funds, enabling him and Mother to live in a grand style." She paused and lifted her curls from her neck in nervous agitation. "So now, with no insurance money or accessible capital, I've got my work cut out for me. And my mother..." She broke off and walked toward Cindy. "You have no idea how terribly she acted during the whole ordeal."

Cindy grimaced. "Oh, yes, I can. Remember, I've seen your mother throw more than one of her tantrums. I'll never forget the fit she pitched when you told her you were going to marry Wes."

"Well, if you can believe it, this one was worse. She was furious when I informed her I was dumping everything in Uncle Charles's lap for a few months and coming to visit you."

"I'm not surprised," Cindy replied grimly.

"Of course, you know she's more worried about having to change her mode of living than anything else. Lightning will probably strike me for saying this, but I don't think my father's death fazed her at all."

Cindy registered a deep sigh but remained silent.

Ali drew a faltering breath before continuing, "She doesn't care about me and never has. She's just interested in what I can do for her. Like now she expects me to be the dutiful daughter and save the company and the Cameron name."

"And how do you propose to do that?" Cindy asked.

"I don't know," Ali replied on a ragged note. "But there is talk that the remaining stockholders are banding together and trying to find a buyer for Cameron. I don't think they will, mind you, but still I feel like I'm living on borrowed time while I'm here."

A puzzled frown settled over Cindy's face. "Just exactly who *is* in control of the company?"

"No one."

"No one?"

"That's right."

"You mean Phillip left no one the controlling stock?" Cindy was astounded and it showed. "What about your mother? Wasn't she upset?"

Ali lifted her slim shoulders in a shrug. "Didn't bother her. As long as she has someone to cater to her every whim, she couldn't care less. She wants none of the responsibility or the bother of operating Cameron, only the benefits. A new dress every day, bridge games, and luncheon dates with her friends are the things that turn my mother on, make her days worthwhile," she finished, her voice dripping sarcasm.

"God, what a waste," Cindy remarked with a disgusted shake of her head.

"Although I was left the largest block of shares, it's still not quite enough to control the company. But Mother and I together have over fifty percent."

"Will she side with you if there's a major confrontation?"

"Who knows?" Ali answered. "At the present time, Uncle Charles, my father's brother, is holding things together until I get back. I just hope Evelyn won't badger him until he's forced to clean out his desk drawer and leave."

"Why would she do a stupid thing like that?"

"Huh!" Ali retorted. "She'd stoop to any level if she thought it would bring me running back to New York. She's afraid I'm going to wash my hands of the company and let it go down the tubes, and then she'd have to live like a pauper since floundering businesses are a dime a dozen."

"Well, are you?"

"What?"

Cindy smiled faintly. "Going to let it go down the tubes?"

Ali pressed her lips together. "No, but don't think that hasn't crossed my mind, because it has," she stressed. "Then reality lands on my shoulders with a hard thump and reminds me that Cameron Cosmetics *is* my life. I could never be happy without the challenge it offers. When I get back to New York I can knock my competitors off their feet with a dazzling comeback."

Cindy grinned and flashed a thumbs-up sign. "Now you sound like the Ali I used to know."

An answering smile crossed Ali's lips at her friend's sudden exuberance. "Although I may sound down, I'm not," she said flatly, the smile having completely disappeared. "I'm never going to let a man use me or take advantage of me again."

Cindy's eyes slanted. "Forgive me if I sound patronizing, but you shouldn't hold the entire male race responsible for what Phillip did to you," she admonished lightly.

"I know," Ali responded, "but I've been through too much. I loved . . ." Suddenly she found it difficult to swallow, to talk.

Cindy held her tongue and sat patiently, giving Ali time to compose herself.

After a moment Ali went on, "I—I loved and trusted my father above all others," she said. "And I thought I knew him like the back of my hand." Her lashes, trimmed with tears, swept upward. "After he was dead and buried, I found out I didn't know him at all."

"Well, I can understand that, even if you can't," Cindy remarked candidly. "After all, you had your life and he had his. There was no reason for you to keep tabs on him after working hours."

Ali's mouth turned downward. "The way it turned out, it seems I should have. But then," she added, with a dejected slant to her shoulders, "I spent all my time in the lab and then went home to my apartment alone. Needless to say, I existed in my own little world."

"You'll hate me for saying this, but what you need is a strong man to put his arms around you and let you draw from his strength. You've been alone too much in your thirty years."

Ali gave a disgusted sigh. "Oh, please, spare me. The last thing I need is a dominating male in my life. Or maybe I should say . . . I don't have room in my life for domestic bondage."

"We'll see," Cindy replied smoothly, completely undaunted by Ali's attitude.

Ali glared down at her. "Don't you dare get any ideas about playing Cupid. My goal is to make Cameron Cosmetics the number one company it used to be. That's all! I don't need or want a *man*." Suddenly, Adam Forrest's taunting face swam before her eyes. She squeezed them shut. Had she finally pushed herself over the brink? she wondered wildly. Was he forever to be her tormentor?

"Hey," Cindy said, throwing a sharp glance at Ali. "Don't pay any attention to my big mouth." She shrugged. "It's just that I want you to be happy—to find someone who'll take care of you, like I have. And maybe settle down with a home and family before you get too old and set in your ways, that is,'' she added with an impish grin.

"Thanks for nothing," Ali replied sarcastically, though a smile tilted the corners of her lips upward.

"Anytime," Cindy countered with a chuckle.

Ali's smile turned into a soft laugh as she began gathering up the glasses and bottle of 7-Up from the table. "What do you say we dump this serious stuff—that we weren't supposed to talk about in the first place—and take a walk outside. I've cried and been over all this mess in my mind so much that I'm sick to death of it."

"But hasn't it helped to talk about it, to get some of the poison out of your system?" Cindy asked.

"Of course, it has," Ali responded softly. "But at the same time, I didn't come here to burden you with my problems."

"Poo," Cindy returned with a flap of an uplifted hand. "What are friends for, if they can't band together and help each other in time of need."

Ali leaned over and gently squeezed Cindy's hand. "Now it's your turn. I want to talk about you, Barry, and the baby."

Cindy's eyes shifted, but not before Ali noticed they had lost their sparkle. "You—you have plenty of time to hear about me and the baby." Her gaze wandered back to Ali, and she smiled. "Let's not get knee-deep in any more 'serious stuff' for a while, what do you say?"

Ali barely managed to hide her frustration. It was obvious Cindy was *not* going to talk about herself or the baby. Suddenly Ali stood up and walked toward the door, feeling the need for a breath of fresh air.

Cindy got up slowly from the chair and followed Ali. "Let's find my better half and see what he's up to. Maybe he'll act as a tour guide." She grinned. "He's much more professional at that sort of thing than I.

"Well, what do you think of the place?" Cindy asked, after they had strolled a while in companionable silence.

"I think it's fantastic," Ali exclaimed excitedly. "I don't know what prompted you and Barry to buy this place, but it was a brilliant move."

Cindy's eyebrows puckered in a frown. "I wish I could be that sure," she responded with a sigh. "In fact most of the time I think we must've taken leave of our senses to bite off such a big chunk, even more so now that I'm pregnant."

Her remark drew an answering frown from Ali. "I take it you're referring to finances."

"Exactly," Cindy said flatly.

Ali shook her head. "How can that be? The place looks like it's filled to capacity with guests." Her eyes again combed the area. The grounds were a beehive of activity with people milling around everywhere.

"Although it may look filled," Cindy said, "it isn't. We have enough rooms to accommodate up to a hundred guests, but here it is the beginning of the busy tourist season, and we have only about half that number signed up for the month of June."

"Well, what about the rest of the summer months? Are they shaping up any better?" Ali asked.

"So far, so good, but still, the reservations aren't coming in the way we'd hoped."

"Maybe you're rushing things a little. After all this is the first summer that the ranch has been under your guidance and management. Maybe you're expecting too much too soon."

Cindy sighed. "Perhaps you're right. It's just that we borrowed extra money to remodel the lodges, buy several new horses, and make other general repairs." She paused and slapped at a mosquito on her arm before continuing, "The previous owners apparently sat back and complacently let the place come tumbling down around their shoulders. We had no choice but to make some repairs. Now, with the economy like it is, I'm afraid we might have bitten off more than we can chew."

Ali was silent for a long moment, trying to decide how to phrase her next question. She decided not to mince any words. "Would you consider letting me loan you the mon—"

Cindy's gasp and horrified expression made further speech impossible. She stopped and placed her hands on her hips in a stubborn stance. "No way would I take one dime from you, Ali Cameron." Even though her words were spoken with authority and seriousness, a smile threatened to pull her tight lips apart at Ali's overblown antics of self-protection. "But thanks for the offer anyway," she added sweetly. "You know I love you. However, Barry and I must learn to handle our own troubles."

"How do you think that makes me feel?" Ali asked bluntly. "Especially after I've spent the last two hours burdening you with all my troubles and now you have the audacity to tell me you have to handle your own."

Cindy suppressed a sigh. "There's a vast difference between acting as a sounding board to a friend and accepting help, especially the monetary kind."

"I understand." Ali's eyes were soft. "But I want you to know that the offer still stands whether you accept it or not."

"Ali."

Cindy's quiet use of her name broke into the silence that had once again fallen between them. She whipped her head around to face her friend.

"As long as we're on the subject of troubles," Cindy was saying, "there's something I've been wanting to tell—"

"Hey, you two. Over here!" Barry's loud, booming voice rang out, causing both women to turn with a start.

At first Ali did not notice the figure standing next to Barry in the pen full of horses, until he turned around.

She froze in her tracks. Adam Forrest slowly unwound his lanky frame from his crouched position beside the lower hind leg of a horse and raised himself to his over six foot height. She couldn't believe it! Her fantasy had come true! She watched Adam stiffen as she and Cindy closed the distance between the men. Then the mocking smile that Ali had come to associate with him slid over his face, his eyes moving over her in one sweeping glance.

Gone were Cindy's words. Gone were rational thoughts. Ali just stood and stared, giving in to the intense feeling of frustration that washed over her. No! Please! Not twice in one day. She blinked her eyes shut, willing him to disappear, but no such luck. When her eyes opened of their own accord, he stood as aggravatingly attractive as ever, possessing the kind of magnetism that could best be described as lethal.

Ignoring the blotches of red that now stained her cheeks, Ali raised her chin and arrogantly returned his stare. Her eyes were once again privy to the dark skin that gleamed against his khaki shirt before traveling down to the jeans hugging his muscular frame. His pants were tucked into grained leather boots, giving credence to his lean indolent grace. Just looking at him, Ali felt a tingling sensation sizzle through her.

"Hi," Cindy quipped, rushing forward to stand beside Barry, although her words were directed to Adam.

"What's wrong with Magic?" Her eyes traveled between both men, concern reflected in them.

Adam forced his gaze away from Ali and looked down at Cindy. He frowned and seemed to have trouble concentrating. "Actually, I'm not real sure," he said. "I stopped by to talk to you about something else, when Barry asked me to take a quick look at Magic's leg." He paused and ran his strong brown hands the length of the mare's leg ever so gently. "She seems to be having a great deal of trouble putting her weight on this leg, but just from the look and feel of it, I can't pinpoint the reason." He continued to run his hand in a soothing manner up and down the leg.

Ali remained silent, completely caught up in the hypnotic motion of his hands as they touched and probed the tender spots without apparently bringing further pain to the animal. In that moment she thought he looked every inch the professional veterinarian. How on earth, she wondered, could she have ever thought he was a hired hand?

"Do you think she's going to be all right?" Barry asked. "Magic is one of our prize horses." He paused and scratched his head. "I'd hate like hell for anything serious to be ailing the old girl."

Adam ceased his adept ministrations to the leg and moved his hand up the mare's smooth flank, giving it a swift pat. "Before I leave I'll spread a tube of liniment on it, and if that doesn't do the trick, call me in the morning; I'll run over between patients and take another look."

Cindy flexed her lips into a satisfied smile and nodded toward Adam. "Thanks. I don't know what we'd do without you," she said with a tiny waver in her voice.

"You might not be thanking me tomorrow when you get my bill," he teased, his eyes alight with devilish merriment.

"Huh," Barry snorted. "I've yet to get one of those bills you're always promising us."

"I wouldn't worry about it, if I were either of you," Adam drawled in a tone that brooked no argument.

"Well, I'm thankful you don't think there's anything seriously wrong with Magic," Cindy intervened, changing the subject. She smiled at Adam. "By the way, what did you want to talk to us about?"

Adam flexed his back muscles as he duplicated Cindy's smile. Then he raised his eyes and flickered them across to Ali.

Ali steeled herself as if for a confrontation but kept her face devoid of all emotion. But she was intensely conscious of Adam Forrest's eyes upon her as he spoke.

"I stopped by to ask you to a barbecue at my ranch tomorrow evening," he said.

A panicky feeling invaded Ali's insides. She held her tongue. *Please, Cindy, say no,* she pleaded silently. The last thing she wanted to do tomorrow was to be around Adam Forrest. She'd had it with this man. Then she brightened. Maybe he wasn't inviting her. But even if he were, maybe she could plead fatigue and get out of it. However, Cindy's next words vetoed that idea.

"Oh, Adam, that sounds wonderful," Cindy exclaimed. "The timing's perfect too." She smiled and threw a pleading glance toward Ali before turning back to face Adam. "This way, Ali will get a chance to meet all our neighbors and friends at one time."

"What about you, Ali?" Barry asked quietly, easing a grin in her direction. "Does this meet with your approval?"

Ali tried to muster a show of enthusiasm. But if her reluctance was obvious to Barry, she was in trouble. Forcing a smile through her stiff lips, she said, "Sounds fine to me. Whatever you two want to do is okay by me." She made it a point to keep her eyes away from Adam, knowing that this would be laced with sardonic amusement.

"Good," Cindy said, smiling. "That takes care of that," she added with an audible sigh of relief. "Now tell me, Adam, what do you want me to bring in the way of food?" She frowned thoughtfully. "I could whip up a blueberry cheesecake, or better still, how about a couple of loaves of homemade bread?"

Adam chuckled and shook his head. "I don't want you to bring one thing other than yourself—and Miss Cameron. If she wants to come, that is," he added, a challenging drawl to his tone.

Ali schooled her features to show none of her inner turmoil. "Why, Dr. Forrest," she cooed in a syrupy sweet voice, "I wouldn't dream of missing your party."

Not about to let her outwit him, Adam's teeth sparkled through his wide smile. "Why, Miss Cameron, I knew I could depend on you to join the ranks of us country folks with true grit."

"How right you are," Ali countered, her voice a perfect imitation of his southern drawl. "If you're going to wade, you might as well go knee-deep." The false sweet smile still clung to her lips.

"I'll remind you of that statement later," he promised softly, making no attempt to hide the fact that he was speaking for her ears alone.

Something in his tone sent a shiver sliding down Ali's spine only to turn into a small fluttering in her midsection. She opened her mouth to counterattack but slammed her jaw shut instead. A verbal fencing match with this man would be as dangerous as poking her hand in a scalding pan of hot grease. How could she expect to win even if she were willing to take the chance? One minute he was taunting her with derision and the next minute he was throwing veiled sexual innuendos at her.

The realization that Cindy and Barry were looking at her and Adam as if they had taken complete leave of their senses brought Ali back to reality. She groped for something to say that would put things back in their right perspective.

Barry came to her rescue. "Ali," he said, "before it gets completely dark, why don't we trek around the grounds so you can see the entire operation." He paused and glanced sideways at Adam. "Want to come with us, Doc, and then stay for supper?" He laughed and turned his dark eyes on Cindy. "No doubt, my favorite girl here can whip up something edible."

"Yes, Adam, why don't you stay," Cindy urged sweetly. "I've got a pot of stew in the fridge that I made last night. It's absolutely yummy, I promise. And to make it even more tempting I'll stir up a pan of biscuits." She smiled at Ali now. "How does that sound to you?"

Ali's tongue prepared to moisten her upper lip as she tried to answer Cindy's question. It did indeed sound appetizing, but not at the expense of having to be under the mocking eyes of Adam Forrest. Was there ever going to be an end to his intrusion in her life? she wondered with a renewed sense of irritation.

Adam, twice within a matter of hours, found himself captivated by this lovely creature in front of him. He stood mesmerized as the tip of her red tongue played about the corners of her mouth. For an insane moment, he wished he knew what it would feel like to have the lash of that tiny instrument against the tender linings of his lips only then to have it venture further into the moist cavity of his mouth. God! he felt his insides cringe. He was behaving exactly like one of the lovesick animals he so often put out of their misery. They weren't able to control their emotions, but by God he was! Or so he thought.

He had always prided himself on being in control and trustful of his basic instincts. He knew exactly what he wanted out of life, especially when it came to women. Yet now as he continued to stare at this one so close to him— so close that her delicate perfume tantalized his nostrils— he wasn't sure any longer. Suddenly he didn't trust himself. The pain he'd suffered at Mary's hands twisted in his brain like corkscrews. He must put an end to this folly now. The rage directed at himself threatened to overpower him.

"I—I'd love to see the rest of the ranch," Ali answered, trying to force her mind away from the frightening possibility of Adam's staying for dinner.

Ali's voice roused Adam with the same effect as having a glass of cold water doused in his face. He had more than stayed his welcome. He pivoted on his heel with the intention of going to his truck, when Barry's words halted him.

"You coming?"

"Thanks, but not this time," Adam responded, careful to keep his tone even and to avoid looking in Ali's direction. "I'm going to grab the ointment out of the truck and doctor Magic. Then I'll be on my way."

"But—" Cindy began with puckered brows.

"Can't stay," Adam declared bluntly, then softened his tone by bestowing a winsome smile on Cindy.

"We'll see you tomorrow night, then," Barry said as he motioned for the two women to fall in step beside him.

Ali listened as Barry and Cindy pointed out various places of interest to her. She hung on every word they said, thereby completely dismissing Adam Forrest from her mind.

She learned there were at least three scheduled and supervised trail rides a day, plus volleyball, badminton, swimming, and a game room filled with the latest video games, not to mention hayrides and square dancing.

"I've saved the best for last," Barry told her as they made their way back toward the lodge. "And that's fishing."

"Fishing?" Ali echoed, a skeptical look on her face.

"Yes, fishing," Barry mimicked good-naturedly. "Boy, do we have the most beautiful and plentiful fishing holes around here. They make the avid fisherman's heart palpitate with excitement."

Ali laughed and shook her head. "Beats me how a person can get his kicks out of watching a poor little helpless fish dangle on the end of a string. To my way of thinking that's cruel and unusual punishment." She wrinkled her nose.

Barry chuckled. "Just wait until you taste one of Cindy's baked trout sautéed in butter and lemon juice. Mmmm, there's nothing like it." He paused and smacked his lips in an exaggerated manner. "You'll be begging us then to take you to the Buffalo River so you can catch a cooler full."

"That's right, Ali," Cindy said with a grin. "They're delicious and more fun than you can imagine to catch."

Ali shook her head. "I don't know about that...."

"Oh, sure you do," Cindy pressed. "We'll schedule a fishing trip soon."

"Don't do me any favors," Ali murmured, sarcasm lacing her voice.

Barry and Cindy just shook their heads and laughed.

The evening continued in the same camaraderie. But after Ali had consumed a bowl of stew and two biscuits, her eyes became heavy as hammers.

"Why don't you go to bed, Ali," Cindy suggested with a smile. "This has been a long, exhausting day for you."

"Indeed it has," Ali responded, stifling a yawn, "but I've enjoyed every minute of it." Well, almost all of it, she admitted silently. If she could have eliminated Adam Forrest's presence, it would have indeed been a perfect day.

"It will be to your advantage if you can sleep late in the morning," Cindy volunteered, "because Adam's parties usually last far into the night."

Ali tried to suppress a groan, but it didn't go unnoticed by Barry.

He looked at her for a moment while he calmly lit his cigarette and then slid the lighter back into his pocket. "Somehow I get the impression that something is going on around here that I don't know about," he said levelly. Now his dark eyes darted across the room to include Cindy in the conversation.

"Not really," Cindy declared, before Ali had a chance to speak. Then she paused with a careless shrug. "The chemical reaction between Ali and Adam seems to be less than perfect, that's all." She frowned.

Barry looked completely dumbfounded.

"What Cindy is trying to say is that your friendly neighborhood vet isn't too impressed with me," Ali said bluntly.

"Now Ali—" Cindy began, "I think you're jumping to conclusions."

"Will you two stop fencing and tell me what the hell's going on?" Barry demanded. The frown creasing his forehead deepened as his eyes jockeyed between both women.

Ali smiled, wishing now she had kept her mouth shut.

"Well—" Barry pressed.

"That's the point," Ali replied. "There's nothing to tell."

Suddenly a teasing glint appeared in Barry's eyes. "Well, now that you mention it, I did notice that Adam behaved a little strangely this afternoon." He paused and ground out his cigarette in the nearest ashtray. "Can't remember, though, when I ever saw Adam run from a beautiful woman."

Refusing to rise to his bait, Cindy threw up her hands in hopeless despair as she uncrossed her legs and stood up. "Before this conversation gets out of hand, I'm going to bed," she said with a grimace. "I'll see you two in the morning," she added perfunctorily.

Now as Ali lay snug within the clean-smelling sheets, instead of sleep overtaking her as she had hoped, she suddenly felt her eyes pop open with renewed vigor. She let her gaze follow the shadows from the outside spotlights as they danced across the ceiling.

She willed her eyes to close, refusing to let her mind wander at will. But the sandman refused to cooperate, and before long she began to backtrack on the events of the day.

No! she berated herself, rolling over and punching her pillow. *I won't think of Adam Forrest. I won't, I won't, I won't . . .*

"Ali—Ali, wake up! It's me, Barry."

Was she dreaming? Or was someone actually calling her name?

The doorknob rattled. Twisting around in the bed, Ali blinked and forced her eyes on the clock beside the bed. Unconsciously she reached for her robe at the foot of the bed and slipped her arms into it.

The rattle of the doorknob grated relentlessly against her senses. She jumped out of bed and crossed the room to the door.

"Barry—?" Ali asked, a feeling of alarm coursing rapidly through her body. "What's the matter?" She opened the door to confront a harassed-looking Barry.

"It—it's Cindy. She's awfully sick." His words were now coming in gasping spurts. "God, Ali, I'm afraid she's going to lose the baby."

Chapter 4

"Oh, no!" Ali exclaimed in a throaty whisper. She squelched the rising panic that clutched at her stomach as the sounds of convulsive gagging reached her ears. Swift as an arrow Ali flew across the hall and into the bathroom, where she found Cindy hunched over the commode, hugging it for dear life.

Immediately Ali opened the nearest cabinet and snatched a washcloth off the shelf. She then doused it with cold water before kneeling down and bathing Cindy's face and neck.

"Shh," Ali said in a soothing tone, "don't fight it, just relax and take long deep breaths."

After a moment Cindy raised red-rimmed eyes toward Ali and with a grateful nod made an effort to rise to her feet. Ali, with the help of Barry, led Cindy back to the bed. After gently smoothing Cindy's limp curls off her damp forehead, Ali positioned herself by the bed, determined to remain until she went to sleep.

There was a worried silence in the room as both Ali and Barry kept the vigil. They were afraid to talk for fear of disturbing Cindy.

As Ali sat with her eyes glued to her friend's pale, washed-out features, she felt tears beginning to prick at her eyes. Something was terribly wrong. Not only was Cindy ill, but there was an unhealthy apathy toward the baby that Ali was finding hard to understand. And Cindy's refusal to talk about it made it worse.

"Do you think she's going to—to be—all right?" Barry stammered softly, unfurling his tired limbs and lifting his chair to place it next to Ali's. Cindy's relaxed breathing now filled the room.

Ali gave him a reassuring look. "I'm sure she'll be fine." She paused, striving to keep her tone light. Barry looked sick with worry. "Did you see how much dinner she ate? No wonder she's sick."

Barry sighed. "I know. I guess I should've said something to her, especially since she's been feeling so rotten lately."

Ali shook her head in bewilderment. "Has she been like this ever since she found out she was pregnant?"

"Yes," Barry responded gravely. "She's had nothing but trouble since day one."

Ali looked perplexed. "You mean she's been vomiting like this from the beginning?"

"Off and on," Barry explained. "Some days she'll feel good, then a surge of nausea will hit her and knock her down again." He paused and rubbed the back of his neck. "Tonight, though, she was sicker than she's ever been. It scared the hell out of me."

"I can understand that," Ali replied lightly.

"And last week she began having dizzy spells," Barry added, new concern roughing his voice. "I'm afraid now for both her and the baby."

"Me too," Ali responded softly as she tried to sift this bad news through her mind and accept it with a calm she was far from feeling. "And to think she didn't even tell me," Ali added in a muffled tone.

"The doctor told her that from now on each month is critical," Barry continued, "although he hasn't actually diagnosed her problem." He sounded sad and broken.

Ali was quiet for several minutes, fighting back the tears. Her eyes shifted again to Cindy's face. "Maybe this time you can get some straight answers from the doctor," she said, raising her eyes to Barry. "What she just went through is extremely dangerous."

Barry's shoulders sagged in defeat. "It seems like when it rains, it pours," he said with a deep sigh. "Knowing Cindy, I'm sure she told you that we've gotten ourselves into something of a financial bind." Following Ali's affirmative shake of the head, he went on with the same heart-wrenching defeat crowding his voice. "And now problems with the baby. I feel like I'm to blame for..."

"Don't, Barry," Ali interrupted, placing her hand on his arm in a comforting gesture. "Don't do this to yourself. I'm sure if she takes care of herself and follows the doctor's orders, the baby will be fine."

"But she's been so worried," he groaned. "She's refused to get excited for fear she's never going to have this baby or that something is going to be wrong with it." His eyes were stricken with pain. "She won't buy one item for the baby nor will she talk about it. When I do manage to get her to say anything, it's like pulling eye-teeth."

Ali compressed her mouth. "I know what you mean. So far, she has refused to discuss it with me." A feeling of guilt shot through Ali. "I can't believe I unloaded my problems on her shoulders this afternoon. I could kick myself now for being so thoughtless."

"Well, don't," Barry said bluntly. "You have no idea how much she's been looking forward to your visit."

Ali smiled. "I hope so. Now that I'm here, will you let me do Cindy's chores? I know she worked a lot with the guests."

"You bet she did," Barry declared. "And I've really felt the pinch, since she's not supposed to lift anything heavier than a dishpan."

A determined look crossed Ali's face. "And I aim to see she does exactly as she's told."

Barry gave a short laugh. "Have you tried telling Cindy anything lately? She's as hardheaded as she ever was."

A hard glint appeared in Ali's eyes. "You just leave things to me. First thing in the morning your wife and I are going to have a counseling session."

Barry rolled his eyes upward. "Good luck," he retorted.

Ali remained with Cindy until she could no longer keep her eyes open. At Barry's insistence she stumbled to her room with his promise to call her if she was needed.

A peek at the clock told her it was now five o'clock. She let out a moan as she crawled between the sheets. Positive that sleep would continue to be elusive, she was surprised when she opened her eyes to a room warmed by sunlight. In a jerky motion she sat upright in the bed, trying to get her bearings. As if programmed her eyes flew to the digital clock. Ten o'clock.

"Oh, no," she muttered aloud, the events of last night crashing down on her head. Cindy. She must check on Cindy without further delay. In one continuous motion she grabbed her robe as her feet hit the floor. She stumbled to the bathroom in her bare feet and began washing her face and brushing her teeth.

"Good morning, sleepyhead."

Ali whirled around, her toothbrush suspended in mid-air and her mouth full of toothpaste. She stared wide-eyed at a grinning Cindy.

"Don't you think you'd better get rid of that glop in your mouth before you choke to death," Cindy advised, propping herself nonchalantly against the door frame. "One crisis is enough for a while, don't you think?"

Ali could only nod her head as she leaned over the sink and rinsed her mouth. Finally able to talk, she turned toward Cindy with narrowed eyes and said, "Well, all I can say is you look none the worse for last night."

Cindy unconsciously brushed her hair away from her face. "I feel weak, but other than that, I'm fine," she said.

Following Cindy's words an awkward silence fell over the room. Ali longed to reach out and tell her friend that she understood, that everything was going to be all right. But for some reason she held her tongue and waited for Cindy to make the first move.

"Ali, I—" Cindy began, only to pause and let her gaze fall to the floor.

Ali's expression softened as she took a step toward Cindy and gave her arm a gentle squeeze. "Why don't we adjourn to the dining room and talk over a cup of hot chocolate." She smiled. "How about it?"

Cindy threw her a wan smile, but the smile fell short of her eyes. "While you finish in here," she said, her voice tense, "I'll put the water on to boil."

Ali quickly dropped her gown and robe in a puddle in the middle of the floor. She rummaged through her suitcase and yanked out a pair of yellow cuffed shorts and a matching terry cloth shirt. Once they were on, she slipped her feet into a pair of leather thongs and quickly ran the brush through her errant curls. Makeup would have to come later, she decided, even though her ghost-like features mocked her through the dressing table mirror.

Turning her back on her reflection, she scurried into the kitchen eager to talk to Cindy. A cup of steaming hot chocolate topped with a marshmallow was waiting for her in the middle of the table as she breezed through the door.

"Mmmm, that smells absolutely divine," Ali said, wrinkling her nose and sniffing the aroma. "If you can't have coffee, hot choc is the next best thing, especially when your eyelids weigh as much as a bowling ball, and you feel like you've been run over by a Mack truck." Ali grinned, hoping to draw a responsive smile from Cindy, but none was forthcoming. Instead Cindy's face fell, and tears rushed unbidden into her eyes.

"Oh, honey, please don't cry," Ali pleaded softly.

Cindy made an effort to gulp back the tears. "I—I should've told you how sick I've been. I'm—I'm so afraid I'm still going to lose the baby." She swiped at the remaining tears on her cheeks with the back of her hand. "The feeling inside me is hard to describe. I can't even make Barry understand." She paused as if groping for the right words to convey her inner turmoil. "It's almost like I'm afraid that if I talk about the baby, it'll disappear." She spread her hands over her stomach. "I know you think I've blown a fuse in my brain with that kind of talk, but..." She let her voice trail into thin air, as if she didn't know what else to say.

Ali gazed at her, sympathy blanketing her features. "Don't you dare worry for one minute about not telling me." She took a sip of the hot liquid. "Oh, at first I was mortified when Barry told me and a little hurt that you hadn't wanted to share your problems with me, but now that I know the mental and physical anguish you've been going through, I can understand."

Cindy flashed her a tumultuous smile before her expression became sober once again. "I—I want this baby more than anything else in the world," she stammered brokenly.

"I know you do," Ali responded softly, "and I want you to have this baby with all my heart." Ali forced a bight smile to her lips. "So why don't I get dressed and drive you into town to the doctor. It will ease your mind to have him give you a quick exam, especially after all that vomiting. And if I were you, I'd make him give me some answers."

Cindy took a deep breath. "I'm going, but you needn't worry about driving me. Barry has to pick up a load of supplies that came in by bus this morning. Anyway, he's determined to talk to Dr. Hanson himself."

"Good," Ali said, feeling somewhat better now.

"While we're gone, why don't you relax, take it easy. Remember Adam's barbecue is tonight."

Ali turned horrified eyes on Cindy. "You've got to be kidding."

Cindy looked puzzled. "No, I'm perfectly serious. Why?"

"I can't see how you could even entertain the thought of going to a party as sick as you've been. That's why!"

Cindy's shoulders slumped. "You're probably right, I shouldn't go. But I think it would do me good to sit around and just visit." Her brow puckered. "Of course it all depends on what Dr. Hanson tells me." She paused. "If I can't go, I'm at least going to send a pie."

"But...Adam told you..." Ali threw up her hands in despair.

Cindy laughed, easing her pale and pinched features. "Come on, my friend, out with it. Don't sputter."

Ali couldn't help but smile in return. "All right, hard-head, have it your own way."

"Good," Cindy declared, "I'm glad that's settled."

But it wasn't settled, not as far as Ali was concerned. She had succeeded in cramming thoughts of Adam Forrest and his forthcoming party to the back of her mind and slammed the door. Since Cindy had become so desperately ill during the night, she had been positive they wouldn't be going near Adam's ranch. Now with this sudden turn of events, she felt both a sense of apprehension and elation attack her nervous system. Why did he have the power to make her feel this way? The possibilities were endless, but none of them gave her any satisfaction.

"You *are* going with us tonight, aren't you?" Cindy was asking now, a frown raising her eyebrows.

Ali started. "I—guess so."

"For a moment there, I wasn't so sure," Cindy replied, "when you got that certain look on your face." She smiled. "I was positive you were gearing up for a fight to the bitter end."

Ali shrugged her shoulders. "I wouldn't embarrass you by not going, especially if it means that much to you."

Cindy reached for the pot and filled a cup with the steaming liquid. "What I want is for you to have a good time, to meet our friends." She paused. "And—to kill the hostility that has cropped up between you and Adam."

"Well, you'll be wasting your time. I'm simply not interested in Adam Forrest," Ali stressed firmly.

Cindy hid a smile behind her hand and wisely held her tongue.

The sunlight was becoming swallowed up by the evening shadows as Adam Forrest's ranch came into view. Barry brought the Suburban to a standstill behind countless other vehicles already lining the circular driveway. Ali forced herself to concentrate on the country and western music that graced the air and fought to push aside her moody thoughts.

She hadn't wanted to come, but she couldn't bring herself to disappoint Cindy or risk upsetting her further. The report from the doctor hadn't been good. The doctor had finally told Cindy that she suffered from kidney poisoning, or toxemia. Without confining her to bed, he had nevertheless cautioned her again against doing anything strenuous. He had gone on to tell her the end result of toxemia was premature births.

Cindy had taken the news well, having already made up her mind to follow the doctor's orders implicitly. "Now that I know what's wrong, I can concentrate on getting well," she had told Ali.

"Ali, isn't this great," Cindy was saying. "Adam is probably a millionaire several times over, but you'd never know it by the way he acts. He's the most generous and down to earth person I know.'

Ali forced herself to acknowledge Cindy's praises of Adam Forrest.

"It definitely seems as if he has the best life has to offer," Ali muttered, striving to keep Cindy from picking up her sarcastic tone.

But nothing escaped Cindy's mink-like hearing. She grinned. "You know what I think, Barry," she said, ignoring Ali and turning to face her husband. "I *think* the lady doth protest too heartily."

Barry laughed and threw Cindy a backward glance before slamming the door and making his way around to their side to help them out of the car.

Ali held on to Barry's hand for a moment to help steady her suddenly wobbly knees. She refused, however, to give in to the feeling of weakness that was so totally out of character for her and baffled her so completely. Squaring her shoulders she made herself stay in perfect step with Cindy and Barry as they walked at an unhurried pace to the front door of the ranch-style brick home.

Peering closely at the structure, Ali thought it extremely modern but on closer scrutiny, she noticed it had a touch of turn-of-the-century Victorian, southern Victorian to be exact. A side veranda graced with detailed gingerbread handwork decorated the front of the house. It was utterly charming, and Ali fell in love with it on sight.

Barry touched her arm and smiled. "There's no reason to go inside now," he said breezily. "Let's go join in the fun." His smile widened into a full-fledged grin as he guided her and Cindy along a brick path that skirted the house.

Even before they rounded the corner, Ali heard the loud hum of voices, boisterous laughter, and the clatter of chairs. These sounds were vying to be heard above the electrifying sound of one of Kenny Rogers's latest hits.

Barry tentatively touched Ali's arm again, gesturing her forward. "Come on, let's find Adam and then I'll introduce you to our friends."

Ali remained rooted to the spot but flashed Barry a smile. "Why don't you two go ahead." She paused and spread her hands. "I need a minute to digest all this," she added breathlessly.

Cindy laughed. "Suit yourself," she said. "Join us when you get ready."

Left to her own devices, Ali drew a shaky breath and gazed about her. The party was in full swing. People in groups, dressed in jeans and western shirts, were scattered across the grounds, drinking, laughing, and having a good time.

Her eyes, wandering to the left, focused on a huge swimming pool surrounded by a redwood deck. There were several heads bobbing up and down in the water, their laughter bouncing through the air. A large flagstone patio, alight with torches flickering with bold brilliance in the late evening shadows, was connected to the house. A six-piece band, dressed in typical western garb, was assembled on a raised platform, playing with enthusiasm for several couples who were shuffling their feet in perfect rhythm to the latest craze in western dancing—the Cotton-Eyed-Joe.

Numerous tables with red-checkered cloths dotted the perfectly manicured lawn. Adjacent to the tables were several men, obviously ranch hands, clad in enormous white hats and butcher aprons. A vapor of steam floated through the air from the large stainless-steel covered pans. Their aroma would put the most expensive New York restaurant to shame.

Her eyes combed the rolling hills cluttered with grazing cattle in the distance. No wonder Cindy's voice had been full of envy and awe when she had mentioned Adam's dazzling wealth. He did indeed appear to lead a charmed life, she thought, not without a touch of envy. Even though Ali had been a part of and now owned stock in a large cosmetics conglomerate, she had never experienced this type of unconventional wealth. She was indeed seeing what fairy tales were made of.

Suddenly, the whooping and shouting coming from the makeshift dance floor claimed her attention. She jerked her head around and stared at the participants with a whimsical expression on her face. Unconsciously Ali smiled and began tapping her foot in time to the music.

As soon as Ali had rounded the corner Adam saw her. His first thought was to drop everything and migrate toward her. Then he cursed himself for entertaining such a thought. Again he asked himself, what was there about this woman that drew him toward her like a violent undertow? It had to be the sensuality that radiated from her every pore. Dressed in a pair of tight designer jeans that molded her derriere like second skin, she looked regal standing there with her sun-lightened brown hair caressing the porcelain delicacy of her cheeks. The blouse she wore was a bright orange and navy plaid tucked in at the waist, giving emphasis to her perfectly shaped breasts.

Just looking at her caused the blood to drum through his body. Physical. That's all it was, he told himself. A physical fascination—pure and simple. But it made absolutely no sense. A grave error in judgment had almost cost him his sanity and threatened his manhood to such an extent that he was still unwilling and unable to make any commitments.

Love was something he no longer believed in, except where animals were concerned. They never let him down or disappointed him. They took a human at face value and loved them no matter what. Humans were sadly lacking in this trait, he thought, especially women.

No, Ali Cameron was definitely not for him. She was forbidden fruit. She had her own problems to cope with and he had his. And he knew with a devastating certainty born from experience that he didn't need her in his life. It was a complication he could do without.

Yet, watching her booted foot keep time to the music and the capricious expression mirrored on her face, he wanted to taste the hidden delights of her body with an insatiable hunger.

Refusing to listen to warning bells clanging in his brain, he found his legs carrying himself toward her. After all she was his guest, he told himself. Didn't good manners dictate that he at least welcome her to his home and to his party? Of course they did, he readily assured himself as he made his way across the lawn, not stopping until he stood behind her.

"They don't indulge in this kind of dancing in the big city, do they?" he asked softly, his words easing through her thick mane of curls to stroke her ears.

Ali's shoulders froze as did her feet at the sound of Adam's voice so close to her ears. Goose bumps rippled across every inch of her skin. She twisted her head at an angle and stared up at him, meeting the tantalizing fragrance of his cologne head on. It tickled her nose as it permeated the air around them. Suddenly Ali felt claustrophobic as his tall muscular frame towered over her, and her eyes collided with his. She had the distinct suspicion there was an insult hidden underneath his even tone. But still she couldn't understand why he baited her this way.

"No—no, they don't," she got out when she could drag sufficient air into her lungs.

"I didn't think so," he responded, continuing to hold her under his cool appraisal.

She wanted desperately to move, run, or do anything that would enable her to rip her eyes away from the sprinkling of dark hair that was visible through his open collar. The urge to reach out and run her fingers through the wiry mat was so strong, she jerked her head back around and faced the dancers.

His drawling voice continued to assault her senses. "I'm an excellent teacher," he said.

Realizing he wasn't going to disappear merely because she wished him to, Ali swung on her heels and confronted him.

"Are you now? I would never have thought it." Her own voice was laced with mockery.

He eased his shoulders back. "Why?"

This was a dangerous game she was playing, she cautioned herself as her eyes were held spellbound by the play of muscles that rippled beneath his cotton shirt. She tried in vain to ignore the unwelcome racing of her pulse.

"I'm—I'm not sure," she finally answered. "Maybe it's because you don't seem to be a patient man."

"Oh, really." He released his breath sharply. "I'm sure you must have something concrete to base that assumption on," he said, the timbre of his voice low and challenging.

Ali's skin burned. Why did she allow herself to get into a verbal fencing match with this man? Why didn't she just politely walk off and join her friends, leaving him to his own devices? *Because Ali Cameron,* an inner voice whispered, *he fascinates you. He's like no man you've ever known. You'd like nothing better than to learn what lies under that cool, closed veneer of his. To have him drop his guard and touch... Don't be ridiculous! Get hold of yourself!*

"Ali—"

At the quiet use of her name, Ali's thoughts splintered like shattered glass.

"Uh—what?"

"Damnation," he muttered softly. "Forget it. Company's coming."

His sharp tone cleared the starry haze that surrounded her with the swiftness of a heartbeat. She heard Barry and Cindy's laughter even before they came to stand beside her.

"Well, I see you two have made friends at last," Cindy remarked happily, completely oblivious to Ali's uneasy features.

Although Adam returned her grin, his eyes remained sober and unyielding.

"Adam, if it's all right with you," Barry said, "we came to steal Ali a minute and introduce her to Marge and Perry and several others."

Adam arched a cynical eyebrow. "Be my guest," he drawled. "I was just welcoming—Ali to the party along with offering to teach her how to dance country-style." His tone dripped with infuriating superiority.

Ali was convinced now that he was baiting her and enjoying every minute of it too.

Anger made her face take on the hue of red roses. But before she could give him a verbal lashing, Cindy chimed in, "Great!" She ventured a look in Ali's direction. "You *are* going to let him show you, aren't you?"

Ali blinked in surprise. "No—actually I'm not the least bit interested in learning the Cotton-Eyed-Joe," she answered primly, instead of venting the anger that smoldered inside her for fear of creating a scene and embarrassing her friends.

"Oh—well, maybe later you'll change your mind," Cindy murmured hurriedly, trying to cover the awkward moment that had descended on them following Ali's words.

Ali kept her eyes averted. "Maybe."

"I, for one, am not worried about dancing," Barry declared in a booming voice. "For starters I want to take my second best-girl and show her off." His eyes were twinkling merrily as he reached over and drew Ali close to his side. "If you'll excuse us, we'll be on our way."

The next hour found Ali shaking hands with what seemed like several hundred people. Everyone was friendly and made an effort to make her feel part of the lively group. Under their kindness she felt the chill from Adam's arrogance begin to evaporate.

But as she flitted from one group to another, she felt Adam's eyes on her. Like a moth drawn to light she found her eyes locking with his more times than she cared to count.

Several men asked her to dance but she refused them, very politely. Even Barry's invitation to teach her the simple steps of the Cotton-Eyed-Joe was declined. She noticed, however, that Adam's impressive figure was frequently among the dancers. And each time he was partnered by the same woman. This had to be Molly Deavers, the one Cindy had told her about. No matter how hard she tried, she couldn't control her curiosity. Her eyes followed their every move.

It was obvious they were on extremely familiar terms. The woman kept gliding closer to Adam as if she resented even the air between them. As Ali watched Adam twirl her around the patio in time to a fast-moving ballad, she gave Molly Deavers her undivided attention.

She appeared to be close to Adam's age. Ali had to admit, though grudgingly, that she was attractive. Her dark hair shaped her rounded face in soft casual waves, calling attention to her large eyes. Her figure was gently rounded, quite the extreme opposite to her own tall, rather thin one. But where she, Ali, was amply endowed in the chest, this woman who looked up at Adam so adoringly was just the opposite.

"If you won't dance with me, then let's track Cindy down and get in the chow line," Barry said, effectively slicing into her thoughts. "I'm famished. How about you?"

Ali turned her gaze away from the dance floor and favored Barry with a grin. "So am I," she answered shortly. *And to hell with you, Adam Forrest!*

Barry responded with a smile. "You go ahead and get in line while I pull my wife away from a gossiping bunch of women." He began shaking his head and muttering beneath his breath as he took off across the grounds.

With the food line moving faster than anticipated, Ali stepped aside to wait for Cindy and Barry to join her. The hickory-smoked smell of the barbecued beef tickled her nose, creating a rumbling in her stomach. She knew it would be suicidal to even taste the highly seasoned food, but she was sorely tempted to do so anyway.

Out of the corner of her eye Ali noticed Adam as he milled around, greeting and visiting. Although it galled her to admit it, he was indeed a fine specimen of a man. No wonder Molly Deavers hung on to him like poison ivy to a tree. He exuded the type of charm that kept women coming back for more. Except her, of course. No matter how sexually attractive she found him to be, he was definitely not for her.

Realizing that she was staring at Adam, she made an effort to drag her gaze away before she got caught. But again she was too late. She discovered Adam staring intently at her, his features molded in harsh contradiction; his lips were stern, his jaw rigid. But the look in his eyes was unmistakable. Like experiencing a jolt of electricity, she was aware of the erotic compulsion, the vibration between them.

A part of Ali's mind whispered that she should stand her ground, while another part urged her to escape. She chose the latter. On legs that suddenly felt constructed of water instead of bones, she turned and headed in the opposite direction from Adam Forrest, her breasts heaving as she struggled to pull air into her lungs.

The cool night air fanned Ali's hot cheeks as she wandered aimlessly along the edge of the unlighted grounds.

With dogged determination and willpower she had completely emptied her mind of all thoughts of Adam Forrest. Ali tipped her head backward and gazed at the stars beckoning brightly from afar. Immediately her eyes hunted for the Big Dipper. No starlight night was complete without one, she mused with delight.

Suddenly she knew she wasn't alone. The fragrance she had come to associate with him was the incriminating clue. Even though her heart began knocking against her rib cage, she kept her eyes turned heavenward. But her peripheral vision monitored his tall lanky body as the moon cast him in her view. He halted abruptly within arm's reach of her.

"The party's not to your liking?" he asked with formal politeness.

"No—I mean yes, everything's fine," she answered, striving to control the slight waver in her voice.

Even through the darkness, she felt his piercing eyes. "Then why are you out here alone?"

Ali folded her arms across her chest resentfully and resumed her walking. "If you must know, I was running from temptation," she said, referring to the rich food that had relentlessly tortured her. But the moment the words flew from her lips she regretted them. She stifled a gasp. What if he thought she was referring to him and the volatile look that had passed between them? Even if it were partially true, she couldn't stand the thought of him knowing that he had been successful in needling her.

"And why was that?" he pressed in a smooth voice. But there was a wealth of meaning underlying his words. He had slowed his long strides to match hers and they were now perfectly in step as they strolled under the cluster of trees bordering their path.

Ali was mortified. She hadn't fooled him in the least. But she was determined to save face. Why had he followed her? To do just what he was doing now—ridicule her? Of course, she told herself unhappily. Well, this time she would show him. She wouldn't rise to his bait.

"What I meant to say was, the *food* was much too tempting for me to stay there," she said in what she hoped was a cool and level tone. She totally ignored the loud heartbeats that drummed in her ears.

"Oh, because of your ulcer, you mean?"

She swung around to face him. "How did you know about my ulcer?"

"Barry told me."

"Is that *all* Barry told you?" she asked sarcastically, not bothering to mask her irritation at Barry's loose tongue.

"No," Adam responded coolly, "as a matter of fact, it wasn't."

Ali experienced a sinking feeling in the pit of her stomach. "What exactly *did* he tell you?"

He paused a moment. "Only that you've been ill along with a watered-down version of why you left the Big Apple."

Anger and frustration swept over Ali. "Damn Barry," she muttered aloud, "just wait until—"

"Don't be too quick to blame Barry. It's not his fault. I pressed him to tell me."

Ali was astounded. "You—you did what?"

"That's right. I pressed him for the information."

"But—but, why?" she began stammering, only to let her voice disappear into the gentle flow of the wind.

"Would you believe idle curiosity?" His tone was ironic, and he appeared to be watching her closely.

Ali barely managed to keep a lid on her temper. She couldn't believe the audacity of this man. Well, two can play this game, she thought with a renewed surge of spirit. She'd see how *he* would hold up under the pressure of twenty questions.

"What about you, Dr. Forrest, what are you hiding?" she asked sweetly, coming to rest beside the gnarled trunk of a huge oak tree. She leaned against it negligently and peered up into his face.

If Adam was taken aback at her prying question, he didn't show it, at least not outwardly. His teeth shone in the moonlight as his lips broke into an amused smile. "I see the lady hath claws."

Ignoring his attempt to placate her, she drove on, "Would you believe idle curiosity?" she mimicked.

A chuckle rattled deep in his throat. "I gracefully surrender this round. Okay, fire away," he said, "I'm a stationary target."

Ali thought for a long moment. "Is it because of your ex-wife that you don't like women?" she asked bluntly for the sole purpose of shocking and routing him out of his complacency.

The sharp intake of his breath vibrated through the still night air at the same time his face became a hard mask. Suddenly Ali wished she could recall her words. Regret at having said them overcame her. This time she feared she had gone too far.

"I see that you've also been doing your homework," he said tightly.

Ali felt trapped in a vise of her own making. "Not—not really." She swallowed hard. "Cindy only told me that your wife left you—"

"Just to set the record straight, I sent her packing," he spat harshly.

"So now you look at every woman through jaundiced eyes," she retaliated, squelching the image of him and Molly Deavers closely embracing on the dance floor.

"Not every woman, Miss Cameron, only *your* kind."

Ali's head snapped back as if she had been clipped on the chin. "Why you—you arrogant—" Unconsciously she raised her hand, itching to slap his smug face.

"I wouldn't, if I were you," he drawled in a dangerously low tone as he locked his hand around her arm.

"Let go of me," she hissed.

"All in good time, Miss Cameron. All in good time."

"I don't have to stand here and take this—"

"Oh, yes, you do," he said harshly. "You're on my turf now. Anyway, I think it's time you learned you shouldn't play with fire unless you're prepared to get burned." His last words were uttered only a hairsbreadth from her face. If she moved a fraction, she would rub up against him.

Realizing she had overplayed her hand and was now at his mercy, Ali began to plead. "Adam—please."

"Please, what—" he whispered, his warm breath fanning her cheek.

"Please, don't," she whimpered, trying to conquer the fright that clogged her throat.

"Please, yes," he mocked her. "You've been begging for this from the first moment I met you."

"No—no." Ali moved her head from side to side. "That's not true," she cried. With a sudden movement she felt her back grind into the trunk of the tree. She had nowhere to go. She was his captive.

"Shh, be still," he demanded sharply. "You've been dying of curiosity to know what it would feel like to have an Arkansas hillbilly kiss you, touch you."

"No," she denied again while she still had enough air in her lungs to speak. "I don't want you to touch me!" She couldn't admit even to herself that he spoke the truth. It would leave her too open, too susceptible. She couldn't chance it.

"Lady, you're a damned liar," he rasped as he boldly cushioned his aroused masculinity against her stomach.

"Adam—" she wheezed.

His mouth, as it moved over hers, slammed the rest of her sentence back down her throat. Its firmness plundered her lips with devastating intensity.

The instant his tongue found its way between her teeth and meshed with hers, she ceased to struggle. Spirals of heat traveled through her body and settled in the lower regions, setting her on fire.

His hands slid down her while their mouths clung in hopeless abandonment. His fingers probed each breast, taunting the nipples until they begged to break through the confining garments and know the true touch of his hands.

Gone now was Adam's anger, his intent to hurt. Instead there was a driving need to appease a hunger in his gut that knew no bounds. The warm, intoxicating feel of this woman in his arms made him desperate to prove that she was no mirage, that her taut nipples were indeed pelting his chest with their aroused warmness.

Reluctantly, he tore his mouth away from hers, but not before he drew her close against him so that she was molded to every hard muscle in his body.

For Ali it still wasn't enough. She wanted to be closer, much closer. She wanted to feel skin against skin....

As though he could read her mind, Adam began to slowly unbutton her blouse while his mouth nipped at the swan-like softness of her neck.

Tugging at the front clasp of her bra, her breasts spilled forth to receive the questing gentleness of his fingers. They splayed across the fullness of each breast, revealing their capacity to more than fill his hand. Then he began to rotate the nipples in the center of his rough palm.

"Adam," she breathed, now desperate for him to cure the ache that throbbed between her legs. It was a feeling she had never before experienced. She wound her arms around the back of his neck, no longer bothering to deny that she craved his touch. She held on to him, giving no thought to the consequences.

But Adam was aware of them, brutally aware. For him the situation was nearing a point of no return. Suddenly, furious with himself, an expletive splintered his lips before he wrenched her arms from around his neck and stepped back from her.

The low moan that escaped from Ali's lips almost drove him over the brink! The soft swell of moonlight bathed her features, allowing him to see the agony reflected in her eyes as she stared up at him.

His jaw clenched. "Ali, don't look at me like that," he ground out savagely, "or I'll be forced to give you what you're begging for."

Ali was horrified. Could he possibly think she was used to doing this type of thing?

Adam began to pace back and forth in front of her, dragging his palms down his pants legs. "Dammit, why did you have to come here?"

Tears stung her eyes. Humiliation wrapped its tentacles around her with strangling ferocity. "You—*bastard!*" she cried, as she tried to button her blouse with hands that were shaking.

Managing to gather what was left of her torn dignity, Ali dug in her heel and ran as if the devil himself was after her. She didn't care where her legs were taking her. She just wanted to place as much distance between her and Adam Forrest as she possibly could.

Chapter 5

Slowly the dark blue clouds were dispersing from the sky. Already the muted light of dawn could be seen as it gently cascaded over the clouds bringing with it the promise of a clear and beautiful day.

But Adam Forrest's thoughts, as he leaned over a fence that separated his clinic from his pasture land, were just the opposite from clear and beautiful. They were twisted and excruciatingly painful. Even the peaceful tranquillity of his beloved land proudly spread before him couldn't ease his troubled mind.

He breathed deeply, filling his lungs with the cool early morning air. The fact that he couldn't depend on his proven tranquillizer, his great love for his land, to pull him up by the boot straps plunged him further into depression. From the moment he had set foot on this ground, it had become his life, his salvation—especially after Mary left. Through daily toil he had let the earth soak up his pain and mend the torn fragments of his manhood. This land, to some extent, was intertwined with his blood; it served as an extension of himself.

Now suddenly everything he had worked so hard to build, to say nothing of his coveted peace of mind, was in jeopardy. All because of the appearance of a woman from a different world, a different life, but a woman who nevertheless had the power to make his loins burn with the eagerness of a youth as well as the agonizing frustration of a mature male.

Adam rested his forearms on the top rail of the gate. God! He was tired and weary to the depths of his bones. Since the night of the barbecue a week ago, his insomnia had steadily grown worse, but it was his restlessness and discontent that concerned him.

Even now, the image of Ali Cameron's tall, willowy figure haunted him. Imprinted on his mind with indelible ink was the mat white skin that had emphasized the pain in her dark, slumberous eyes. He cursed the moonlight anew at having allowed him to see her features when he had so brutally broken their embrace.

Now, this moment, he longed to feel again the throbbing roundness of her breasts, to coax their pink crests to diamondlike hardness. And her smell. Lilacs. She had smelled of lilacs. Suddenly, he felt his tongue swell as he remembered the taste of her skin against his lip, the way she had blindly adhered her lissome body to his, the yielding softness of her tights that gave him a preview of what it would be like to have her moistness create a sheath around his pulsating hardness. It would be exhilarating agony.

Dammit to hell! he cursed himself and his thoughts. In his life he had never felt so cornered by the nameless emotions that now raced and collided head-on with the chosen path for his life.

Until he had gazed into Ali's lovely eyes, he had never envisioned anything or anyone interfering with his job as a country veterinarian or his productivity as a cattle rancher.

Molly had always been there when he needed a woman. He cared for her and her son, Chad, but he had made it clear from the beginning of their relationship that he wanted no entanglements, no commitments. Their arrangement had been enough. Until now.

"Damn her!" he swore aloud as he jammed a tightened fist into the upper rung of the gate. Even the feel of the rough wood slicing off the top layer of his knuckles with the precision of a surgeon's scalpel failed to penetrate his entombed senses.

Forget her, Forrest! She's poison—the kind that gets in your bloodstream and plays havoc with your mind. Forget that she wanted you as much as you wanted her. Remember in three months time, she'll be gone. Gone back to a world filled with glitter and glamor. For God's sake man, her come-on to you was nothing but a game to her. Forget about her sweet breasts....

"Adam, Adam! Can you hear me?"

The urgency behind the use of his name snapped him back to reality with startling clarity. He whirled around to encounter the limping figure of his clinic aide hurrying toward him, waving a hand.

Forcing an even tone to his voice, Adam hailed, "What's up, Matt?"

Matt Arnold was huffing and puffing by the time he trudged up the hill and stood at a standstill in front of Adam. "Not sure, Doc," he allowed, tipping his hat back and scratching his head. "But from the way Mrs. Cindy talked on the phone, you'd best grab your bag and head over that way. She sounded a mite upset to my way of thinking.''

Fear knotted Adam's stomach muscles into tight, hard knots as he strode quickly in the direction of the clinic. Matt had to run in order to match Adam's long strides.

''God, I hope it's not another of those senseless accidents,'' Adam remarked grimly, more to himself than to his companion.

Six months ago he had rushed to the dude ranch for just such an accident. A guest had separated himself from the guided-tour group and provoked a horse into exploring virgin territory. As a result the horse had slipped, breaking a leg in the process. The rider had been thrown and had suffered a concussion.

Hurrying through the back door of the clinic, Adam ignored the yelping greetings of wet-tongued boarders as he grabbed his bag off the countertop and marched back outside.

''Matt, tell Margie to hold the fort. I hope to be back in time to keep my office hours. You know where I'll be if another emergency crops up.'' With those words, he jumped into his pickup and was gone.

A twofold sense of fear gripped his insides as the Peaceful Valley Dude Ranch came into view. He dreaded what he might encounter as a veterinarian, but more than that he dreaded coming face to face with Ali. His palms turned sweaty as he curled his fingers around the steering wheel in a death grip.

Shamefully he felt his manhood strain against his jeans. Who the hell was he trying to kid? In spite of the flogging he had just given himself, he still wanted her and was starving for the sight of her. But, after the other night, he had few illusions she would ever come near him again.

God! he thought as the brought his truck to a screeching halt inside the grounds, it was going to be a long, hot summer.

"Ali, come quick," Cindy shouted, "there's been an accident. Barry needs us." The front door slammed shut loudly behind her.

Ali swallowed her fear along with the bite of toast she had just shoved into her mouth and followed Cindy.

"Cindy, for gosh sakes, slow down," Ali hollered as she broke into a dead run in order to catch up with her friend. "You're not even supposed to be out of bed, much less running like you're on fire," she added between spurts of heavy breathing.

Cindy begrudgingly slowed her pace and allowed Ali to catch up with her.

"What happened?" Ali demanded.

"I can't believe it," Cindy cried, "but Magic's leg buckled under her and flung a child over her head, slinging him hard enough on the ground to knock him out."

"Oh, God!" Ali groaned, not knowing what to say to comfort Cindy.

"If that child is seriously injured, I don't know—" Cindy's voice broke off on a sob.

"Shh, take it easy," Ali cautioned. "I'm sure Barry'll have everything under control. Besides, Dr. Hanson would have a fit if he knew you were stirring. I can't believe Barry wanted you to come down to the stables and help him." Ali turned her eyes sharply on Cindy, a question in their depths.

A flush crept up Cindy's face. "Well—uh—," she stammered, "he only wanted me to call Dr. Johns and Adam." She blinked. "Nothing was said about needing my help or yours." Her last words were spoken barely above a whisper.

Ali threw her hands up in utter despair. "Have you lost your mind?" she asked. "You've been dizzy for three days and—"

"I know," Cindy wailed, "but I was feeling much better this morning and I just couldn't stand not knowing what was happening."

Ali's eyes softened as she took in Cindy's pale, pinched features. Then she released her breath slowly, silently. This morning's accident was typical of the way things had been going lately for both her and Cindy. Four days ago now Cindy began having dizzy spells. Severe ones. Another trip to the doctor had curtailed her activities to a greater degree. Cindy bemoaned this sudden turn of events but had adjusted to it extremely well. Ali had used Cindy's inability to work to browbeat Barry into letting her help on the ranch. He had finally agreed, showing her how to coordinate group activities and games for the younger guests.

She had plunged headfirst into the work. It had given her a chance to soak up the sunshine and take advantage of the exercise the spontaneity of youth provided. But more important, working had kept her mind occupied, and off Adam.

She had gone over and over the nightmarish events of Adam's party. She had berated herself repeatedly for allowing him to touch her emotions, *to touch her!* She'd be damned if she'd be a whipping post for his frustrations over his ex-wife. Hadn't she promised herself never again to be at the mercy of a man?

For years her career had been the driving force behind her existence. Male companionship had been a luxury she allowed herself, *not* a necessity. But the moment she had laid eyes on Adam Forrest, something had happened. His bold sensuality had created a need within her, which heightened when he had ravaged her mouth and touched her pliant flesh with his calloused hands. Her senses had clamored for more. She realized he had stirred the embers of her slumbering passion and had fanned a need within her that only *he* could assuage.

Even now, after the way he had rejected her and after a week of branding herself a confused and demented fool, she still craved the sight of him. But under no circumstances could she let Adam know this. It had to be her soul's secret. She simply could not risk suffering another rejection at his hands. She was much too vulnerable.

Adam's tall, commanding figure absorbed her total vision as she and Cindy shuffled around the corner and stepped into the riding ring.

Anger? Where was the anger she knew she should be feeling? Instead, a warm, shaky sensation invaded her bloodstream leaving her weak and suddenly disoriented.

Adam's attention was centered on Magic, the Medfords' prize mare, who lay pathetically inert at the edge of his booted foot. It was obvious even to Ali's unschooled eyes that the horse was in pain. It took Barry and a ranch hand to hold the gentle mare still so Adam could examine her.

While Ali moved aside, not wanting to get in the way, Cindy dropped immediately to her knees beside her husband. She turned tortured eyes up to his face. "What— what about the child? How—how badly was he hurt?" she stammered, fright making her voice sound wheezy.

Barry placed an arm around Cindy's waist, balancing her against his thigh. "It's nothing serious, hon," he explained soberly. "The kid just had the wind knocked out of him. Dr. Johns is with him now." He paused, lowering his gaze to Magic. "I just wish Magic had fared half as well," he added with a grimace.

Cindy seemed to go weak with relief on learning of the child's condition. "Thank God," she mumbled before turning her attention to the horse. With gentle fingers she began to knead the horse's forehead while she talked to her in a soft, soothing tone.

Miraculously, the mare stilled, making it possible for Adam to cut the hairs away from the wound. Ali crept closer but remained silent. She halted adjacent to Cindy's left shoulder and peered over it.

"Oh, no!" she gasped aloud, then jammed her hand between her teeth to keep from crying out again and disturbing the animal. Exposed to her eyes was an oozing gash that spanned the lower half of the mare's leg. Ali felt her stomach turn a double somersault as she watched Adam's fingers probe and test the raw and gaping hole.

Suddenly Magic whinnied pitifully while laboring vigorously to get up on all fours. The excruciating pain the horse was forced to endure tore at Ali's heart. Tears stung her eyes as she kneeled quickly and joined in the effort to hold Magic's heaving and thrashing body steady.

Sniffing back the tears that threatened to blur her vision, Ali's eyes were drawn to Adam's long sensitive fingers as he went to work mending the leg. He worked quickly and silently. She watched as the sweat collected over his jutting brow and then began to trickle slowly down his face. It took all her willpower to keep from leaning over and wiping it off. But when he dug into his bag and came up with a long needle and several vials of liquid, she closed her eyes and prayed she wouldn't be sick. Regaining her composure, she opened her eyes slowly, only this time, she refused to watch Adam's fingers as he manipulated the needle.

She concentrated instead on Adam. Even with his features screwed tightly in concentration and still hampered by the river of perspiration running down his face, she found him to be disturbingly perfect. She noticed, for the first time, the numerous strains of gray hairs that intermingled with his dark ones and how they curled at the nape of his neck.

Every muscle in his shoulders and arms strained against his shirt and they, too, were doused in sweat. His jaw reminded her of a smooth piece of granite. There was a controlled violence about him as he performed his duty as a surgeon.

Was it possible he resented her presence? *That's absurd!* she told herself defiantly. But then she wasn't so sure. Something was wrong. And she knew it wasn't because he was worried about his ability to do his job either. No. He exuded confidence and competence at every turn. And not once had he acknowledged her presence.

Ali was damned if she'd stay where she wasn't wanted. She'd have to be a glutton for punishment to stay anywhere near him after the disgraceful way he treated her the last time they were together. *Would she ever learn?*

Then it was over. Adam had successfully completed his task. The end of the gruelling thirty minutes was met with relieved sighs from everyone, especially Cindy and Barry.

Cindy's eyes were cloudy with tears as she gave Adam a watery smile. "As usual," she whispered, "I don't know how to thank you—"

"Don't," Adam returned brusquely. Then he smiled. "If I can get Magic girl to be as good as new, that's all the thanks I'll need.'

"Adam," Barry asked reluctantly, "do you honestly think she'll ever be fit for the riding trail again?"

"It looks promising," Adam sighed. "Later, though, when she comes around and we get her up, I'll be able to give you a better opinion."

Wordlessly Barry nodded his thanks before extending a hand to Cindy and pulling her up to stand beside him.

Adam's eyes softened on Cindy. "Don't worry about Magic. She'll be fine. You and Barry go on and see about the boy."

"Be sure you stop by the house for coffee before you leave," Barry told him before shifting his eyes to Ali who was still crouched on the ground. "You comin', Ali?"

Barry's invitation was like manna from Heaven. Ignoring the sun's stinging rays that flayed her back and shoulders, Ali grappled to stand on legs threatening to buckle beneath her.

Suddenly a hand shot out and curled around her arm, lifting her with gentle ease to her feet. Ali swung her head back and met the stabbing penetration of Adam's eyes.

"Go ahead, Barry. Ali can come with me."

"No—please, I—I feel sick," Ali said, using the first credible excuse that popped into her mind.

Adam's expression darkened. "What's the matter, city girl," he drawled harshly, "can't stand the sight of a little blood?" His strong fingers gained a tighter grip on her tender flesh. It was almost as if he took perverse delight in hurting her.

Ali stiffened visibly. Her fingers itched to reach up and slap the smirk off his chiseled features. How dare he talk to her like that? She dug her nails into her palms, turning to see if the others had heard his insulting remark. It was then she realized they were alone. Obviously Barry had taken it for granted she would remain with Adam as he and Cindy were already making their way toward the lodges.

Seeing no reason now to mask the fury that surged through her body with vicious force, she jerked her head around to face Adam. Flags of crimson dotted each cheek.

"Get your hands off me and don't ever touch me again," she hissed, her words ripping through the quiet morning like bullets through a tin can.

Adam's eyes fired sparks to rival hers. "If my memory serves me correctly, you didn't mind my touch before," he countered harshly.

Ali's composure snapped. "You're disgusting!" she cried, fighting back the deluge of tears that were lodged in her throat. She then lowered her eyes and began rubbing the spot his fingers had marked on her fair skin.

A muffled curse tore through Adam's lips as he raised his hand to the back of his neck in a weary gesture. Damn! What the hell was wrong with him? The sweet remembrance of her had haunted him relentlessly. Then why did he persist in picking a fight with her every time he was near her? Why didn't he do what he longed to do—grab her and kiss her until they were both senseless?

In the past he'd had no qualms about using women to satisfy his sexual appetite. And Molly was no different. *But Ali was.* That was the crux of the whole matter, he thought with grim honesty. And that scared the hell out of him!

He looked at her now and saw that tears had gathered on her lashes, giving her rounded eyes a haunting beauty. He dragged his eyes away. He wanted to apologize, but he didn't know how.

"Dammit, Ali, I'm—"

"Please—just leave me alone," she said, her voice low and strained.

His hooded eyes were on her again. "That's the whole problem," he murmured in a strangled tone, "you do please me. Too damned much!'' His fingers gently cupped her chin and lifted it, forcing her eyes to meet the melting softness of his gaze.

Ali swallowed hard as the panicky need to escape once again invaded her limbs. But instead she just stood there, looking at him with her heart caught in a ridiculously sweet storm.

"Ali,'' he muttered hoarsely as he slowly lowered his head and began moving a finger the length of her lips.

"Uh, uh,'' Barry coughed, "am I interrupting anything?'' His voice was half amused, half impatient.

Ali's heart dove to her toes at the sound of Barry's voice. Tearing her eyes away from Adam, she breathed deeply in an effort to calm her jangled nerves. But still she could not look Barry in the eye.

A mask of indifference had slipped over Adam's face, replacing the look of passion. He nodded briefly at Barry. "No—you didn't interrupt anything,'' he said gruffly. "We were just leaving.''

Barry was embarrassed. "Well, I just wanted to check on Magic before I headed to the house.'' There was a lengthy pause. "Cindy's already there,'' he said lamely.

Adam smiled and flexed his back muscles. "A cup of Cindy's coffee sounds great to me,'' he said, making an effort to release the biting tension.

Barry's gaze wandered to Magic. "Has there been any change?'' he asked.

Adam shook his head sympathetically. "Not yet, it's too soon.''

They walked back to the house in silence. Ali struggled desperately to reorient her thoughts. What did Adam want from her? And why did she allow him to trifle with her emotions? To needle her so? She wished she understood how his mind worked. Around others he was the epitome of charm. Around her he acted like a bear with a sore paw. She knew he desired her. She read it in the smoldering darkness of his eyes. Then why did he continue to mock her, to ridicule her? What galled her more than anything was that no matter how he treated her, she still wanted him.

Cindy greeted them from the couch. Ali instantly forgot her own problems and centered her attention on her friend.

"How are you feeling?"

"Considering all that's happened today, I guess I'm doing about as well as can be expected." Cindy made a move as if to get up, but Ali stopped her with a tentative hold on her arm.

"Stay put," Ali ordered. "I'll serve the coffee."

"Yes, ma'am!" Cindy said, raising her hand in a mock salute.

Ignoring Adam as best she could, Ali played the hostess. While the men discussed the events of the day, she poured the coffee and put a frozen pan of cinnamon rolls in the microwave. Although she never once let her eyes stray toward Adam, she was not immune to his probing glances.

As she placed a double serving of hot rolls in front of him while refilling his coffee cup, she made a conscious effort not to touch him. But his presence dominated the room. His cologne, mixed with the perspiration that still clung to his body, wafted towards her, causing another surge of primitive emotions to course through her.

"Thanks," he mumbled, dark brows quirking above his lean brooding face as his eyes met hers.

"You're—welcome," she replied shakily. Determined to give herself breathing room, Ali quickly prepared a tray and carried it across the room to Cindy.

Cindy frowned. "Is a cup of hot chocolate all you're having?"

"I'm not hungry," Ali smiled. "Remember I was eating breakfast when all the hullabaloo took place."

Another frown fell over Cindy's face. "I'll be so glad when things begin to take a turn for the bet—"

"Hey, honey," Barry called, interrupting her sentence. "It just dawned on me tomorrow night's that damned hayride."

"Oh, damn," Cindy muttered, and looked at her husband who was now moving from the kitchen to the den, Adam following closely on his heels.

Ali looked puzzled. "What's the big deal about a hayride?"

"The big deal," Cindy explained patiently, "is precisely this: I'm supposed to supervise our first big ride for nearly fifty kids."

Ali rolled her eyes upward and then laughed. "Someone else will just have to take your place."

"Who, for instance?"

"Barry?" Ali replied quickly.

Barry shook his head. "Can't do it. I'm taking a group of adults on an overnight camping and fishing trip."

Ali played with her lower lip and turned her dark eyes on Barry. "Surely you have an aide who's capable of the task." She spread her hands. "There's no way Cindy can go," she declared adamantly.

"You're right about that," Barry responded, "but at the moment, I can't think of anyone on our staff who's responsible enough to handle the rowdy youngsters. But don't worry, I'll come up with a solution."

"What about me?" Ali asked.

"You!" Barry and Cindy cried in unison.

Ali stiffened. "Why not? I'm perfectly capable of supervising a group of young hooligans."

Cindy cocked her head to one side, a doubtful expression covering her features. "Oh, Ali, no, we couldn't allow you to do that—"

Barry turned abruptly toward Adam, who had been sitting quietly taking it all in. "Would you by any chance—" Then he stopped midsentence, a flush crossing his cheekbones. "Ah, forget it. It was a crazy idea anyway," he finished contritely.

"I think it's a great idea," Cindy chimed in enthusiastically, knowing exactly what had been on her husband's mind. "Would you consider it, Adam?"

Ali's next breath hung in midair, but somehow words tumbled from her lips. "I'm sure Adam has more important things to do." She refused to look at the man only a stone's throw from her.

"If you don't mind," Adam said with pointed amusement directed toward Ali, "I'm perfectly capable of speaking for myself." He paused significantly. "And yes, I'll do my part to help with the hayride."

Ali gulped down a mouthful of hot chocolate, but it went down her windpipe the wrong way. She began coughing heartily, while her face suffused with wild color. God! Talk about embarrassed. Out of the corner of her eyes she could see Adam's eyes dancing with devilish laughter. When she had at last regained her composure and crushed her frustration, she injected a calm note into her voice she was far from feeling. "Barry, I'm certain I can hack it alone," she said, completely ignoring Adam's spoken consent.

Barry smiled indulgently. "I'm sure you could, but since Adam's volunteered, we might as well take him up on it."

"Whew!" Cindy exerted gleefully. "You two are an answer to my prayers. Now I can rest with ease and pamper my little one here." She laughed as she patted the rounded contour of her stomach.

"That's right, little mama," Adam declared firmly, "your first priority must be the baby and leave the rest to us."

Defeat settled heavily on Ali's shoulders. If she voiced any further objections, she just might force Cindy into going on the hayride. She couldn't take that chance. As long as Cindy needed her, she wouldn't let her down. But by the same token, she wasn't about to let Adam Forrest use her as a punching bag. Tomorrow night she vowed she would hold on to her cool even if it killed her.

"Well," Barry said as he stood up and grabbed his hat from the back of the couch, "it's about time I had another look at Magic." He bent over and kissed Cindy on the cheek. "See you later, hon."

"I'll go with you," Adam said, "but only for a moment. I'm sure I'll have a full clinic when I get back," he added as he ambled his way across the room to stand by the door.

Ali kept her gaze averted. She refused to be the target of those mocking eyes anymore today. Tomorrow would come soon enough.

"Ladies, thanks for the goodies and the company," Adam said, acting the epitome of charm, before closing the door behind him and Barry with a jarring slam.

Somehow Ali pulled her shell-shocked body together and made her way into the kitchen where she stripped the table of the dirty dishes.

"Forget those dishes for now," Cindy urged, following Ali into the kitchen. "They're not going anywhere. Why don't you go for a swim." She paused. "I'll join you after I've rested a while longer.'

Ali pushed her tousled curls behind her ear. "I'll have this mess cleaned up in a jiffy," Ali stated firmly. "You just go crawl into bed and don't worry about a thing."

Cindy hesitated, shifting from one foot to the other. "Ali—you're not mad at me, are you?"

There was a moment of silence. "No—I'm not mad at you."

"Are you sure?"

"Yes, I'm sure.'

"I'll see you later then," Cindy responded lightly.

The moment Ali heard Cindy close her bedroom door, she began to attack the kitchen with a vengeance. It was a wonder she hadn't broken the plates into a million pieces as she stacked them on top of each other and then slammed them down on the counter.

"Why didn't someone suggest they just cancel the damned hayride?" she muttered to herself as she began cramming the dishes in the dishwasher.

What did one wear on a hayride with fifty young "darlings?" What else but the proverbial sloppy jeans and sweat shirt, Ali told herself with a heartfelt sigh. She flung several pairs of jeans past her in the closet before sighting her oldest and most beleaguered pair.

Snatching the garments off the hangers, she donned them quickly. She was already late. In fifteen minutes she was due to meet Adam down by the stables. She had made the mistake of chatting too long with Cindy while she dressed to go visit with friends for the evening.

Quickly she brushed her tangled curls, securing them away from her ears and forehead with a wide yellow ribbon. After tying the ribbon on top, she shifted her bow to the back so only the band was visible. She added only slightly to her eye makeup and frosted her lips with gloss. After spraying herself with her favorite fragrance and slipping into her boots, she was ready. She deliberately refrained from adding any blusher to her cheeks. They were already too pink, she noted, but refused to dwell on the reason.

The late summer evening smelled fresh and cool as Ali made her way toward the designated meeting place. She spotted the haywagon immediately only to stop dead in her tracks. "Oh, no!" she cried disbelievingly.

Instead of the truck-pulled wagon she had envisioned, a team of mules was hooked up to the massive flatbed wagon that was surrounded by high split-rail sideboards. It was filled with mounds of hay. She knew now why Barry and Cindy hadn't wanted to answer her questions concerning tonight's venture. A smile played around her lips. They were afraid she'd change her mind and refuse to go. Well, she'd show them and Adam Forrest too. This city girl was tougher than they thought.

She leaned over and placed her face next to the sweet-smelling hay and took a whiff.

"Good evening."

Ali jumped at Adam's words and spun around. "Goodness," she croaked, throwing her hand up to her heart, "you scared me.'

"Sorry."

She licked her bloodless lips. "That's—all right." To her dismay, a faint tremor ran through her voice. She prayed Ali hadn't noticed. Despite her promised detachment, his presence filled her senses. Her brain hadn't been able as yet to erase the memory of how his mouth had felt against hers or the way his fingers had nurtured her nipples to budding hardness...

"Well, what do you think?" he asked, a challenge lurking in the hidden depths of his eyes.

"I—I think it's going to be great fun," she replied quickly, her body locked in a stubborn stance.

"We'll see," he countered tauntingly. "Wait here then while I round up the driver and the kids. An aide has them grouped together in the rec room reading them the riot act."

She watched Adam's disappearing figure with an empty feeling inside her. She knew she'd scored a victory. From the curt tone of his voice he had obviously expected her to complain about the primitive conditions surrounding the hayride. Why then didn't she feel a sense of satisfaction at having won that round?

Left to her own devices, she leaned against the wagon's wooden frame and waited impatiently for Adam. She didn't have to wait long. He appeared shortly, followed by at least fifty exuberant youngsters. She marveled again at how devastatingly handsome he was. His eyes and face were brimming with undisguised laughter from something the cherub-faced little girl skipping beside him was saying as she matched his pace step by step.

Ali's heart began clanging like wind chimes on a blustery winter's day as Adam stopped near her, his face still soft with traces of laughter. *Why hadn't I noticed his dimples before now?* she wondered in total bemusement.

Unconsciously moving to the side, she watched as Adam herded the majority of the excited children into the wagon. Her eyes were riveted to the sinewy strength of his arms as he lifted child after child, too young to climb by themselves, onto the hay. Suddenly a statement her beloved grandmother made to her once flashed across her mind, "A man who loves animals and children is a man to be trusted."

At once Ali realized she was not doing anything to help. Rousing herself into action, she moved quickly to Adam's side. Before she could say anything to him, however, he turned and looked down at her, a brooding expression having replaced his smile.

"Ready?" he clipped.

"Yes," she replied stiffly, feeling the sting of his censure.

"Are you sure, city girl? This is the way we do things in the wild west—primitively."

Deciding to ignore his baiting, she tossed him a radiant smile. "This is one city girl who's looking forward to her first hayride—primitive or not," she stated emphatically.

At that precise moment, Adam was feeling *primitive*. He was positive the hottest stretch of desert he knew could not compete with the intense heat that rushed through his body. Raking his eyes over Ali's face, he thought she had never looked lovelier. The sun had lightened her hair until it was the color of pure honey. Her skin no longer looked pale. It now had a healthy, vibrant cast to it. Her faded jeans pronounced every curve as they adhered to her slender thighs and long, trim legs. He tried not to stare at the burgeoning fullness of her breasts as they rammed in obvious agitation against her lightweight sweater. He swallowed convulsively and jammed his hands in his pockets to keep from grabbing her.

Was there a chance that perhaps he had misjudged her? When she had smiled at him just now, she almost seemed innocent, untouched. Could it be possible that she wasn't like Mary—brittle and sophisticated, unwilling to compromise or adjust to change of any kind? That underneath all her outward calm and sophistication lay a warm, unselfish woman?

Whoa, Forrest! Stuff it. You're asking for all kinds of trouble with thoughts like these, he warned himself with irksome candor. But no matter how hard he came down on himself, it didn't stop him from wanting her....

The sound of loud giggles brought him back to reality abruptly. He whirled around in time to see Ali making an effort to get on the wagon. Several of the older boys had hold of her by the arms and were struggling to pull her forward. One of her legs was bent at the knee with the booted toe positioned at the edge of the wagon while the other leg grappled to attain the same stance, giving the kids leverage with which to pull her.

"Goddammit, Ali," Adam thundered, quickly covering the distance between them, "if they don't pull your arms out of their sockets, you're bound to slip and break your fool neck."

At the sound of Adam's voice, Ali craned her neck around to call for help. "Adam—please," she gasped between spurts of laborious breathing.

"Turn her loose, boys, I've got her," Adam declared sharply, standing behind her.

The boys let go of her immediately. The muscled strength of Adam's stomach tensed as her backside plowed into it. He then gripped her firmly around the waist. "Now drop your leg and rest your entire weight against me," he ordered calmly.

Needing no second invitation, Ali let her leg plummet to the ground and, like a limp sack of flour, crashed into Adam. His arms circled her and cradled her close, bearing the full weight of her quivering limbs.

The air left her lungs as her body made solid contact with his. A curl of desire snaked through her, pumping new life into her body. But still she was powerless to move, to speak. She was trapped by his enveloping warmth.

He, too, stood motionless, taut, as if every muscle and bone in his body was stretched to the breaking point.

Unconsciously she moved. Suddenly, electrically, she became aware of the pulsating hardness of his manhood as it stirred against her buttocks.

"For God's sake, Ali," he rasped into the delicate folds of her ear, "don't move."

Chapter 6

Ali stood transfixed, barely breathing, aware of nothing but the thudding sound of her heart.

"Hey, Doc, we're ready," one of the youngsters cried from the front. "What's taking so long?" The other forty-nine followed suit and began clamoring excitedly.

The spell was shattered. Suddenly Adam dropped his arms from around Ali's waist and then gently but firmly pushed her away from him. Ali bit her lips to stifle a cry as a feeling of intense embarrassment stole over her, flagging her cheeks in a bright red color. She had the urge to run, hide, or simply disappear. She dared not look at Adam for fear of seeing the mocking ridicule she was sure would be lurking in his eyes.

She need not have worried. Adam seemed as determined to avoid her as she was him. Out of the corner of her eye, she noticed he had already put distance between them. He was on the other side of the wagon diligently checking the side railing for loose boards.

"Ma'am, would you like me to help you on the wagon?"

Recognizing the drawling voice of the driver, a camp aide, Ali turned and gave him a weak smile. "Thanks, I'd appreciate it."

"My pleasure." He grinned and tipped his hat to Ali after she was knee-deep in hay, before moving in a lazy gait toward the front of the wagon.

Ali spotted a place to sit in a deserted corner at the back of the wagon. None of the kids had claimed this section, all wanting to be as close to the sides and the end of the wagon as possible. She collapsed against the headboard and buried her posterior deep in the hay.

Suddenly the wagon lurched and then slowly, with grinding sullenness, began to creep forward. Ali watched from her secure position as Adam jumped on the end of the moving wagon amidst the laughter and shouts of the children. He then squatted down beside the two teenage aides responsible for planning the games and the songs in order to keep the youngsters occupied and out of trouble.

Ali had gone weak with relief when Cindy had told her that *all* she and Adam would be required to do was to make sure the "darling little monsters" didn't kill each other or themselves. Having never done this sort of thing, she hadn't known what would be expected of her.

But now she had the urge to join the group closest to her and take part in their fun. Anything, she reflected wryly, would be better than her own thoughts. Just thinking about the way she had nestled in Adam's arms like a homing pigeon coming to its nest made every hair on her head stand on end. Even though the encounter had been a brief one, spanning only a matter of seconds, it was long enough for the impact of his surging passion to sear through her pants and brand her with a desire so hot it threatened to engulf her. She struggled to disperse these unsettling thoughts, refusing to acknowledge even to herself that Adam Forrest was slowly but surely becoming an obsession with her.

The sound of the youngsters' laughter was infectious and diverting. Ali forced herself to concentrate on the words of the song they were belting out in their high-pitched voices as the slow-paced mules clipped along the designated path.

She couldn't help but smile as she recognized the raucous ballad "Ninety-Nine Bottles of Beer on the Wall" now being sung by every child and aide on the wagon. Stretching her legs to a more comfortable position, Ali blinked her eyes shut against the evening twilight and listened to the happy, soothing voices that rivaled the leaves rustling gently in the evening breeze.

"Mind if I join you?"

Ali's heartbeat became frantic. "No—no, of course not," she said, wrenching the words through the dry roughness in her throat. She gazed up at him.

Adam hesitated for a split second and stared at her under bushy brows. He seemed to be trying desperately to read the expression in her dark eyes, even though the murky shadows hovering around them proved to be a strong deterrent.

Ali dipped her head with the pretense of removing a piece of hay that had poked through her jeans and was prickling her thigh. She heard his sigh as he lowered his body next to hers. Although she was able to keep her eyes away from him, she wasn't having as much luck controlling her body. Her stomach began rumbling uneasily and the pulse at the base of her neck was beating wildly.

Neither spoke. An awesome and intense silence fell between them. Ali was almost afraid to breathe for fear of adding to the already explosive situation. It didn't take her long to realize, however, that she couldn't take this type of pressure much longer. Her stomach had shifted from uneasiness to the old familiar stinging and burning feeling.

Pressing her palm to her temple, Ali turned toward him and forced useless words through her stiff lips, saying the first thing that came to her mind. "Tell me about your—your work."

A smile suddenly slid across his beautifully chiseled mouth. "I was just about to ask you the same thing, about your work, that is."

"Oh," she articulated with difficulty, suddenly tongue-tied with his abrupt change of mood. But she wasn't about to look a gift horse in the mouth. She parted her soft lips into a smile, every nerve in her body tuned in to his nearness.

"Is it exciting?"

"What?" she asked lamely, forcing her thoughts away from his bulging thigh that lay near her slender one.

"Your work. Do you enjoy it?" he repeated a trifle impatiently, but a heartstopping smile tempered his tone.

"Yes, I love it. My entire life is centered around my job," she stressed adamantly, refusing to stop and question the note of defiance she heard underlying her words. "I'm determined to make Cameron Cosmetics the first-rate company it used to be."

"I see," he stated flatly.

But Ali could tell by his tone that he didn't see, that he didn't understand. He hadn't fooled her. The contempt was there.

Although his words stung, she kept her voice even. "I don't think you do." She paused. "However, what you think is of no importance to me," she added pointedly. *But dammit,* she confessed silently, *she did care what he thought. And that was her downfall.*

Ali heard his ragged breath, but when he spoke his voice, too, was even. "What are your chances for recovering from the blow your father dealt the company?"

Her chin went up a fraction. "Unfortunately the battle is all uphill," she replied. "But I'm mulling over an idea that just may change my luck," she added.

"Have you always been interested in—cosmetics?" he asked, noticing how the moonlight turned her eyes into shimmering pools.

"No—" she answered reluctantly. "I got my master's degree in chemistry, and there was a time when I thought I would go into medical research of some kind." She shrugged. "But my father changed my mind. He finally persuaded me to come into business with him. Back then Cameron was a small, insignificant company."

"Have you ever been sorry—sorry you didn't go into, say, cancer research?" he questioned soberly.

"Oh, at times," she admitted truthfully.

"Like now, for instance?" he prodded.

A deeply drawn sigh expanded Ali's lungs. "Especially now, but not enough to call it quits." She smiled. "For one reason, I could never leave the Big Apple." She tried to catch Adam's reaction to her confession, but the inky blackness surrounding them kept her from reading his facial features.

"What do you do with your spare time in the city?" he asked, sounding interested.

"Huh? I have very little spare time. But when I do get a moment to call my own, I take care of chores around the apartment." She shrugged carelessly. "You know, the usual, washing, cleaning, watering plants—"

"I'd hate that kind of life," he responded bluntly.

"How do you know? Have you ever tried it?"

"Hell, no! And don't intend to, either."

Ali pursed her lips. "Don't knock it till you've tried it," she quipped irritably.

"God forbid!" he laughed. "Give me the clean air, the trees, the moon, the stars. All those good things that make life worth living."

"New York has all that." She smiled sheepishly. "Well, all but the clean air and the trees, that is. But I still love it," she added hurriedly before he could interject another sarcastic remark. "I love the glamor, the melting pot of people." She sighed. "Of course, I abhor the crime, the drugs, and the prostitution, but somehow I've learned to tolerate the bad and dwell on the good."

"Tell me about your family," he demanded abruptly as if suddenly tired of the subject of New York City.

Ali hesitated, raising her eyes to gaze at the stars and the full moon shining so bright and pure. Adam was right. She had never seen anything lovelier than the brilliant beauty of this star-studded night.

Feeling Adam's eyes on her, Ali drew her mind out of the clouds and made an attempt to answer his question. "You don't really want to hear about my family," she hedged. "My father, you already know about. And my mother—" Her voice faltered. "You sure don't want to hear about her."

"That bad, huh?"

"Worse."

"What seems to be her problem?"

"Greed."

Adam laughed. "You don't mince words, do you?"

"This may sound terrible to you, but if there was ever a flesh and blood barracuda, it's my mother, Evelyn. She tries to bend everything and everyone to her will. If she can't, she simply devours them."

"She sounds like a lovely lady," Adam remarked sarcastically.

"Oh, you don't know the half of it. She is gnashing her teeth because I came to Arkansas. She's convinced I'm placing my own needs above those of the company. What she's really afraid of is that she'll have to go on the welfare rolls." She ended her tirade on a bitter sob and then felt sudden remorse and embarrassment at having bared her soul to him. What had come over her? She couldn't ever remember being this loose-tongued with a virtual stranger. But then, she couldn't label Adam Forrest a stranger either, not when he had touched her so intimately....

"Ali—" Adam breathed, acutely aware of the hurt and anger that was embedded deep within her. He longed to hold her close. But, sweet Heavens, not because he felt sorry for her but because of what her warm body pressing against his side was doing to him. He wanted to feel *all* of her lush softness next to him, not in anger, as before, but in a hot shared passion.

She blinked at the softly spoken use of her name and turned toward him blinking again, trying to bring his face into focus. He seemed much closer now, different somehow. Then she knew; it was the tortured sound in his voice.

The hard slam of her heartbeat crashed against her ribs as she suddenly became frightened by this new, gentle Adam Forrest. Ali fought to remember where she was, to remember that she was in the company of fifty boisterous youngsters, who still sang at the top of their lungs. Hearing their loud voices reminded her that they were oblivious to her and Adam's presence. The children were having too much fun to notice the two of them stowed away in the corner. A tremor shook her body.

"Cold?"

She tried to speak but the effort was futile. She nodded her head.

"Well, if that's the problem, I can solve it easily," Adam said, a husky timbre to his voice.

Ali felt an odd thrill of apprehension jump into her stomach when he abruptly left her side, scooted over, and grabbed a blanket off the stack piled up in the opposite corner.

As if programmed, Ali leaned over slightly and let him drape the blanket around her shoulders. He then placed his arm around her, at the same time pulling the other end of her blanket over his shoulder and letting the remainder of it fall across the front of them.

Ali's senses were going haywire. His strong arm reached out and hauled her close against his side. Her body jerked as if she had been plugged into a live electric socket.

"Better, hmm," he murmured, shifting his position so that Ali's head settled against his chest. Impulsively she snuggled deeper to draw from his warmth. Adam's hand began to caress her arm with the same vibrancy and urgency as their heartbeats.

She blocked everything out of her mind except this man who held her in the folds of his arms as if he never intended to let her go. All five of Ali's senses were tuned in to his every move, his every heartbeat. *Kiss me!* her mind screamed. *No, don't!* it yelled back. Suddenly she knew she was on a collision course; she'd be damned if she didn't and damned if she did.

"Ali—" he whispered as his fingers began wandering over the planes of her face, fluttering across her eyebrows, her eyes, before making their way down to her lips. He then began to outline their tumultuous fullness with sweet, gentle strokes. They parted unerringly for him, bidding his index finger to invade their inner softness.

Ali ceased to breathe for the span of time he traced, massaged, and sought to pilfer the honeyed sweetness. This erotic endeavor feathered an ache in places that had never been awakened in her body. She sensed, too, that Adam was holding on to his control by a mere thread. The knotting hardness of his muscles was a dead giveaway.

Then in one swift motion, his finger fled her lips and cupped her chin, tilting it back. His warm, minty breath brushed her mouth as he spoke. "Your sweetness is ripping my guts to tiny shreds."

His mouth seared hers with determined accuracy. It was not a gentle kiss. He purged her lips of all their moistness before relentlessly pursuing the nectar beyond. She returned his kiss with a fervor to match his own.

He finally released her mouth only to bury his lips at the base of her throat. He rained light kisses up and down the side of her soft neck while his free hand began to sensuously stroke the delicate bones protruding through the skin on her upper chest. It was not an aggressive assault, but a gentle, compelling one that built a tormenting need within her.

When his hand grazed the top of the swelling fullness of her breast, it stilled. His aching groan teased her delicate ear, yet he didn't venture farther. It was almost as if he waited for her permission.

Echoing his groan with one of her own, Ali reached up, trapped his hand, and placed it on her breast, fusing them together. This was a new experience for her, to be the aggressor. It was a tantalizing venture. *What could be the harm?* she asked herself, bemused by her drugged senses. This was what she'd been wanting ever since he had first touched her. So long as it went no further...

Her initiative evoked a shuddering response in Adam. His hands roamed her breasts leisurely until he began to

unfasten the button that would free them to his touch.
Then they began to shake. With no bra for a deterrent,
they spilled freely into his seeking hands.

"God, Ali," he grated hoarsely, "your breasts are just
right." He tutored a tender crest into yearning hardness.
"Each one fits my hand as if it were made for it."

Through trembling lips, she managed to whisper,
"I'm—I'm glad they please you."

"Ali—please—touch me," he demanded with gentle
persuasion, following a moment of heavy silence. "No one
can see through the blanket," he added with a scraping
urgency in his voice.

Fiercely, she shook her head, her heartbeat knocking in
time with her knees. "No—" She couldn't breathe. "I—
I—" Her voice faltered. Panic seized her. At no time during her adult years had she ever *touched* a man. Her one
brief encounter with sex had been with her fiancé, Wes, the
night before he left for Vietnam. It was a totally unhappy
and unsatisfying experience, leaving her disillusioned and
confused. She hadn't invited a man's touch since. All her
efforts had gone into a career... until now.

Taking her hesitation for acquiescence, Adam took her
quivering hand in his and placed it on him lovingly. Instant heat leapt between them. But instant panic flung Ali's
heart up to her throat, almost choking her. She quickly
moved her hand to Adam's waist and clung to him.

"Oh, Ali," he breathed against her lips while his heart
threatened to explode within his chest, "don't be afraid."
He was drowning in her silky softness, in her intoxicating
kisses. She completely hypnotized him. He knew he should
call a halt to this madness—the kids were their responsibility—but he was powerless to move. She was so sweet,
felt so right in his arms and so unawakened that he could
almost believe she was totally unskilled in the art of love-

making. Her timidity in touching him had been a shock. It only made him want her, to show her what love was all about. But he knew with a devastating certainty that though he may yearn for this woman, he could never have her. His stomach lurched violently. He was terrified to take a chance. . . . *Damn you, Mary! for making me less of a man.* Still, he couldn't let her go.

It was Ali who broke the embrace. Adam's control was tenuous at best. Suddenly frightened of him, the situation, and her own driving need, she stiffened and dropped her arms from around him.

"Adam, please, no more," she whispered, surprised to find tears streaming down her cheeks.

Adam released her, though not before he felt the moisture against his face. A shudder shook his body as he struggled to regain his control. "Shh," he said, "I understand, and I don't blame you. I promise, you have nothing to fear from me," he finished on a strained and bitter note.

Ali turned aside and leaned her temple next to the hard post, dashing back the tears from her eyes. The instability of the past few months rendered her hopelessly incapable of dealing with a complicated man like Adam Forrest. She couldn't begin to sort out her feelings for him, nor what she wanted from him.

Intensely aware of his physical attraction, remembering how he had made her feel only moments before, she longed to tell him she understood, that she didn't fear him, but an inner caution held her back, urged her to guard against being too compulsive.

Still a deep-seated need drove her, a need to keep their communication lines open. She twisted around toward him. "Adam, I—" she began. The remainder of the sentence never passed her lips. Adam was no longer beside her. She saw the back of his tall figure as he made his way toward the front of the wagon.

Ali slumped against the railing, fighting the feeling of desolation that promised to overwhelm her.

Ali trudged down the slightly steep mountain path, watching carefully where she placed her next step. She had twisted her foot against a sharp rock on her way up, giving her a scare. She was enjoying this trek through the woods in the cool afternoon breeze. The minute she had finished judging a swimming contest and substituting in a volleyball game, she had treated herself to this time alone.

A fleeting smile crossed her lips as she conjured up in her mind's eye the horrified expression that would be on her mother's face had she seen her sophisticated daughter bouncing up and down on a volleyball court with a screaming bunch of teenagers. But she had loved every second of it.

Noticing she was nearing the end of the path, Ali paused and gazed about her. She breathed deeply, hoping this quiet time would help soothe her jumbled thoughts. How calm everything seemed. How peaceful. She could lose herself among the tall, billowy hardwood trees as they swayed gently in the breeze. And the sound of the gurgling mountain stream that she had just minutes before dipped her hands into was an added tranquillizer.

Physically Ali had never felt better. She knew, even without consulting a doctor that her ulcer was healing. Her life in the midst of these mountains was so far removed from anything she had ever known. Her days were full and brimming with her involvement in the children's activities and keeping Cindy company. Yet she never felt tired or irritable as she did in the city. Under the gentle tutelage of the summer sun and the unpolluted air, she was learning what it meant to be truly alive and free. If only she could force her soul to mend along with her body, she would have it made. She longed for peace of mind. Unfortunately, it continued to elude her. In its place reigned confusion and self-doubt.

It had been over a week since the hayride. And not one word had she heard from Adam. Adam. Even his name had the power to make her heart tremble. This past week her thoughts had flown to him during every waking moment—the shape of his face, the softness of his hair, the tender touch of his hands on her breasts, the way he had moaned when she had touched him. Oh, God, these primitive images were eating away at her insides. She kept telling herself she didn't want to get involved with him. Yet her traitorous body made a mockery of her determined words.

Okay, so she was attracted to him. She wouldn't deny that. But what good would this confession possibly do her? Obviously he wasn't stewing over their "little encounter." He hadn't even bothered to call or see her since then. Not that she thought he would, she quickly reminded herself. But she couldn't help but be miffed by his indifference. Nor could she keep from wondering if during his absence he was taking his frustrations out on Molly Deavers. God, just the thought had the effect of an arrow piercing her heart.

When they were together, it seemed as if their personalities were in total conflict—satin rubbing against granite. *But when they touched,* it was like satin against silk—perfectly compatible.

Seeing the grounds of the ranch come into view, Ali vowed to lock her thoughts of Adam in the back of her mind and throw away the key. Why should she continue to torture herself so about a relationship that had no future?

Adam's life was here in Arkansas with his ranch and animals and hers was in New York with her cosmetics. The revival of Cameron Cosmetics had to be her first priority. Until now, she had never met a man she thought worth more attention than Cameron. Yet sexually compelling though he might be, Adam Forrest would definitely not come before Cameron.

With that thought uppermost in her mind, she let herself quietly in the back door. Suddenly realizing she was hungry after her day of strenuous activities, she made her way into the kitchen for a light snack before dinner. Grabbing a bowl out of the cabinet, she opened the refrigerator and helped herself to an assortment of chopped fresh fruit. She fell into the nearest chair and began munching thoughtfully.

"How did your afternoon go?" Cindy asked from the doorway as she watched while Ali toyed with her bowl of fruit.

Ali looked up with a start and forced a smile. "Fine, just fine. But I should be asking *you* that question." She couldn't help but notice the darkening circles under Cindy's eyes that were more noticeable with each passing day. The baby's health was a constant nagging worry to both her and Barry.

Cindy smoothed the worried frown on her brow with her fingertips. "Well to tell you the truth, this hasn't been one of my better days." She hesitated. "My dizzy spells are getting worse."

Ali's already floundering spirits took a further nose-dive. "Have you called the doctor?"

Cindy shook her head. "No," she whispered, lowering troubled eyes to Ali. "I know what he'll say. He'll tell me to go to bed and stay off my feet." Tears trimmed her lashes. "And you know better than anybody that I've been doing exactly that."

"I know you have," Ali agreed softly, concern darkening her gaze. "But maybe it would be a good idea if you call him anyway. He might want you to come into the office."

"Oh, Ali," Cindy sobbed, "I'm so afraid I'm going to lose the baby."

"Shh," Ali pleaded as she jumped up from the chair and moved to stand in front of Cindy. "You'll make things worse by crying." Ali paused and embraced Cindy tightly. "All it will do is drain your strength."

"I—I know," Cindy gulped, laying her wet cheeks against Ali's shoulder. "But sometimes I can't help it. I'm so worried about the baby, Barry. . . and me." Her voice broke off on another sob.

Ali patted her on the back and began talking to her in a soft but firm tone. "First of all you're *not* going to lose the baby. As for Barry, he's doing fine, other than worrying about you, of course. Together we're going to see you through this." She paused again and delved into her pocket for a tissue. "Here, take this and mop up those tears."

"Oh, Ali," Cindy cried, "I don't know what I'd, we'd do without you."

"Probably just fine," Ali smiled as she walked with Cindy to the nearest chair and helped lower her cumbersome body onto it.

"You stay put, my friend," Ali ordered, "and let your motor idle while I pour you a refreshing glass of 7-Up." Ali forced a lightness into her voice that she didn't feel, hoping to dispel Cindy's gloomy mood. Between thoughts of Adam's virile body driving her crazy, coupled now with Cindy's worsening condition, it wouldn't take long for her ulcer to start acting up again, she thought.

After placing the refreshing drink in front of Cindy, Ali chatted about the day's events, giving Cindy time to gain control of herself. Finally satisfied that Cindy could be left alone, Ali said with a smile, "I think I'll take a quick shower and change my clothes before dinner."

Cindy returned her smile. "Go ahead. I'll probably sit right here until Barry comes in." Her eyes became shadowed again. "I—I hope you're not working too hard. You came here to rest and relax—" She tightened her lips. "I feel so frustrated because I can't do my part. I—"

"Cool it!" Ali interrupted. "If I didn't enjoy helping I wouldn't. You know that. But honestly, I love it here and love doing what I can to help." She reached down in passing and yanked an errant curl. "So don't let me hear any more apologies from you. Is that clear?"

"I read you loud and clear," Cindy replied with a grin. "Go on and take your shower. Don't forget Barry's grilling steaks for dinner tonight," she added just as Ali was leaving the room.

Ali yanked the grimy shorts, shirt, and underwear from her body the second she closed her bedroom door. The intense heat combined with the unusually high humidity made her skin feel sticky and clammy at the end of the day. A long relaxing bath loomed as a special treat.

She filled the tub with water as hot as she could stand. As she began to scrub her body, now tanned a golden brown, a silent "ouch" crossed her lips. She was feeling the twinge of muscles she didn't even know existed. After rinsing the sweet-smelling lather from her body and hair, she climbed out of the tub and toweled herself dry.

Entering the bedroom again with the towel tucked securely around her, she sat down at the dressing table and within thirty minutes had dried her hair and had made up her face.

Deciding comfort was definitely the order of the evening, she chose to wear a white piqué sun dress with thin spaghetti straps, instead of the proverbial jeans and shorts. For a reason she didn't wish to pursue, she felt the need to do something to give herself a lift. The simplicity of the dress made wearing a bra impossible. Her firm, uplifted breasts combined with the thickness of the fabric made this oversight unnoticeable. It was impossible now for her to look at her breasts without hearing the husky drone of Adam's voice as he stroked their velvet softness and said, "Each one fits my hand..." Suddenly she became short-winded at the sensual memory. Then she realized where her thoughts were heading... *Don't Ali! Don't do this to yourself.*

Quickly she reached for the curling iron and touched several silky curls with it, ignoring the slight shake of her hand. Pleased with the way her shining hair fell in waves around her shoulders, she picked up her favorite bottle of perfume and misted herself with the light but rich fragrance.

She then snapped off the light and stepped out, squaring her shoulders determinedly. She *would* be pleasant company the entire evening, she told herself. Not once would thoughts of Adam Forrest and his absence rise unbidden to shadow her evening. Time was passing much too quickly as it was. She couldn't afford the luxury of wallowing in her own self-pity. Cindy needed her too much, and she wasn't about to let her down.

Ali rounded the corner into the den. For the second time that day, she saw her good intentions disappear with the quickness of leaves in a windstorm.

Adam Forrest was sitting in a chair listening to Barry's every word. She stood motionless while the room spun before her eyes. She blinked several times and took gulping breaths to try to alleviate the cold ball of panic that was forming at the base of her stomach. Knowing that she couldn't stand there like an idiot forever without being seen, she ventured on unsteady legs into the room. It took all the willpower she could muster to face him. She straightened, gathering the torn edges of her pride together.

Before Ali could say a word, Adam looked up and saw her. A hush fell over the room. Their eyes collided head-on, each fighting their own private battle. The melting hunger mirrored in Adam's eyes was intensified by the same hunger in Ali's.

Then slowly he unfolded his wiry length from the chair and stood. His gaze never wavered.

Ali's eyes continued to devour every magnificent inch of him. He looked strong and fit as usual, dressed in a pair of tan jeans and a cotton sports shirt. His cologne, effective but elusive, did nothing to lessen her lightheadedness as it drummed her senses. It was the shock of seeing him. But was there something different about him too? He seemed tense, uncertain, vulnerable. Or was her imagination simply running away with her? These possibilities circled her brain until they were laid to rest by his quiet voice.

"Hello," he said.

"Hello." The wheezing sound coming from her throat was not at all like her own voice.

"How've you been?" His eyes were disturbingly intent.

"Fine." Her response was stilted. She wanted desperately to appear indifferent, but she was finding it extremely difficult, especially when her eyes were glued to the crop of dark body hair just visible above the unbuttoned neckline of his shirt. She didn't want to be aware of this or anything else about him. But she couldn't seem to stop looking at him, and her mouth felt dry as sawdust.

"I was just telling Barry that I was hoping to persuade you to have dinner with me."

His flagrant audacity and the frankness of his approach threw her completely off balance. How dare he think he could ignore her for over a week and then come waltzing in and casually ask her out to dinner? She clamped her jaws together tightly to keep from blurting out exactly what he could do with his dinner invitation. She remembered just in the nick of time that Barry was a party to their exchange, a very interested party too, and she had no intention of having a verbal mud-slinging match with Adam in front of him.

Ali thought quickly. "I'm sorry, but I promised to help Barry grill the steaks we're having for dinner tonight." She knew her excuse was lame, but at the moment it was the best she could do. She shot a look in Barry's direction imploring him to back her up.

"Oh, Ali, don't worry about that," Barry said, completely oblivious to her silent plea. "I can handle it by myself. You go ahead and take Adam up on his invitation," he added with a grin.

Ali ground her teeth together. "I—I still don't think—"

"I'll tell you what," Barry interrupted heartily, "I'll leave you two alone to sort this out. I've got work to do." He paused at the door and addressed Adam. "You're welcome to stay and eat with us, you know." He smacked his lips playfully. "I don't need to remind you how delicious my steaks are."

Adam smiled but shook his head. "Thanks, but I've already prepared a meal of vegetables out of the garden, plus I've got steak, too," he added with a wider smile, displaying his dimples to the fullest.

If only he were to smile at her like that, Ali thought with a silent groan, she would be tempted to grant him anything.

"Ali, for what it's worth, you'd be crazy to pass up Adam's offer for a home-cooked meal. He's a better cook than Cindy and me put together." These timely words of wisdom were flung over Barry's shoulder as he exited the room.

"He gives good advice," Adam said softly, his eyes slanted. "And he's right, I can put the best chow on the table you've ever eaten."

"Adam . . ." She couldn't care less about food. Instead she longed to ask him why he hadn't made any attempt to see her for over a week. Her nerves were now tiny pinpoints of pain. Had he been with Molly?

"You've got to eat, don't you?"

"Yes—but."

"Dammit, Ali, don't make me beg."

Her insides wrenched violently. Adam Forrest beg! Unheard of! Incredible! What had possessed him to make a statement like that? she wondered. Why *had* he come after her? What did he want? And even more disturbing, what did she want from him?

"No—no. I—I don't want you to beg," she said at last when she was able to speak coherently.

Adam took a step closer, then stopped. His eyes were narrowed, dark, and sensual between his thick eyelashes. He remained silent while he jammed his hands into the pockets of his jeans and looked down at her. This action tightened the material across his muscled thighs, calling to her attention his arousal now taut and visible against the unyielding tension of his pants.

It brought to mind the intimacy they had shared on the hayride. She felt the trap closing... An affair? Could that possibly be what she wanted and needed to purge this man once and for all from her mind?

"If you don't hurry and give me an answer, I'm afraid everything will be burned." He paused and suddenly a mischievous glint appeared in his eyes. "Including the house."

Ali gnawed uncomfortably at her lower lip. She wanted to go. She wanted to be with him. She could no longer deny, even to herself, the excitement his sudden appearance had engendered, but at the same time there was a marked sense of fear coursing through her limbs. Still she hesitated.

As if sensing her uncertainty, he stated quietly, "Remember, you can trust me."

With those words, Ali's final resistance crumbled. Her lashes swept up. "All right," she whispered, "I'll come."

Chapter 7

They rode in silence. Adam was aware of Ali's presence beside him and with every heightened nerve in his body. He had to make himself concentrate on his driving rather than on her fragile profile. But he didn't have to look at her perfect features to see her. They were engraved on his brain: the lucid brightness of her eyes, the delicate curves of her cheekbone, and the soft fullness of her lips, made even more memorable by the taste of her shimmering burgundy lips.

As the fragrance of her perfume brushed his nostrils, he wondered how he had let a week pass without seeing her. Now that she was with him, that week seemed almost like a lifetime. Thoughts like these were dangerous and self-destructive he knew, but he could no more wipe them from his mind than he could stay away from her. He was positive if he could take her just once, he could get her out of his system. It was a pressing and consuming thought.

Following the hayride, he had tried to drown the sight, smell, and touch of her by plunging wholeheartedly into his work. His clinic load had been usually heavy, for which he was thankful. However, he had gone through his clinic routine—surgery on Monday, outpatients on Tuesday, and regular office hours the rest of the week—as if he were in a daze, or more apropos, a programmed robot. For once, nature had cooperated and had not plagued him with an overabundance of new births or tragic accidents. The only injury of any consequence had been an old tomcat's left ear. He'd had to sew it back on after it was left dangling following a scuffle with a female cat. He could have performed that surgery blindfolded, if he'd had to.

Even Molly—oh, God, Molly. His heart lurched at the thought of her. The stricken expression in her eyes when he had repulsed her effort to make love still haunted him unmercifully. A horrendous fight had followed his rebuff with nothing having been settled between them. She didn't understand what *had* happened to him or what *was* happening, and he couldn't tell her.

Had it only been three days ago that it had happened? He gripped the steering wheel so hard, he felt his knuckles crack. But dammit to hell, he couldn't help himself. After experiencing a taste of Ali's sweet lips given in gentle abandonment, he could not stomach the thought of touching another woman. In fact since Ali had come into his life, a month ago now, he hadn't been able to touch Molly.

Having already experienced gut-wrenching suffering at the hands of a woman, he was aware that he was skidding on a treacherous road of thin ice by feeding his obsession with Ali. But even that cold and clinical warning couldn't budge him from his determination to have her—to feel, taste, and explore every delectable inch of her body no matter what the cost.

It was that compulsion which had driven him like a starving man smelling the scent of food to see her, to plead, if necessary, for her company this evening.

Now as she sat quietly, elegantly beside him, he wasn't sorry he had listened to his heart instead of his head. Live for today had been his motto since Mary's selfishness had ripped his complacent life into tiny pieces so long ago.

He would not, could not think about the future. He would take this moment and savor it, letting tomorrow take care of itself.

"I hope you like roast and gravy with potatoes and carrots cooked with it," he said with a little boy's eagerness, a grin slashing his lips. "Plus I've cooked purple hull peas from the garden," he added before Ali had time to respond.

She noticed they were entering a private road that led to his ranch. Again the breathtaking loveliness of the immense pastureland, thick with clumps of tall trees massed together at various intervals, gave her a thrill. This time of the evening when the sun was losing its stinging power was her favorite of the day. To her everything was at its best.

She turned with a start, feeling Adam's eyes boring into her. His lips parted with a tentative smile to reveal small, white teeth. "Purple? What kind of peas did you say?"

An indulgent smile tugged at his harshly etched lips. "Purple hull," he repeated, stressing each syllable.

Ali's frown deepened. "Whatever the color, purple, green, yellow. I still don't know what kind of peas they are," she countered lightly. God! what a ridiculous conversation they were having. Was it merely a buffer for the tension that crackled between them? she reflected anxiously. Could it be possible that Adam was as uptight and uneasy as she?

Suddenly he threw back his head and laughed aloud, his vivid eyes narrowing into tiny slits.

"Well, city girl," he announced after his laughter had faded into a winsome smile, "you're about to find out what real food tastes like. Think your system can handle it?"

Wordlessly she nodded. Her system could handle the food all right, she thought. But she wasn't so sure about handling his brand of blatant charm. It was sending a riot of emotions clamoring throughout her body. Her pulse was pounding and her head felt dizzy as if she'd just consumed a glass of potent wine. She circled her suddenly dry lips with the moist tip of her tongue.

Adam stared at her a moment longer, seemingly enthralled by the play of that tiny instrument as it flavored her lips with glistening enchantment.

"Let's go in," he murmured brusquely, before quickly opening the door of the Mercedes and exiting from it. He then strode around the hood of the car and opened the door for Ali.

Silently they made their way up the steps and into the house. The moment she entered the front door, Ali remembered she had never seen the inside of his house. Now as her eyes surveyed the softly lighted interior she was pleasantly surprised. Even without a woman's touch—or so Ali assumed—it was tastefully and beautifully decorated. To the right of the entry hall was a large den. As Adam propelled her into the room, Ali was captivated by what she saw.

A thick, creamy-brown carpet covered the floor, giving one the impression he was walking on air. Dominating the middle of the room was a massive, circular open fireplace. Spanning the entire right wall was a ceiling-to-floor window, divided at intervals by narrow strips of paneling that matched the walls.

Ali's breath caught as she crossed the room and took in the magnificent view. The mountains and the rolling hills of the mown pasture were still visible in the deepening shadows of the early evening.

To her left was his study. Bookcases lined the walls, providing the backdrop for a stunning hardwood desk that occupied the middle, near the fireplace. Pictures and other memorabilia lined the vacant walls and tall lifelike plants gave the area a touch of hominess.

"Well, what do you think?" he asked, coming to stand behind her.

Ali's eyes reverted to the outside view. "It's absolutely breathtaking," she exclaimed with awe in her voice. She was reeling from the lazy luxury of the wide open spaces compared with what she was used to in New York City. The beauty of this place could become a part of one's blood, she thought with a strange wistfulness.

"If you'd like, I'll show you the rest of the house before we have our dinner." He sounded both pleased and eager that she liked his home.

As she paid close attention to the warm colors and the plush but comfortable couch, chairs, and ottoman that sat in elegant grace around the fireplace, she thought he had something to be proud of. But that was before she saw the formal dining room, the bright orange and yellow kitchen with every conceivable appliance and convenience known to man, and the two bedrooms and connecting baths. They reeked of furnishings and decorations chosen with money as no object. Each contained the best that money could buy. Being no stranger to the best, Ali knew that Adam

Forrest's home surpassed anything she'd ever had in the city.

"Now," he was saying, his warm breath fanning her ear, "I'll show you my bedroom."

Ali's heart began to thud in her chest as she swung her head around, fastening her eyes on him. The moment she entered the room, the king-size bed leapt out at her. But Adam's face was stoic as he calmly pointed toward the wall, his voice full of pride.

"I wouldn't take a million dollars for these."

Covering the wall opposite another fireplace and bookshelves was an assortment of photographs of all sizes and shapes. Many were framed, some were not. Ali's first impression was that of a jumbled mess.

"What in the world—?" she began as she wandered up to take a closer look.

A proud gleam danced in his eyes. "This entire collection is a picture of almost every animal I've doctored since I set up practice here." The light suddenly left his gaze. "Unfortunately I can't tell you I was able to save or even heal each one, but I've certainly had more in the winners column than in the losers."

For some unknown reason, Ali felt unbidden tears form on her lashes. "Oh, Adam, I think this is marvelous."

"Do you really?" He grinned sheepishly. "Most people would probably think I was crazy if they were to see this. I'm glad you don't," he added softly.

They stared into each other's eyes for what seemed like an endless time, before both jerked away awkwardly.

"Take this little fellow, for instance," Adam said at last, pointing with his index finger at an old and crinkled picture, devoid of a frame, but with the cutest cocker spaniel puppy in it she'd ever seen. "His name was Barney." Ali noticed his eyes clouded again as he said the word *was*.

"Several years ago a car ran over Barney, mangling him badly. He was my first patient," he added, digressing from his story for a moment. "It took five hours of tedious surgery to set all the broken bones in his tiny body. It was a miracle but Barney pulled through and lived to the ripe old age of fifteen. However, a month ago yesterday, his owner brought him to me to bury. He'd had a heart attack in his sleep and died peacefully."

"Oh, Adam, I'm sorry," she said, her soft words breaking into the poignancy of the moment.

He smiled at her easily, causing her heart to turn over in her breast. "Don't be," he replied. "Barney lived a long good life. His owners even fed him filet mignon."

Ali shot him an incredulous look. "Surely you're joking."

"Nope," he said, grinning. "Couldn't be more serious. So you see, you don't need to feel sorry for Barney. He had the best of both worlds."

Ali laughed, suddenly feeling a warm glow on the inside. "If only we could all be so lucky," she remarked.

"While we're on the subject of food, I'm starving. How 'bout you?"

"Lead on, I can't wait to sample those purple peas."

His narrow lips spread into another amused smile. "What are we waiting for then?" he said, taking her arm and leading her in the direction of the kitchen.

The minute they entered the bright, functional kitchen, Adam went straight to the stove. "Have a seat. Chef Forrest will have a perfect meal in front of you in a matter of seconds." He grinned at her boyishly.

When he smiled at her like that, she would willingly become his slave. No wonder, she thought, Molly Deavers and every other single woman in the area were vying for his attention. He had everything—looks, money, a lovely home, and when he wanted to turn it on—a devastating charisma.

"Are you sure there's nothing I can do to help?" Ali's eyes were wide and luminous as she looked at him. "Believe it or not, Dr. Forrest, I'm quite good at the culinary arts," she volunteered.

"That may be so, but tonight you're my guest." He began pouring grease into a skillet. "I'm even going to fry you a quick batch of okra."

"You won't hear me argue. I don't know when I've had such a good deal," she said saucily.

Adam felt his pulse rate zoom as he paused, hands rendered useless, and raked his eyes over her, beginning with her animated face. Was she actually flirting with him? God, but she was lovely! Her hair curled in shining softness around her ears with wispy tendrils caressing her cheeks with every movement of her head. He felt an urgent need to bury his face into its fragrant sheen. The sun dress she wore, leaving her honey-gold arms and shoulders open to his naked appraisal, did nothing to scale down her voluptuous figure. If anything, it enhanced it. Then without apology or trepidation, his gaze targeted and clung to the swelling mounds of temptation that were silhouetted beneath the airy garment.

Ali, too, remained stunned, unable to move against the surging heat of his gaze. His eyes, like glittering coals, were reminiscent of a banked-down fire. She felt her nipples spring and a fiery liquid flow to the center of her being, making it difficult to remain still in the chair.

Ali smelled it before she noticed it. Her eyes widened in horror.

Following her line of vision, Adam whipped his head around and encountered the hot burning grease in the skillet. It was spluttering and crackling and wasn't far from catching on fire.

Still rooted to the chair, Ali watched as Adam grabbed a pot holder off the rack beside the stove and lifted the pan off the stove.

"Damn!" he exploded as he covered the distance to the sink in two gigantic strides and threw the pan into the stainless steel sink. He then ran hot water in the skillet showering the room with a puff of steam.

When everything seemed to be finally under control he turned back to Ali with a mortified and embarrassed look on his face.

They looked at each other for a moment and then both burst out laughing.

"Well, so much for my ability to show off." His smile was lopsided. "That's what I get for not paying attention to what I'm doing."

"The rest of the food is still okay, isn't it?" she asked when the hammering of her own heart had subsided. Suddenly it struck her that she was out of her depth with this man. His unpredictability was a disturbing force which she didn't quite know how to handle. Nevertheless, she couldn't deny the weakness and excitement his changeable mood engendered.

"What would you like to drink?" he was asking now. "Milk or water? I know coffee and tea are both no-nos."

She battled against her tumultuous thoughts in order to answer him coherently. "Uh, milk will be fine." Then she made a face. "But I can't tell you how much I dislike having to drink that stuff."

He laughed as he began pouring her a tall glass of the creamy liquid. "Here, drink up and stop complaining. It's your ticket to a clean bill of health."

Ali threw him an exasperated look but remained silent, watching him dish up the roast and trimmings onto a platter. He sauntered over to the table and set it down.

"Well, what do you think? Does it tempt your palate?" His eyes swept her gracefully as he so obviously waited for her compliments.

She closed her eyes slowly, sniffed the aroma through her nostrils. "Mmmm, it smells absolutely divine."

"Great!" He grinned. "Now all that's left is the peas and rolls. Oh, and the deviled eggs. I almost forgot about them. I decided to have those instead of a green salad."

"At least let me get the eggs while you take care of the rest."

"Okay."

She spied the tray of stuffed eggs near the back of the refrigerator. After uncovering it, she carried it to the table and set it down amid the other dishes. A smile broke across her lips as she paid attention for the first time to the table. Before, she had been too busy looking at Adam. Now she noticed how beautifully it was decorated.

A vase of fresh-cut flowers dominated the middle of the table, further complemented by the place settings of fine china and silver. On the right sat a crystal wineglass.

"Let's eat," he said softly, coming up behind her, catching her unaware. She felt the brush of his warm breath against the nape of her neck as he pulled the chair out and indicated with a mocking bow that she should be seated. Goose bumps tickled her spine as she thankfully lowered her trembling legs into the chair.

After seating Ali, he reached for the bottle of chilled wine and filled both their glasses. He then took her plate and began heaping it full of the delicious meat and vegetables.

She stared at him aghast. "There's no way I can eat that much food."

His lips twitched. "Sure you can."

Leaving no room for argument, Adam sat down and began filling his plate to the same capacity as he had filled hers.

Ali just shook her head as she placed her napkin in her lap and began eating.

A comfortable silence fell between them as they both began to munch heartily on their food.

Suddenly Ali stopped chewing. She knew even before she looked across at Adam that he was watching her. For some unknown reason she felt her face flush with color.

A lazy grin stole over his lips. "Well, what's the verdict, city girl?"

"It's as delicious as I knew it would be." She wrinkled her nose mischievously. "I've even taken a liking to these strange little peas," she said as she stirred them around on her plate.

"I'm glad." His eyes held hers. "These groceries will help heal your ulcer."

Refusing to discuss her health, she changed the subject quickly by asking, "Do you cook for yourself like this often?" She pushed aside visions of him and Molly enjoying a cozy dinner for two just as *they* were doing now.

"Not hardly, although I do try to eat at least one well-balanced meal a day. But with my hectic schedule, it's not always possible." He shrugged. "My animals have to come first."

"How long have you had a clinic?" Suddenly she was hungry for information about him. She knew nothing except the little Cindy had told her.

"Only about eleven years," he responded. "I had to give Uncle Sam four years of my life in exchange for a college education."

Ali looked nonplussed. "What about your parents, weren't they able to help with your education at all?"

Suddenly his face took on the image of a granite sculpture, anger in every line of it. "I *had* no parents."

Wordlessly, Ali stared at him, not knowing how to interpret his blunt statement or how to respond to it. It was obvious from his clipped tone and the hardness etched in his face that he had no intention of discussing his past. *Had no parents.* How heartbreaking. How lonely. His plight tugged at her heartstrings, and she yearned to reach out and smooth those harsh lines carved around his eyes and forehead. But she knew he would resent her sympathy, resent her for offering it. He was too proud.

Almost as though he sensed her helplessness and confusion, a shutter fell across his eyes and with it, his features lightened considerably.

"Care for some more roast?" he asked, slamming the door on that subject.

"No—no," she said, swallowing the desire to question him further. In no way had her curiosity been satisfied. But all she said was, "I'll have another helping of peas."

After that, the conversation reverted to impersonal subjects. He entertained her royally with anecdotes concerning his wet-tongued patients. She in turn answered his questions about her work, enlightening him on the finer points of putting a cosmetics line together.

As they talked, she was extremely conscious of everything about him: the way the knit shirt hugged his broad shoulders, the magic scent of his cologne, the way his long sensitive fingers curled and uncurled around the stem of his wineglass, and the ever-present visibility of the fine dark hair trapped in the open V neck of his collar. But, dear God, thoughts like these were driving her crazy. And all for naught, because nothing could ever come of her fascination with him. *Back off, Ali,* she warned herself. *Before it's too late. Adam Forrest is a complication you don't need.*

"I hope you've saved room for dessert," he said after they had downed the last drop of wine.

"Oh, no, I couldn't—"

"Please." He smiled. "If you knew all the trouble I went to just to prepare this concoction—"

She laughed. "All right. You win. I'll at least sample it."

"Fair enough."

"Shall I help you dish it up?"

"Nope. You just waddle into the den and make yourself comfortable. I'll follow shortly." His gaze rested softly on her, his eyes heavy-lidded and smoky.

Ali stood rooted to the floor. It seemed as if in that moment his eyes blazed a trail through her soul, destroying every defense she had erected against him, leaving her insides a quaking mass of jelly.

Somehow she found the strength to jerk her eyes away from his and make her way into the den, albeit on numbed legs. She grabbed a couple of the large pillows off the couch, backed them up to the hearth and collapsed lethargically against them, the plush carpeting cushioning her backside.

Her head now spinning dizzily, she closed her eyes in an effort to regroup. *Damn!* she thought. She had consumed far too much wine. Not only was it making her head spin, but it was making her much too vulnerable to Adam's potent charm.

It had been years since she had even thought about a man in terms of sex. Looking back she couldn't remember one she had dated who had turned her on sexually. She had prided herself on not needing or wanting a man in her life. But now, after all this time, and when she had more problems than she could cope with, she was suddenly attracted to a man to such an extent that she thought of nothing else except him, and what his hands and lips felt like on her body.

"Wake up, sleepyhead. You're not about to get out of tasting this delicious tidbit."

Ali's eyes flew open in time to see Adam set two oversized pieces of pie on the nearby coffee table, along with two glasses of wine.

She smiled lazily and blinked her gold-tipped eyelashes. "What kind of pie is that?"

"It's blueberry cheesecake topped with whipped cream."

Adam had grabbed two pillows and was now stretched out on the carpet next to her within easy reach of the pie.

He bowed his arm at the elbow, letting the palm of his hand cradle his head. He looked up at her between his thick lashes. "Do you want your pie first or another glass of wine?" he asked, his voice a lazy drawl.

"No—no more wine—please," she said. "I've had enough as it is. But I will sample the pie."

Adam sat up and reached for the plates and handed one to Ali. After a long moment he remarked, "It must be good. You haven't said a word since you swallowed your first mouthful." He smiled as he watched Ali take another generous bite of cheesecake.

"How were you able to eat yours so fast?" she asked, eyeing his empty saucer.

He patted his stomach and reclined into the same relaxing position only this time closer to Ali. His eyes were warm and teasing. "Easily," he said. "I have a penchant for good food and beautiful women—one woman in particular, that is."

Ali almost choked on the last succulent bite of pie before setting her dish aside.

A suffocating tension suddenly filled the room, rivaled only by the breathless silence that had fallen between them. The danger of the situation affected every nerve in her body. Her ears picked up the sounds of the crickets chirping through the open patio door beyond the den. Her peripheral vision noted that only one lamp was burning, its glow casting a warmth over the room.

Perfect for a seduction!

"Comfortable?" he asked softly as he began to brush his thumb sensuously against her jawline.

Ali gasped for sufficient air to breathe in a suddenly close room.

"Did you know you had whipped cream on your lip? Here." He smiled, as he gently wiped the corner of her mouth with his thumb.

"No—no, I didn't," she stammered, her voice annoyingly husky.

His eyes were pinned to hers as his thumb traveled with a butterfly touch across her lips. "And here," he added thickly.

Ali's insides quivered as she made an attempt to lift her hand to remove the unwanted culprit.

"No, don't," he whispered, folding her hand in his free one. "Let me."

Ali was powerless to move as he lowered his head and licked the cream off her lips with his tongue before laying his lips against hers.

It was a gentle kiss, achingly sweet and simple. Her heart pounded as she wrapped her arms around his neck and clung to him.

"Ah, Ali..." he said unsteadily as he pulled his lips from hers so as to shift into a more comfortable position. Holding her close he scooted down farther on the carpet, taking her with him. They faced each other on their sides with their heads against the same pillow.

"Please ... Adam ..." she choked, "I'm ..."

"Frightened?" he whispered, finishing the sentence for her. His lashes screened eyes that were dark and disturbingly intense. "God ... if it's any consolation to you, I'm just as frightened as you are. Believe me, I'm not used to doing the chasing."

She searched deep for the oxygen to speak. "Is...is that what you're doing...chasing me?" Her commitment not to get involved with this man was drowning in the feelings he aroused in her.

Her question startled him, made him think. Absently his finger continued its caressing motion up and down her bare arm.

What was it about this particular woman that aroused him so fiercely and made him want her so desperately? Was it because her kisses drove away the hunger that gnawed at his guts, a hunger which as yet had no identity, and drove away the loneliness that ruled him day and night?

But it didn't matter, not a whit, he told himself urgently. What mattered now was Ali's warm, pliant body next to his, responsive to his driving need. Tomorrow would be soon enough to question his temporary loss of sanity.

"Call it what you like," he whispered against her lips. "All I know is that I want you so much that I'm shriveling up and dying on the inside. I want to hold your naked body in my arms and kiss every inch of your silken flesh."

"Adam, this is insane. I shouldn't ... we shouldn't ..."

"I know," he groaned, his brandied breath intermingling with hers. "But I can't stop now. And I don't think you can either."

Ali drew back, her eyes falling beneath his piercing gaze. She couldn't stand to think he was reading and comprehending the confusion that was plainly written on her face. She was trembling like a leaf. Dear God, what was wrong with her? Why wasn't she behaving like the mature woman she knew herself to be? Adam was right, she did want him. She wasn't going to try and fool herself any longer about that. So what was the problem? Then suddenly she knew.

Fright. She was frightened that she wouldn't please him. Frightened that he would in some way find her lacking. After all she knew virtually nothing about pleasing a man. What if she failed to bring him satisfaction? Yet how could she give herself to a man who had ridiculed her, mocked her, and made her burn with anger? Even as she cursed the frailty of the human body, she admitted yet another truth: She longed to experience the hot, sweet ecstasy that she knew only his touch could provide. Just this once...

"Ali," he murmured, lifting her face toward him with hard, warm fingers. There was no mistaking the question in his eyes.

"Why are you fighting me?" he pressed, when she made no effort to answer him. "Please...let me make love to you." His voice throbbed with suppressed emotion.

"Ali...?" He said her name again at the same time his hands descended on her shoulders and began untying the straps on her sun dress.

She was lost. It was too late now to stop his questing fingers even if she'd wanted to. She felt paralyzed with pleasure as his eyes seared a path across her breasts bared now to his ardent inspection.

"Oh, Adam," she whispered, "I—I hope I won't disappoint you."

"You're—beautiful. Perfect," he whispered achingly. "You could never disappoint me."

His name was a sigh on her lips as he claimed them in a long, drugging kiss that sent tremors through her heart. His fingers journeyed tenderly down the side of her throat, onto her nipples, now nodules of sweet, pointed flesh.

Dragging his mouth away from hers, he dipped his head and kissed the underside of her breast, letting his tongue slide across to the honeyed delicacy of her nipples. His hand stroked her hip, moved across to her buttocks where he then paused and lifted her skirt, allowing him access to her soft supple skin.

Ali moaned with rising desire as she felt his fingertips on her calves, then move to the insides of her thighs. There he teased, caressed, taunted until she felt them part of their own free will. She offered no protest when his hand dove beneath her buttocks and slid her panties from her long slender limbs.

"Ah, Ali, you feel so good, so right," he breathed as his fingers began to move over her once again, working their magic in tune with his hungry kisses plundering her mouth.

His breath came in short hot spurts as he pulled back and peered deep into her eyes, testing her reaction to his questing fingers.

Ali gasped and clutched at Adam's shoulders, digging her nails into them. "Adam! No...please...yes!" No one had ever touched her in this way. His fingers felt like hot pokers as they melted into her, setting her on fire.

He ceased his movement at her moaning gasp.

"Relax, sweet baby. I won't hurt you. Just let it happen."

She dug her nails deeper into his back as his fingers moved slowly, languidly in and around the pulsating velvet of her.

"Yes, oh, yes," she said in a voice she didn't recognize as her own. There was no fear. No inhibitions. She yielded to pure feeling, blocking out everything else.

Suddenly he pulled her next to the thrust and potency of his arousal. With the tender lash of his tongue assaulting her nipples, he began to move persuasively against her.

His clothing was no deterrent for his hardness as it stirred the embers deep within her womanhood. Her mind splintered into a million different directions as he increased his pace, striving to drive her to the edge of a sweet madness, thus knocking down any remaining walls between them.

Her moans filled the air as she clawed at his back in bold urgency as wave after wave of liquid, like hot rich cream, replaced the blood in her veins and flowed from the inner softness of her. When it was over, her once rigid body slumped with the gentleness of a limp rag doll against the length of him.

Still too bemused and drugged from what had just happened, Ali was only vaguely aware of being lifted with ease from the floor and carried into Adam's bedroom.

As he deposited her on the bed, he whispered into the fragrant strands of her hair, "That was just an appetizer. Now you're about to taste the full course."

Chapter 8

The bedroom was steeped in the glowing brightness of a full moon. It paraded quietly over Ali's body, allowing Adam to feast his gaze on her beauty as he stripped the remaining garment from her, flinging it to the floor. Shedding his own clothing with the same adeptness, he joined her on the bed.

With nothing between them but the sweet mountain air pouring in from the open window, Adam again took the liberty of perusing her limbs with his hot eyes. He felt his breath become tangled in his throat at her ethereal loveliness. The firm, uptilted breasts with their dusty pink buds, the exquisite curve of her hips, the golden nest of curls that twined between her thighs, the flawless finish of her skin, all were as perfect as he'd imagined them to be.

The fire in his loins suddenly rushed to his head, making him dizzy and irrational. He thought he'd die from wanting her.

"Oh, sweet, you're lovely," he whispered. "I want to kiss you everywhere...everywhere. Do you understand?" His voice had dipped to a decibel below a whisper.

Ali's wordless nod collided with his seeking lips as he moved closer, curving his hands into her hair. He sank into the parted softness of her mouth and began to weave his tongue around and around, exploring every crevice, before moving to the back of her mouth and exploring its sweet contours.

Ali circled his waist with her arm and pressed herself against him. Then she began to kiss him back, roaming the inside of his moist cavity as though she owned it. As their tongues sparred, Ali felt that his mouth was now an extension of hers and not separate flesh.

Finally lifting his head, Adam leaned over and latched on to a nipple, teasing the already swollen bud to stonelike hardness.

"Oh, Ali, you completely enchant me," he groaned as he nipped his way around each breast and downward to the buttonlike indentation in her stomach, downward still to mesh his lips in the tangled curls of her rose-petal softness.

Low whimpering sounds escaped from her lips as he worshipped her there. He loved those sounds, loved watching her go wild under the expert tutelage of his mouth.

As unbelievable sensations raked her body, Ali couldn't comprehend what was happening to her. She'd had no idea the loveplay between a man and a woman could be so perfect, so beautiful. The way Adam was exploring her body, making her aware of every nerve in it was the most exciting and wonderful thing that she had ever experienced.

Suddenly she had the urge to bring him to the same height of satisfaction that he had brought her. She was no longer worried about not pleasing him, or making any mistakes. Under his patience and guidance, she had blossomed into an eager, confident woman.

When at last he raised his head and looked into her dazed pupils, she smiled at him with a question on her lips.

"Are you sure?" he asked hoarsely.

"I'm sure," she whispered in return.

He was laying on his side now, all six-foot-plus of him open to her gaze. He lay motionless, allowing her to do as she pleased. Her hands wandered through the dark wiry mat on his chest, finding the tiny buds nestled within.

"Ahhh..." he breathed as she pulled, tweaked, and gently pinched them until they grew hard and strong against her soft palm. From there she moved lower amid more of the same bristly fur that covered his flat stomach. But when she traced the dark shadows still lower she paused.

"Please...don't...don't stop now," he moaned urgently.

With disturbing accuracy, she reached out and claimed what she so avidly sought. His response was instant.

"Oh, God, yes!" he said huskily.

Suddenly high with the power she held, she went to work in earnest to try and burn into his mind the memory of her lips and hands. She wanted to make sure he would never forget her as she was certain never to forget him.

"Oh...I can't stand any more," he gasped, stilling her hand at the same time he rolled over and parted her legs, positioning himself between them.

Unconsciously and with awed tenderness, Ali reached out and wrapped her fingers around the throbbing hardness of him and lured him to the entrance of her warm femininity.

"Ali...God...yes! You're driving me crazy," he ground out hoarsely and kissed her deeply.

Swiftly she edged her hips down to more easily accommodate him as he began to slowly bury himself within her. Exquisite agony coursed through her as she felt him expand and touch her everywhere.

"Oh, baby, you're so tight, so small." He closed his eyes and probed deeper, encouraging her with sweet words to move with him. Convulsively she tightened her hold and placed her lips on his, which ignited a fusion so intense, so shattering, so wild that when the final explosion came it was more wondrous and fulfilling than either of them had ever dared to dream.

Sated, lethargic, and drowsy, Ali lay deep within the haven of Adam's arms listening to the now quiet beating of his heart. All too soon, time brought them back to reality, though she fought it.

She would be content to lie beside his man forever. He had brought her more joy in the last few hours than she had known in her entire life. His gentle but fiery possession of her had made her achingly aware of just how empty her life was. He had struck a chord deep within her, so deep that for a moment it had seemed as if their souls had touched.

Suddenly, she bit down on her lip to keep from crying out as the disturbing thought of leaving Adam rose up to haunt her once again. But a lone tear escaped through her tightly closed eyelids. Why did she torture herself this way? *Fool!* she chastised herself. *Relish the moment. This moment. With this man.*

"Ali?" He spoke softly into her ear, his warm breath kissing her cheek, "Is something wrong?"

It was uncanny, Ali thought with a shudder, how he was able to read her mind, sense that she was upset. Unknowingly tears began to roll down her cheeks.

He turned and propped his head on his hand and looked down at her. His heart constricted as the moonlight, dancing across her features, highlighted her tears. Dear God, what had he done? Had he hurt her? He had tried his best to be gentle; he'd been as gentle as he could. But this was one time he hadn't been able to control his lovemaking. It had controlled him, as well as every waking moment of his life since he'd met her.

It wasn't because her breasts were perfect and drove him wild with temptation, or that her skin was softer and silkier than any other woman's he'd ever known, or that her mouth tasted like sweet honey, or that the fragrant valley between her thighs was tighter and hotter and welcomed him with unselfish anticipation and delight. All those things were true, but they still did not tell him why she was special to him, special in such a way that he was terrified to define, while at the same time he couldn't seem to stay away from her.

Now as he reached out and trapped a tear with a warm fingertip, an aching need, followed by guilt and remorse, swept through him.

"Ali, look at me."

As if pulled by a magnet, she opened tear-stained eyes and gazed up into Adam's slate-colored ones.

"Did I hurt you?"

"No... no," she said evasively.

"Are you sure?" he pressed, not convinced she spoke the truth.

She shook her head.

He sighed. "Are you always this tight?" Even as he asked he felt a hammering behind his temple and a sudden expansion of his loins. Just the thought of how well and securely she fit him and how repeatedly he had been able to empty himself into her, made him want to take her again with a yearning urgency. But not until he got answers for the nagging questions that plagued him.

He whispered again, "Tell me, Ali," before lowering his hand to caress that part of her body which had him completely obsessed. There he began to leisurely stroke, tease, and plunder at will.

"I...I can't say," she whispered as she gave in to the increasing heat coursing through her body.

Adam fought for his next breath. "You...you haven't known many men then, have you?"

"Only...only one. And that was years ago." *A lifetime ago,* she added silently, incoherently. His talented fingers were making it impossible for her to think, much less speak.

Even Adam was finding it difficult to keep his mind on what she told him. He, too, was fighting a rising tide of desire so intense it threatened to push him over the brink.

"Somehow I knew you were untouched." He brushed his lips against hers. "I'm so glad I'm the one who awakened you to what it can be like between a man and a woman."

"Oh, Adam...I am too."

His lips took hers again in a long, steamy kiss. She wound her arms around him, scaling his back and shoulders, and clung to him.

His hand continued to stroke the heart of her, making sure she was ready. She strained against him, begging him to bring an end to her agony.

"Please...Adam!"

Only then did he enter her and this time there was no pain, just intense pleasure.

"Oh, Ali, love..." he moaned as he shuddered and took her fiercely, carrying her with him to the uppermost peaks of joy.

Later and with regret, Ali felt him slide from her while still cradling her close in his arms. With a contented sigh she snuggled deeper into his embrace.

Tomorrow would come soon enough. And with it, more doubt, recriminations, fright, maybe even shame and resentment. But for now—there was only Adam.

"Did you have a good time last night?" Cindy asked as Ali made her way into the den around ten o'clock the next morning.

Ali felt her face burn as she turned her back on her friend and crossed to the front window. The day was beautiful, but she hardly noticed. Her mind was in utter chaos.

"Well?"

Ali turned and forced a smile on her lips. "Sorry," she said. "I wasn't ignoring you. It ... it's just..."

"What?" Cindy was relaxing among the soft cushions on the couch, her eyes steady on Ali's pale face.

Ali's lashes fluttered to her cheeks before she answered. "Yes," she admitted soberly, "I had a wonderful time."

A tiny frown creased Cindy's forehead. "Then why the long face, my friend?" Her face brightened suddenly. "You know I'm delighted."

"Oh, Cindy, don't be," Ali wailed. "Right now I don't need any more complications in my life."

"And Adam's a complication?"

Ali thought for a long moment, refusing to admit the truth even to herself. "He very well could be," she replied, her mouth twisting strangely.

Suddenly a dancing gleam appeared in Cindy's eyes. "Wouldn't it be wonderful if—"

"No!" Ali cut her off mercilessly. "Don't even think like that. My life's in New York with Cameron Cosmetics. That's where my roots are and that's where I'll return."

"Ali—"

"And speaking of cosmetics," Ali went on as if Cindy had never spoken, "an idea has been growing in my mind for some time now. I'd like to talk it over with you." She paused briefly. "Actually, it's for a new line of perfume. It's been churning—"

"Ali, stop it!" This time it was Cindy who did the interrupting. "Remember what Dr. Todd told you. In case you don't, I'll remind you. He told you to forget about your work, New York, and everything else connected with it while you're here."

A tremor ripped through Ali. "I know he did, but that's just not possible, Cindy. Not realistic. I know it and you know it." She *had* to get her mind on something else besides Adam Forrest. She just had to.

"You're right, of course," Cindy responded bleakly. "It's just that I'm selfish and enjoyed having you here so much."

"No more than I enjoy being here," Ali returned softly, "but I still love my work and I must remember my priorities."

"I know." Cindy sighed. "Don't pay any attention to me. It takes very little these days to upset me and get me all weepy."

"Are you feeling any better this morning?" Ali asked, thankful for the change of subject.

"A little. But I noticed when I first got out of bed that my feet and ankles were swollen." She grimaced. "I guess it's another 'stay flat on my back' day for me."

Ali pointed a finger at her. "And you'd better not fudge it, either. Barry has my activity schedule all mapped out for the remainder of the week, so everything's under control."

Cindy lowered her eyes. "What about Adam?"

"What about him?" Ali flashed.

"Ali!"

She held up her hands. "Okay, okay. You've made your point. He's planned a picnic for the end of next week, when he gets back from Houston."

Cindy looked surprised. "What's happening in Houston?"

"I'm not exactly sure." Ali looked down at her watch. "His plane should be landing in about an hour." She shrugged. "The trip has something to do with a cattle virus that is sweeping certain parts of the country. A group of ranchers and scientists are meeting to try and find a solution to the problem."

Adam had waited until the wee hours of the morning, when it was time to take her home, to tell her that he was leaving. He had told her he didn't want to go, but the meeting was important and he had no choice. Her heart had plummeted to her toes when he'd added that he'd be gone nearly a week.

But neither had voiced their objections; they had nursed them in silence. It was almost as if they had been afraid of bursting the bubble of warm contentment dashed with a sense of expectancy that hovered over them following their long hours of lovemaking.

Just the thought of last night and how she had been so eager to please as well as receive brought another flush of red to her cheeks. She turned quickly back toward the window to keep Cindy's inquisitive eyes from seeing the guilty blush.

"Well, I can't say I'm surprised," Cindy said. "Adam carries a lot of influence in these parts both as a veterinarian and rancher." She made a face. "So naturally every time there's a crisis, the cattleman's association calls him."

Ali made her features as placid as possible before turning around to face Cindy again. She did not want to talk about Adam, or think about him. The feelings he had evoked in her and what they had experienced were still too new, too fragile to be shared even with Cindy

Desperation underlined her words when at last she spoke, "Please, Cindy, I don't want to talk about Adam." She threw Cindy a pleading look. "You—you understand, don't you? I..." Ali's voice faltered and she couldn't continue.

Cindy's eyes softened. "I understand. Just remember I'm here if you need me. Now," she said, moving carefully over on the couch and patting the empty place beside her, "sit down and let's hear all about that new idea for a perfume."

"I have about thirty minutes before I have to meet Barry," Ali responded, trying to muster up a show of enthusiasm. "That should be more than enough time."

Although Cindy knew nothing about the glamor industry, she listened with fascination to Ali's every word. Ali was pleased as she watched Cindy's animated features. She needed this, Ali thought. It helped to take Cindy's mind off her problems and relieve the boredom of inactivity.

The remainder of the week passed in much the same manner. Ali spent time with Cindy, she slept, she rested, and she took long walks. But never once did she escape thoughts of Adam. They pursued her relentlessly. She chided herself over and over for having created another monster in her life by letting Adam become too important to her. It was imperative that she hold on to her obligations, her duties, and her commitments. It would be suicidal, she reminded herself severely, to heap another complication on top of the ones she already had, especially one with far greater repercussions.

Granted, Adam might want her now, and she him, but how long would it last? Another two months? Then it would be time for her to return to the city—to another life, another future. And she knew what would follow—pain, disillusionment, heartache. Those emotions would indeed be a high price to pay for a few days and nights in the arms of a man who could never again give himself to any woman. The shadows of his past were still too much of a reality to expect that type of commitment.

No. She would not believe and could not believe that she was in love with Adam Forrest or he with her. She was not ready to tag her feelings for him with that definition. Dared not. If she were to do so, she would make herself more vulnerable and defenseless than she already was.

Yet she admitted with aching honesty that she was not ready to give him up or to let him go. So with each passing day her emotions became more jumbled, more disruptive. And she found herself counting the hours until Adam returned.

Today wrought no changes. To silence the taunting voice that seesawed back and forth inside her head, she had thrown on a pair of cut-off jeans, a yellow knit halter top, jogging shoes and socks and made her way through the grounds to haunt her favorite trails in the dense woods.

Now with a mile of brisk walking behind her, Ali still felt at loose ends, unsatisfied. Sighing, she tugged disconsolately at the damp tendrils of loose silky hair that clung to her neck. By the time she entered the back door of the house, she was hot, sticky, and tired.

Just as she reached her bedroom and was about to close the door, the doorbell chimed musically. Reluctantly, she trudged to the front of the house and pulled the door open. Suddenly her heart leapt to her throat and lodged there. She was totally unprepared for the sight of Adam. He loomed large as life, a hesitant smile on his face.

She could do nothing but stare at him. She had never seen him dressed in anything other than jeans and a casual shirt. Now he was wearing a silk dress shirt, its tie askew, and a pair of slacks, minus the matching jacket. Even though his face looked tired—she could have sworn the grooves around his mouth were deeper—and paler, he was, nevertheless, a welcome sight.

"May I come in?" he inquired in a strained voice, his eyes returning her steady gaze.

Wordlessly she stepped aside and lowered her eyes, embarrassed by her unsophisticated appearance. And she'd wanted to look her very best for him, she thought in frustration.

Raising her head, she watched him covertly, as they both stood silent, unmoving.

"Did I interrupt anything?" he asked at last, when the silence stretched between them.

Ali nodded her head negatively. "No... no. I was just getting ready to take a shower."

Adam's eyes darkened suddenly at this admission and fell to her chest where the halter top left very little to the imagination.

Now it was his turn to lose his capacity to speak. He was too busy staring at her breasts floating free beneath the dampened flimsy fabric. Her nipples seemed to taunt him as they pouted with provocative invitation, challenging him to respond.

He sucked in his breath sharply and barely managed to keep a lid on his control. He was fighting the temptation to grab her and crush her limbs against his. God! How he had missed her. He hadn't been able to keep his mind on the meetings. What little he'd participated in had been forced. Thoughts of Ali had filled his every moment, making him restless and uninterested.

No matter how much he had chastised himself, and he *had* called himself a damned fool many times during those long hours of lectures and testing sessions, none of these warnings seemed to have penetrated his hard head. So what had he done? The first chance he'd had to leave, he'd taken.

And now, before having even gone home, he was standing in front of Ali with the blood surging hot in his loins. *Dammit man! Get hold of yourself!* he cursed silently.

But he couldn't. She was in his blood.

"Er . . . do you want to go into the den? Do you . . . I mean . . . would you like something to drink?" She licked her lips nervously. "Coffee maybe?"

His sudden return was not lost on Ali. She didn't know how to respond to it. But she could still see the fire that kindled in his eyes as they zeroed in on her breasts. They sprang to life and rubbed against her garment. God, she wished he'd kiss her—not just wished—but ached for it. Then suddenly a knot formed in her stomach.

Adam remained where he was, clenching and unclenching his fists. "No . . . I don't want anything to drink."

The tension in the room had grown so thick that it could be cut with a knife. Neither was prepared to make the first move. Both were too insecure, too afraid. Afraid of breaking the fragile threat that held them so tenuously together.

"I . . . I see. I just thought . . ." She broke off, suddenly aware she was rambling nervously.

"Ali—!" His voice was hoarse with emotion.

She held every muscle in her body rigid until she felt them cry out for release. Glancing around helplessly she finally voiced her tumultuous thoughts, "What do you want, then?" Her pulse raced as she looked him in the eyes, begging him to put an end to this foolish game.

His response was instantaneous and total. "Goddammit, I want you," he grated coarsely.

That was all Ali needed. As if she had suddenly sprouted wings, she closed the distance between them and found herself closeted warmly within his strong arms.

For a breathless moment their collective heartbeat was the only sound in the room. Then with gentle hands he moved her back, creating enough space between them to swoop down and claim her lips as his own. For long drugging seconds, he feasted upon their sweetness. It seemed as if he were starved for the taste of her. While their mouths were fastened one to the other, Adam's hands began to slide over her supple curves, from her shoulders down to her waist, her thighs, and then eventually lower to cup the underneath of her buttocks, making her keenly aware of the urgency of the situation.

She was drowning in physical sensations and there was no doubt about Adam's desperate need of her.

"Oh, Ali, you have no idea how much I've missed you," he groaned into the delicate linings of her ear. "Or how miserable I've been."

She could feel him tremble as she clasped her arms tightly around him as if she never intended to let him go.

For a stirring moment they remained locked in each other's arms. At last, Adam lifted his head and gazed down at her. "Where's Cindy?"

"She's gone...that is, Barry's taken her to the doctor."

There was another moment of tense silence.

"When are they due back?" The timbre of his voice was low and shaky.

"Any time now," she answered, lowering her thick eyelashes.

He drew a ragged breath before dropping his arms and stepping back. "In that case, we'd better get the hell out of here." His tiny smile was rueful. "If not, Barry and Cindy will catch me in the act of ravishing your delectable body."

Although Ali felt a flush sting her cheeks, his words were like warm brandy; they went straight to her head, making her reel with both excitement and fear. But she thrust the fear aside, positive that she still owned the key to her heart, and let the excitement take over.

She looked up at him. "What do you suggest, then?" she asked, her tongue appearing to moisten her lips.

His eyes dropped to her soft mouth, before sliding to her breasts and lingering there. "Let's go on that picnic I promised you," he said, his breathing ragged.

"Now?"

His eyes were smoldering as they held her saucered ones captive. "Why not? We have several hours of daylight left." A grin softened his features. "We can call it a dinner picnic, and you're already dressed and ready to go."

"Are—are you sure that's what you want to do?" she stalled, suddenly aware that she was again caught in the swirl of his sensual charm. Every time he got within touching distance of her, she responded to him with the same subtlety as walking through a glass door.

"Is that your way of telling me you don't want to go?" His tone was terse.

"No—no," she stammered, "it's just that it's obvious you've just arrived home."

"Dammit, Ali," he exploded, raking his hands through his already unruly hair. "Don't do this to me! I came straight here from the airport because I couldn't wait another goddamned minute to see you." His eyes narrowed into tiny slits. "If you think this is any easier for me, then you're dead wrong. All I know is that I want you so much it's taking precedent over everything else." He paused, taking in the horrified look that crossed her face at his sudden tirade. He smiled then, dispelling immediately the harshness of his countenance. "I'm sorry—it's only that—"

"I'll go."

Her quietly spoken consent aborted his sentence and caused his jaws to click together. A brilliant light sprang into his eyes.

"I'll—I'll leave Cindy and Barry a note." Then she hesitated. "I really should take a quick shower and change my clothes. It'll only take another minute."

"Don't worry about how you look. All you need to do is grab your bathing suit." He grinned. "A dip in the Buffalo River will adequately take the place of a shower. Now run and leave that note," he added. "I'll be waiting."

Chapter 9

Adam pointed the car in the direction of his ranch. Glancing at her briefly he said, "You do realize, don't you, that we can't have a picnic without food?" His eyes danced impishly. "And I sure as hell don't want to swim in my Cardin suit."

Ali slammed her palm against her forehead, radically illustrating her mortification. "Why didn't you say something?" she cried. "I could have thrown together sandwiches and . . . and, or chicken," she sputtered.

"Don't worry your pretty head." He grinned as he brought the Mercedes to a halt in front of his house. "Everything's under control. While you were getting ready, I phoned my housekeeper, Mattie, and told her to rustle up some grub."

Ali relaxed and answered his grin with one of her own. Then she had the grace to look sheepish. "Well," she admitted, "I'm glad one of us used his head." Suddenly she felt happy, carefree, and curiously light-headed. It was uncanny, she thought, how being around Adam could turn her world topsy-turvy. She wished she could blame this feeling on his clean masculine smell, his gentleness, or his big, brawny body. But she couldn't. Of course, these physical attributes were important, but it was the man himself who fascinated her.

"Want to come in while I change clothes and get the picnic basket?" Adam asked, nudging her.

She cocked her head sideways. "No—no. I don't think so. I'd rather stay here and soak up more of this gorgeous day."

Adam studied her for a moment through slitted lids. "Don't go away," he ordered, reached out and tracing a finger down the length of her jawline. "I'll be right back."

When Adam returned a short time later, Ali's heart was still hammering at an accelerated speed. She found that she could not take her eyes off his beautiful body as he slung his ditty bag in the back seat alongside hers. He placed the picnic basket between them in the front seat.

He had changed into a pair of loose athletic shorts over a bathing suit. The pull of the double fabric made her more aware than ever of his potent masculinity. Although he had on a shirt, it was completely unbuttoned, displaying the carpet of dark hair flecked with gray on his chest, hair that she had wound her hands through until he had groaned in pleasurable pain.

"Ready?" he asked. Now his gaze lingered on the rosy flush of her cheeks, a sharp twinkle in his eyes.

Damn him! Ali thought. He could read her mind like a book. In order to save face, she began rearranging the cover over the basket before lifting it over the seat and placing it on the rear floorboard.

Once the Mercedes was on the road, she relaxed some-what and turned her attention out the window. Adam was quiet as he tooled the car in a southward direction on Highway AR7. His adherence to the fifty-five mile an hour speed limit gave Ali a chance to view the scenery.

Never in her life had Ali's eyes feasted on anything quite as magnificent as the wild and rustic terrain. The mountains were overpowering as they towered over and around them like a steel cloak.

Turning to face Adam, she asked, a breathless excitement in her voice, "Are we getting close to where we're going to swim and picnic?"

"Yeah," he replied with a smile. "You're about to see another favorite place of mine on the Buffalo River," he went on. "Every time I'm able to get away from the clinic I come here to relax. I mostly fish or take a float through the mountains and the forested hills."

Her eyes sparkled. "Oh, that sounds wonderful. Could we do it this afternoon, the float trip, I mean?"

"Not today," he said quickly, and then grinned indulgently when he saw the crestfallen look that suddenly appeared on her face. "Next time, I promise. I'll take the day off and we'll get a much earlier start."

She smiled. "I'll hold you to that promise."

His voice dipped low. "I wouldn't have it any other way."

In a moment, the Buffalo River came into sight, claiming Ali's attention. She felt her excitement mount as Adam pulled the car into an access road and shut off the motor.

"We'll take the rest on foot," he said.

Ali quickly glanced down at her feet decked casually in a pair of thongs. "Not far, I hope."

His eyes twinkled. "Nope, just a short distance to a primitive and secluded stretch along the bank where we'll be completely alone."

Suddenly his eyes grew darker, deeper and shone with an emotion she didn't understand—dared not understand.

"Lead—lead on," she finally managed to eke out.

The trek through the woods along the river was as short as Adam had promised. Suddenly Adam came to an abrupt halt in a grassy clearing beside a gurgling stream adjacent to a beautiful waterfall. It was like a miniature Garden of Eden, Ali thought as her mouth gaped open and her eyes widened in amazement.

"Isn't this place great?" he asked as he set the basket down and shook open the quilt to spread it on the grassy knoll.

"I can't believe this." Her curls gently kissed her cheeks as she swung her head around to face him. "I feel like a princess in a fairy tale." She grinned. "Or better still, I think I know what Eve must have felt like when she entered the Garden of Eden."

"Oh, Ali, you're beautiful. Did you know that?" he murmured hoarsely. His eyes were like shimmering diamonds as they explored her body, leaving everything awakened in their path. Her lips parted softly, invitingly. Her breasts swelled with longing as her legs threatened to buckle beneath her from the intense heat that gathered at the very heart of her.

"Adam—"

"I'm aching to hold you," he whispered and closed the short distance between them.

"Oh, Adam," she whimpered, her mind spinning in giddy circles.

He placed a strong arm around her then and dipped his head and covered her mouth with his. Ali's lips opened and blossomed beneath his gentle onslaught, giving as greedily as she took.

Then suddenly he disengaged himself and stepped back, an arm's length away. His harsh breath rang through the silence. "Believe it or not, I didn't bring you to my private paradise just to seduce you." His visage was tense, his eyes piercing as he strove to regain his control and quiet his still racing pulse.

You're a damned liar, Forrest! he added silently. *That's all you've had on your mind for an entire week.* But thank God, he'd had enough sense to use tact and finesse in covering up his bold intentions. He'd hate like hell to have to turn around and take her back home because of his brutish behavior.

Ali was struggling to come to terms with his apparent rejection of her. But then his words suddenly penetrated her shattered emotions, sending a warm glow through her. He wasn't rejecting her, he was placing her feelings above his own.

"Let's walk a while, shall we?" he asked, his voice still rough around the edges, though the muscle no longer ticked in his jaw.

Ali complied silently, eager for an outlet of her own physical agonies that lay smoldering underneath the hesitant smile she threw him. Slowly but careful not to touch each other, they strolled down a slight embankment to the water's edge and paused. Ali's eyes swept over the eerie beauty of the free-flowing river, the breeze deliciously cool on her bare skin.

Ali kept her eyes glued to her surroundings, even though she knew Adam watched her. The air was thick with strangling tension. They were both aware of the sexual time bomb that ticked between them, each afraid to move or speak for fear of setting it off.

Suddenly Ali groaned inwardly. Why must there always be this feeling of crushing panic when she was with Adam?

Why couldn't she merely accept that she was hopelessly addicted to everything about him and let it go at that? Anyway in another month she would be leaving. Leaving! That thought ripped through her like a bullet through a plate-glass window. She had to bite down on her lower lip to keep from sounding her despair aloud.

"Ali—" he began, almost as if her agitation had communicated itself to him. But then he turned away abruptly, the remainder of his sentence dying on his lips.

Suddenly frantic to ease the tension, Ali scampered closer to the water and poked a foot into it.

"Ouch!" she gasped. Whirling, she faced Adam who was trying his best not to laugh.

Ali cocked her head sideways. "Why didn't you tell me the water was freezing?" She tried to keep her lips from bending into a smile.

"Well, for one thing," he drawled in a lazy, indulgent tone, "you didn't give me a chance." He grinned openly now. "And for another, I happen to know it's not cold. In fact it's just the right temperature for a long leisurely swim."

Ali grimaced and flung a tumbled curl out of her line of vision. "Do you really intend to swim in that ice water?" She paused and looked down at the clear, rippling waves. "Brrr—just the thought makes goose bumps run up and down my spine. See," she said flinging out an arm toward him in an effort to prove her point.

"Oh, no," he laughed, shaking his head and completely ignoring her outstretched arm. "You're not about to get out of taking a dip. You'll love it once you get used to it."

Ali was far from convinced, but she wasn't about to argue with him and break the easy camaraderie that bounced between them. This was another of those rare times between them. She wanted to savor every moment of it as the time loomed closer like a threatening thundercloud when they would have to part and lead their separate lives again.

"I'll race you to that winding bend," he said. "And back," he added with a jesting grin across his face.

"Huh, some contest, but you're on!" she shouted as she kicked off her thongs and began running full speed ahead, taking Adam completely by surprise.

"Why, you little minx!" His words, however, were nothing but an echo through the surrounding mountains as he tore off in hot pursuit of her.

Halfway to the designated point, he caught up with Ali and sped past her with an egotistical grin on his face. But he had to truthfully admit it was no easy feat.

"Damn," he said, his breath coming in huffing spurts, "for a city girl, you're in excellent shape."

Ali threw him a grin and kept moving.

Having reached the bend in the river, they whipped around without stopping and headed back at a jogger's pace, making conversation possible.

Ali smiled, her feet springing in perfect rhythm with his on the carpet of thick grass. "Are you forgetting that I've been taking Cindy's place around the camp?" She paused, drawing the clean air deeper into her lungs. "I can swim, play volleyball and square dance with the best of them now." She wrinkled her nose. "All that has done wonders for my stamina."

To prove it, she flashed him another saucy grin and upped her pace.

"Show off," he retorted teasingly.

Ali reached the pallet and plummeted down in an exhausted heap. Adam, only a few steps behind, flung himself down beside her.

With a groan Ali rolled over on her back and closed her eyes, trying to ease the thumping of her heart and ease her erratic breathing.

"Not quite as good as you thought you were, are you?" Adam teased warmly.

Ali's eyes flew open to find him leaning over her. He was so close she could count the tiny lines that were carved at the corner of each eye. The fluttering screen of his dark eyelashes claimed her full attention while she groped for something profound to say.

Suddenly Adam snaked a finger out and began to gently caress her cheek.

"I think it's great the way you've pitched in and helped Barry and Cindy."

Ali swallowed hard, making a conscious effort to concentrate on what he was saying. "You—you sound surprised," she said.

Adam's eyes probed hers. "Well, I have to admit I was," he confessed, before removing his finger and drawing back.

"Why?" She raised up and propped herself upon her elbows, not looking at him, staring out across the water.

"For one thing, I figured you would be too high and mighty to dirty your hands."

That stung but Ali managed to keep the lid on her emotions. After all he no longer felt that way, or so he intimated, but still he hadn't been able to disguise the bitterness in his tone or keep the pulse from jumping at his temple.

Instinct told her that for whatever reason, he linked her with his past. But why?

Pushing this dreary question aside, she forced a degree of coolness into her voice. "Just to keep the record straight, I never at any time considered myself too good to help my friends.''

His eyes softened. "Don't you think I know that now. You've more than done your part to help them through their hard times." He spoke heavily. "And I appreciate it too. They're dear friends and I hate to see them frustrated and unhappy." He paused a moment. "I know what living hell that can be."

Then lines of sorrow and resentment clouded his features. For a moment his mask had slipped and Ali was privy to a glimpse of the real Adam Forrest. It touched her deeply, for she too had known what it was like to experience heartache and despair.

"Adam, what is it about your past—your ex-wife, that haunts you so?" she asked impulsively, then at once was sorry. A brooding scowl suddenly darkened his face.

"I don't want to talk about it," he replied flatly.

"I—I understand," she whispered when she was able to get past the lump in her throat. To her dismay, her eyes slowly filled with tears. Quickly she looked away.

"Oh, Ali—God, I'm sorry," he groaned as he reached out and cupped her chin, gently turning her toward him. "I didn't mean to snap at you, but what you're asking of me is impossible." He paused and drew a long shuddering breath. "We each have crosses to bear; let's not spoil this beautiful day by forcing me to air my dirty laundry."

"Adam—" There was a waver in her voice as warm tears overflowed the shadowed rims of her eyes.

"Ali, Ali, never let me make you cry," he whispered brokenly, his lips achingly near her own. "I'm not worth it."

She never knew who first initiated the kiss. Before either of them could stop it, their lips met softly, deeply. Then again. Desire sprang between them, jolting every nerve in Ali's system. Adam's sinewy body crushed her into the soft fabric of the pallet where he began planting small kisses over her face, her eyes, her cheeks, the corners of her mouth. When at last he returned to her lips, he kissed her with devouring intensity. And she responded instantly, her mouth flowering into his, stroking, nibbling, receiving his tongue simultaneously with the giving of hers.

His hands roamed over her, seeking, pressing, feeling. She clung to him, gently squeezing his shoulders and the hard muscles of his back, moving downward to knead the cheeks of his buttocks.

Gasping, Adam yanked his mouth from hers and without haste began to undress her. Her eyes never left his face. She saw a longing and a need in his eyes, a powerful yearning that lit his face with breathless anticipation.

He quickly stripped off his clothes, peering down at Ali in the dim light of the late afternoon like a Greek god. She treated herself to a bold glance of his beautiful body beginning at the top of his head down to the tips of his toes.

"Oh, Adam," she whispered, "you're perfect."

"Not nearly as perfect as you," he whispered in return. "You're like a fever in my soul, burning hot and out of control." He sank down beside her again.

She reached out and buried a hand in the curls on his chest. "I've—I've never just thrown caution to the wind and done anything like this." Her eyes darted from right to left as if she expected someone to intrude on their private haven.

"Don't worry," he assured her quickly, "no one will ever find us here, I guarantee it."

Her lower lip caught in her teeth. "Are you sure?"

"Mmmm, positive," he muttered indistinctly as he was nibbling on the tender spot at the side of her neck.

She felt the sudden need to postpone the shattering climax of their lovemaking and strove to convince herself that she wasn't just one in a long list of many to share an afternoon like this with him. Molly. Had he brought Molly here? The thought of following in her footsteps caused her stomach to revolt. She had successfully managed to keep thoughts of Adam's mistress at bay. But now they surged to the forefront of her mind with renewed vigor, representative of a serpent in this tranquil Garden of Eden.

She had to know. "Have—have you ever brought Molly here?" She waited for his answer, her heart in her throat.

"No," he replied simply, his breath warm and tantalizing as his lips grazed her mouth. "I've never brought another living soul here."

His words made her heart sing. She smiled sweetly and gave herself up to his ardent lovemaking.

He explored her body leisurely, deliberately, first with his eyes, lingering on her breasts, enhanced by the dusky pink nipples, now swollen peaks. Then his hands searched and probed before finally targeting the satin fold between her legs with his lips and tongue.

Ali's gasp did nothing to deter his hands and mouth. They played her body like a loving musician plays his most treasured instrument, with love and skill.

She dug her fingers into his hair as his lips returned to hers. He pelted them with short, sizzling kisses. She was oblivious to everything: the warm gentle breeze as it caressed her skin, the flow of the river as it rippled peaceably by them, and the force of the nearby waterfall as it pounded down the mountainside. Even the slow erosion of the sun's stinging rays failed to puncture her blissful haze.

She explored his body as thoroughly as he had hers. She felt primitive, wanton, daring, as she slid a hand down the flat planes of his stomach, then lower to surround his swollen pride.

"Oh, Ali—wonderful," he said, his voice low and grating.

Feeling dizzy with power, she hesitated barely a second before dipping her head and touching him with her tongue.

A sharp gasp spilled from his lips. God! He felt himself drowning in the tender torment she was heaping on him. Never in his wildest dreams and fantasies could he have ever imagined the erotic pleasure that her tongue was bringing to him. So hotly exciting. So habit-forming.

"Now—Ali—now," he demanded urgently, pulling her atop the length of him.

It was her turn to gasp as her sweet softness enfolded the driving force of him. Moving within her, Adam's hands traveled over her limbs, encouraging, pressing.

Their coupling was quiet, almost euphoric. He paced their rhythm, enjoying the feel of himself throbbing and expanding within her.

His lips sought and found a nipple until all consciousness fled, and he spilled into her with loving force. Ali's groans matched his as waves of desire racked her body and transported her to another world. He clasped her tighter as he reached the same pinnacle of bliss. Together they floated and soared and then crashed back to earth with a matching cry on their lips.

At last, he tenderly rolled her over and placed his head on her breast. He had not eased his hold on her, having flung one of his legs over her thigh.

He wished he could hold her forever—that he never had to let her go. And he knew now it was more than just desire that made him feel this way. *Love?* Could it be love? A deep shudder shook him and a pain stabbed at his chest.

Oh God, please, don't let me be in love with her. Moisture dotted his upper lip.

Blind, searing panic twisted through his body. He couldn't love her. Her life was in New York, and she would never willingly give it up. He wouldn't ask her to, couldn't ask her, but neither was he willing himself to settle for less. It was a hopeless situation and it was slowly chopping his heart and his life into tiny pieces. And he was deathly afraid that when she left she would take the most important pieces with her, leaving him only a broken shell of a man.

She stirred, disturbing his chaotic thoughts. Stretching like a lazy cat, she looked up at him, a question in her eyes.

"What time is it?" she asked.

"Time? What's time? Who's counting?"

She smiled contentedly. "Not me."

He bent down and nuzzled her neck and whispered near her ear. "How would you like to take that shower you've been wanting under the waterfall?"

Ali jerked her head up and looked at him as if he'd lost his mind. "Are you serious?" Her eyes were wide and still somewhat glazed from the warmth of their lovemaking.

She had no idea how lovely she looked at that moment. But Adam was very much aware of it. Suddenly, he longed to take her just as she was, her slender naked limbs heightened by her firm, uptilted breasts, her tousled and unruly curls, her deep smoldering eyes, take her and mold her into a lifelike statue. Then she would be his and nothing could ever take her away from him.

But, no, that wouldn't make him happy for long, he thought crazily. It was her warmth, her flesh and blood beauty that made her so desirable, so appealing.

And she was his now for the taking. He must not squander the time they had left.

"Adam—can we really?" She halted. "I mean, will it be all right?"

He threw his head back and laughed delightfully. He then dipped his head and gave her a quick kiss on the lips. "We can do anything we damn well please. Come on," he said, jumping up and pulling her with him, "let's go."

Like two kids they scampered hand in hand the several yards to the nearby waterfall that continuously wreaked its vengeance against the rocks.

"Oh, Adam," Ali exclaimed, "are you sure we—we won't drown?"

His lips twitched. "I'm positive, honey. You can trust me. Now give me your hand and I promise, you'll love its stinging spray against your body. It'll make you feel alive."

Ali stepped closer, but still she hesitated. She shot a look at Adam who stood watching her with a sweet smile on his face.

Then she knew. She loved him, *loved* this sometimes hostile, sometimes gentle giant of a man who cared more for animals than he did people. This insight rocked her on her heels, for she knew she would never get over him—never get him out of her system.

"Well?"

"All right," she acquiesced in a subdued voice.

But her heart was no longer in it. She had changed. She no longer wanted to be a part of this playful romp under the waterfall. She wanted to crawl off by herself and ponder her plight. She hoped Adam would see her reluctance and suggest leaving.

He didn't.

Clutching her hand tightly within his, he pulled her with a resounding laugh of pure pleasure underneath the gushing flow.

"This will wake you up," Adam exclaimed exuberantly as the force of the waterfall claimed them.

Before she could stop herself, Ali squealed with laughter, lifting her face upward to meet the onslaught of the water. Suddenly she hated herself for frittering away even a second of their precious time together. Knowing that she loved him, she would be a fool not to fill each second to the brim with memories. Memories that would have to last her a lifetime.

The pattern was set for the next hour. Not even the lateness of the waning day altered their play.

They laughed like two children with a bright new toy. Adam stared at her with glazed eyes as she stood under the misty spray of water, at her body wet and gleaming, her nipples hard and inviting, and beyond to her stomach and thighs. To him, she was the loveliest creature that ever walked the face of the earth. His hands literally shook as he stepped closer, letting his hands follow the same path as his eyes.

"Do you like this, darling?" he asked huskily.

"Oh, yes, yes!"

His fingers felt like tiny spears everywhere, from her shoulders down to her toes, up and around her hips, her buttocks, before he centered his ardent attention on the secret place between her legs.

"Adam—please—it's my turn."

She rubbed his bronze skin down his hard belly to his surging passion, then around to the back of his thighs where she lingered until she heard his agonized cry and felt a tremor shake his body.

He turned and pulled her into his arms, their bodies melting as one as his mouth covered hers. Then drawing back he moved them to the edge of the falls where he slowly lowered their bodies into the overflow pool.

"Adam?"

"Shh," he whispered and then drove into the depths of her with probing gentleness. With the sand as their bed and the erotic dance of the water as a shield, they soared to the stars and beyond....

No words were necessary as they made the short journey home. Ali, exhausted, curled up next to Adam and rested her head against his shoulders. She was spent and happy and all she could think about was that she still had several glorious uninterrupted weeks with him.

Adam, as he looked down at Ali nestled next to him like a warm kitten, wondered how in the world he was ever going to let her go.

"God, Ali, am I ever glad to see you," Barry declared forcefully, bounding down the front steps the minute Adam's Mercedes pulled up in front of his house.

Fear clutched at Ali's heart. Cindy. Something had happened to Cindy.

Without waiting for Adam to come around and open her door, she slid out of the car straight into Barry.

"Cindy?"

Barry shook his head. "Cindy's fine. It's your uncle." His brows knitted together in a dark frown. "He's been ringing the phone off the friggin' hook."

Fear of a different kind squeezed Ali's heart. She paled visibly. "Did—did he tell you what he wanted?"

"You're damn right he did. He expects you to be on the next flight to New York City."

Chapter 10

Impossible!

She couldn't return to New York. Not now! She couldn't leave Adam, not after the day's startling revelation. Nor could she leave Cindy in her condition. Yet she still had her responsibilities, she reminded herself severely. Responsibilities, she prided herself, that she alone could handle. Something must have gone terribly haywire, she thought, for Charles to call her and issue such an ultimatum. Or else her mother was behind this sudden emergency.

Ali dared not look at Adam who was now walking stoically beside her up the front steps, while Barry held the door open. She fought back the tears of frustration on her eyelids.

Cindy stood in the middle of the den, her face pinched and pale. "Ali, Charles is on the phone," she said, a dismal note in her voice.

"Now?"

"I'm afraid so. He just this minute called again and I told him to hang on, that I thought you were driving up."

With a tight smile Ali all but stomped to the corner of the den where the phone lay on its side. She stared at it for what seemed like eons but in actuality was only seconds. Suddenly she had the urge to slam it down on the receiver.

Then maturity and sanity surfaced. Again, she reminded herself that New York *was* her home and with it went her commitments. Suddenly it dawned on her, as she continued to stare at the coiled black instrument, that she wanted the best of both worlds, Adam Forrest *and* Cameron Cosmetics. Was it possible to have both? she wondered. Or was she living in a fool's paradise by even entertaining such a thought?

Realizing she couldn't postpone the inevitable any longer, she raised the receiver to her ear.

"Hello, Uncle Charles," she said.

"Ali, honey, can you hear me?"

"Yes, yes, I can hear you just fine."

"Good," he said. "Now we can get down to business. How soon can you get out of that godforsaken place and get home?"

Blind panic rose in her throat. "What's—what's happened? Is it Mother?"

"No—no, nothing like that." His deep sigh vibrated through the line. "It's the other stockholders, Ali. They have joined together and have found a buyer for Cameron."

A knife turned in her stomach as she practically fell into the chair by the phone.

She gripped the receiver until her hand turned numb. "And—Evelyn? How does she figure in all this?"

Another sigh vibrated through the long-distance wires. "I might as well tell it like it is," Charles said. "Evelyn is straddling the fence. One minute she's ready to give her consent and the next minute she's not." There was a moment of silence before he spoke again. "I think if you would come home and soothe the board's ruffled feathers along with your mother's, everything will be all right. That's why I want you to be on that next plane." He paused. "Unless of course you don't care what happens to the company."

"You know that's not true," she snapped, anger making her voice waver.

"I thought not," he replied, barely loud enough for Ali to hear. "But unfortunately it's not me you have to convince."

"Dammit, Charles, can't you stall them? Give me a little more time? I've got a great idea for a new perfume line that's just about completely worked out in my mind. In fact tomorrow I was planning to jot down my ideas on paper and send them to you."

"I don't know, Ali," Charles began, uncertainty deepening his voice.

"Please, Uncle Charles," she asked, stopping just short of begging.

"Ali, you know I would do anything I could for you, but this time I'm not so sure."

Her throat stung with suppressed tears as she made an effort to keep her eyes off Adam who was across the room making a pretense of listening to Cindy's solemn voice. She knew they were trying not to listen to her conversation, but it was impossible for them not to understand the gist of what was happening. She noticed Adam's visage becoming darker by the minute.

Forcing her mind and heart away from him, she turned her attention back to Charles and asked, a dejected note underlying each word, "It's that bad, huh?"

"It's that bad," Charles repeated heavily.

"Oh, Uncle Charles—" Her voice broke on a sob. She felt the trap closing. . . .

"Ali—my dear, is there some reason why you can't come home?" He paused significantly. "I mean, you're feeling better, aren't you? At least Evelyn seemed to think so, judging from the note you sent her." He paused again, sounding thoroughly frustrated. "Don't you think it's about time you leveled with me, honey?"

She ran a hand tiredly over her eyes. "I can't. Not now." Her voice was devoid of all emotion.

"Dammit, Ali . . ."

"I'll let you know tomorrow," she said tonelessly.

"Ali, don't you dare hang up," he sputtered.

"Goodnight, Uncle Charles." Her hand shook as she leaned over and placed the receiver back on the hook with a clunk.

There was a dead silence in the room. The three on-lookers no longer bothered to hide the fact that they heard every word of her heated exchange with her uncle.

For a moment Ali was too numb, too shaken to move. Why? she cried silently, did this have to happen to her now? Oh, God, it would absolutely be like separating her heart from the rest of her body if she had to leave Adam. Even if there were no promises, no pledge of allegiance from him, no future, she still couldn't give up one day of their remaining time together.

"Ali—"

Cindy's weakly controlled voice pulled Ali out of the vortex of her tortured thoughts. She shook her head. Her eyes, instead of focusing on Cindy, bounced once again to Adam. Icy fear clutched at her insides as she saw the harsh scowl that marred his handsome features, contorting them into a menacing mask.

Feeling as if she had just received another punch in the stomach, Ali slung an arm across that area of her body and tried to ward off the threatening nausea. Surely this dark stranger couldn't be the same one who had only a short time ago treated her to another glimpse of Heaven in his arms?

Jerking her eyes away from him, Ali concentrated on Cindy.

Her heart received another jolt when she saw the rivers of tears flowing down Cindy's pale face. Barry sat next to her on the couch with a comforting arm around his wife's shoulders.

Completely ignoring her shaking legs, Ali quickly covered the distance between her and Cindy and knelt down in front of her friend.

"Oh, honey, please don't cry," Ali pleaded, for lack of anything else to say, unable to cope with the rising tide of emotions.

"That's right, honey," Barry chimed in, "you're borrowing trouble. Before you go all to pieces, let's wait and see what Ali has to say."

But Cindy refused to be pacified. "You're not going back to New York now, are you?" Her eyes were wide with fright as the tears continued to drench her face.

Ali swallowed convulsively as she got up from her crouching position and sat on the couch next to her.

Still Adam remained quiet, keeping his vigil across the room, an arm dangling negligently from its position on the mantel, a booted foot propped on the hearth, and his face expressionless. To all intents and purposes, he appeared calm and uninterested in what was being said, but Ali's instincts told her differently. He was coiled tighter than a rattlesnake and equally as dangerous.

"I—I don't know," Ali said at last. "I—I don't know what to do." She dragged a nervous hand through her curls. "Things are in turmoil in New York and everyone's depending on me to straighten it out," she finished on a bitter note.

"Ali, please, don't go," Cindy begged in spite of Barry's attempt to calm her down. "You—you promised you'd stay until the baby was born." Cindy's voice held sheer panic.

"Darling, get control of yourself," Barry demanded softly. "You have me. You know I'll take care of you." He seemed unsure how to cope with his distraught wife.

Cindy looked up at him with her heart in her eyes, squeezing his hand that lay on her shoulder. "I know you will," she gulped, "but I'll need Ali too."

Ali chose her next words carefully, realizing that Cindy was close to becoming hysterical. "Look," she said, projecting as much firmness into her voice as she could muster, "you know I would never desert you. If—and remember I said if—I do go back to New York, it will be for only a short time. I will come back, I promise," she stressed quietly. Then as if pulled by a force she couldn't control, she looked at Adam. *If only he would ask me not to go.*

But he didn't. Instead he straightened up to his full height and slashed his eyes up and down her body, his upper lip curled backward.

"Let her go." Violence burned in his voice as he turned his attention to Cindy where his eyes softened for a moment. "We don't need her."

The next thing Ali heard was the hard slam of the front door followed by Cindy's raking sobs.

Without even as much as a backward glance, she whirled on her heels and made a dash for her bedroom. Along with her stomach, her heart had taken another severe beating. But this time, she was terribly afraid she would never recover.

The bright sunlight paraded across Ali's still form with a vengeance. Groaning, she rolled over and buried her face in the pillow. Even through her semiconscious state, the events of last evening swamped her. *It was just a bad dream,* she told herself as she slowly pried her eyes open. But then with full consciousness came the brutal pain. And Adam's face. It was no dream. The pain was too excruciatingly real for that.

What now, she asked herself as she flopped over on her back and stared up at the ceiling. If she *were* to decide to fly home this afternoon, would she be able to convince Cindy that she was indeed coming back? The way things stood at the moment, she thought not. Cindy was much too hyper and ill and wasn't responding to the medication as they all had hoped. Her dizzy spells were coming on more frequently now as were her trips to the doctor.

From that standpoint it was not a good idea for her to think of leaving even for a day. Emotionally Cindy was clinging to her, mainly because she was a woman and could better understand the trauma that Cindy was going through.

But on the other hand, Charles and her mother would be absolutely livid if she ignored their summons as would the corporate board. So how could she sit back and knowingly antagonize the people she would have to work with when she *did* go back? And *how* could she even think about putting Cameron Cosmetics and its future security in jeopardy? Her idea for the perfume line was a brilliant one. Once she presented this to the board members, she was positive they would no longer consider placing Cameron on the chopping block.

Her mother, even as greedy as she was, would be no problem. She would see to that. Besides Evelyn only needed reassuring that she, Ali, didn't intend to let the company sink. But her new idea and her enthusiasm would convince her mother that she wasn't about to give up without a fight.

So why wasn't she up now, getting dressed, and explaining patiently to Cindy why she had to return to New York without further delay?

Realizing that the answers to these questions weren't to be found lying in bed, she hauled her weary body up and pushed aside the feeling that she had just fought the Battle of Armageddon. But then she still had one more battle to fight—perhaps the most important one of her life.

Cindy was preparing breakfast when Ali walked into the kitchen dressed in a salmon-colored linen suit.

Cindy's face paled when she looked up and saw Ali. "You have decided to go then?" she asked, but it was more of a statement than a question.

Ali hugged Cindy fiercely for a moment before letting her go. "I have to, you know that."

Cindy nodded wordlessly as she stirred the eggs in the pan perfecting them to a bright and fluffy texture.

"But first, I have to talk to Adam," Ali blurted out. "I—I can't leave without trying to make amends."

Cindy immediately removed the pan from the flames and set it aside. "You care about him, don't you?" she asked softly.

Pride made Ali hesitate.

"Ali, answer me."

Ali blinked and forced her gaze back to Cindy. "Yes, I care," she replied hesitantly, "but as you well know, any type of relationship with Adam is headed on a collision course."

Cindy looked at her curiously. "Why do you say that?"

"How can you ask me that?" Ali demanded, exasperation crowding her voice. "You, better than anyone, know that Adam wants no serious commitments." She shrugged carelessly though her heart was cracking. "Anyway it's a hopeless situation. My life's in New York and his is here," she added flatly.

Cindy sighed. "But you're still going to try to talk to him before—before you leave?" Her eyes were beginning to fill up with tears.

"Oh, Cindy, don't, please, don't make me feel worse than I already do."

"I'm—I'm sorry," Cindy sniffed, "don't mind me."

"While you're eating your breakfast, I'm going to call Adam." She paused and laughed without humor. "I'm probably the world's biggest fool, but here goes."

Moments later, with her hands trembling significantly, she dialed Adam's number.

The phone rang several times before a female voice came on the line and said, "Forrest residence."

"May—may I speak to Adam, please?"

"I'm sorry, but he isn't in right now."

"When do you expect him back?" She drew an unsteady breath.

"I'm not sure, ma'am. Would you care to leave a message?"

"No—no, I don't think so," Ali said dully. "Thank you, anyway."

"You're welcome."

The resounding click on the other end of the receiver was the only sound in the room. Ali just stood there holding the phone, letting the tears saturate her face.

You're a damned fool, Ali Cameron. Let him go. He does not want you! Why can't you get that through your thick skull? You're just a fancy diversion—a good lay. Nothing else.

Suddenly and frantically she began dialing directory assistance to get the number of her favorite airline. When Cindy ventured into the room a short time later, she was still fuming over the fact that she couldn't get a plane out of Fayetteville until late the next afternoon.

"Damn," she muttered aloud in frustration.

"That bad, huh?" Cindy asked.

"Worse."

"I take it you didn't get hold of Adam."

"You're right, I didn't, and I can't get a plane out of here until tomorrow."

"Have you called New York and told them?"

"Not yet. I'm just not up to that right now," Ali declared tightly.

"Since you're not going anywhere today, why don't you ride into Fayetteville with me and Barry? He has to pick up some more supplies." Her sad eyes had suddenly come to life. "There's a good restaurant where we can have lunch. How about it?"

Although eating was the farthest thing from Ali's mind, she hated to disappoint Cindy, and anyway she hadn't anything better to do with her time except fret over Adam and his whereabouts. And that, she told herself, would accomplish nothing. So, mustering a show of enthusiasm, she agreed to the outing.

"Ali, I hope you like Chinese food," Barry remarked as the three of them now strolled down Main Street.

His question jarred Ali out of her deep thoughts. "That's fine with me," she replied. "I want you and Cindy to please yourselves."

Barry smiled but cast a glance in Ali's direction, a strange look on his face. "Are you all right?" he inquired thoughtfully.

She smiled in return, relaxing her face somewhat. "No, I'm not, but hopefully I will be after I talk to Adam."

"Why don't you try calling him from the restaurant?" Cindy suggested. "You'll have plenty of time while we're waiting for our food."

Ali lowered her eyes. "I'd—I'd rather wait, I think. Since I'm not leaving until tomorrow, there's still this afternoon and tonight."

"Are you sure?" Cindy asked as they reached the restaurant and were about to enter it. The smell of oriental food swamped Ali's senses.

"I'm sure," she emphasized, plastering a bright smile on her lips. It wasn't fair, she told herself, to burden Cindy with her problems and she had no intention of putting a damper on her friends' day by wearing a long face.

"Let's eat then, shall we?" Barry chimed in.

The inside of the restaurant was surprisingly large and tastefully decorated. They were shown to a table at the far side of the main dining room, overlooking an enclosed garden with the mountains as a background.

A waiter promptly provided menus, and Barry asked both women what they would like to drink.

"I think I'll just have a glass of ice water," Ali answered politely.

"Sounds good to me," Cindy responded.

"Make mine iced tea," Barry told the waiter. "We'll be studying the menu while you're taking care of our drinks."

Shortly the waiter returned with their drinks. He immediately took their order and left them alone.

While they waited for their food to be served, they chatted about some funny incidents that had happened to the guests, the coming baby, and Ali's work at Cameron.

Ali was amazed that she was able to respond in a halfway intelligent manner, especially since her thoughts were so scrambled. Barry and Cindy, however, seemed to sense this and went out of their way to shower her with questions. Although she tried to paint a glamorous and exciting picture of what she did on a daily basis at Cameron, she found it extremely difficult to do so. The excitement and enthusiasm just wasn't there. Even when she found herself giving them a detailed account of the new perfume ideas and her game plan for winning the board's approval, she had to force her thoughts not to wander and to inject a smile where none was forthcoming.

Cindy sighed and shifted her weight in the chair, obviously searching for a more comfortable position. "Compared to your life, mine seems terribly mundane," she mused, but the sweet look she threw Barry counteracted her words, telling Ali she wouldn't trade places with her for anything in the world.

Ali's stomach knotted with jealousy as she viewed her friends' closeness. Then feeling ashamed, she quickly took a bite of her peppered shrimp dish before answering Cindy. "After being here for over a month, I've about come to the conclusion that I'd much rather live your mundane life, as you call it, than mine." She paused and smiled. "Anything beats the pressure I'm under twenty-four hours a day. Ulcers are all I have to show for my hard work," she added. She tried to keep the loneliness and bitterness out of her voice, but from the sympathetic looks on Cindy's and Barry's faces she didn't think she'd succeeded.

"You're welcome to stay here, you know," Cindy offered quickly.

Ali tugged painful fingers through her hair and smiled. "You've no idea how often that thought has crossed my mind."

"Maybe if you and Adam—" Cindy began.

Ali looked away. "Now, Cindy, don't get your hopes—"

Suddenly her next words died on her lips as her gaze just happened to sweep past the front entrance. Her breath became trapped in her heart, allowing neither to function properly.

Adam, looking devastatingly handsome in a powder-blue casual suit, was making his way toward a table, preceded by Molly Deavers and her son.

Ali's instant reaction was to jump up and scream *No! You can't do this to me! To us!* But of course, she didn't. Instead, she swallowed the bile that rose up in the back of her throat and watched the beautiful rays of her imagined rainbow disintegrate and disappear before her eyes, leaving a dark, meaningless void in its place.

"Ali, what the hell?" Barry muttered. "Pardon my triteness, but you look like you've just seen a ghost."

Her mind grappled to gather her scattered wits together so that she could speak. But instead, she continued to sit like a zombie and stare at Adam who was now sitting at a table across the room, his profile outlined for her perusal.

She longed to turn away, to scorn him as he had so obviously scorned her. But she couldn't. It was as if she were hell-bent on punishing herself for falling so foolishly in love with this moody rancher or tender veterinarian. Which one was the real Adam Forrest? But now she would never know, she thought bitterly as she watched Adam lean over and patiently help the small boy with his cumbersome menu. Adam's smile was warm as he chatted with the child for a moment before turning his attention to the mother. From where Ali was sitting his smile appeared equally warm as he bestowed it on her.

Ali continued to sit immobile, her eyes fastened on the intimate interplay at the far table. Her insides burned as though a hot knife had seared through them. Again her heart cried at the injustice of it all. What had she done or said to make him turn on her like this? If this was what being in love was like, she wanted no part of it.

"Dammit, Ali," Barry growled as he leaned across the table and shook the hand that was squeezing a portion of the tablecloth in her fist. "Are you sick?"

The touch of Barry's hand served to pull her out of her stupor. He and Cindy were both craning their necks in the direction of her stares, but because of the crowded dining room and the buffet with its long line, they were unable to see the object of her scrutiny.

"Ali, please tell us what's wrong," Cindy begged, her eyes wide and troubled.

Ali pressed her palms to her hot cheeks as she tried to swallow the sob which stuck like a tight knot in her throat, "It's—it's Adam. He—he—er just came in with Molly and her son."

As if on cue, both Cindy and Barry turned and strained their necks in search of Adam. They spotted him now with ease.

The silence drummed loudly around them as they each made an effort to eat the food that remained heaped on their plates. Then Barry and Cindy began talking at the same time.

Suddenly Ali's fork clattered on her plate. "If you'll excuse me—" the words were wrenched out of her "—I think I'll go to the ladies' room."

Unconsciously her gaze once again sought and found Adam. Choosing the same moment to let his eyes wander, their glances locked and held.

Had Ali not been so distraught herself, she would have noticed the shock mixed with bewilderment that settled over Adam's features. But Ali noticed none of this. She was too busy trying to keep her legs from folding beneath her and to curb the ferocious pounding of her heart.

After a fleeting moment, Ali ripped her gaze away and made her way carefully, with her shoulders erect, toward the outside hall and the ladies' room.

Adam, as he watched Ali's regal departure, felt his own heart react with an excited surge, only to have it then crash to his toes in deep despair. Her presence had caught him completely by surprise. He had assumed she would be well on her way to New York City by now. Obviously, she had changed her mind. He wondered if it were possible that he had anything to do with it. No, he told himself viciously. The pain and vulnerability he had seen in her eyes made him realize tenfold how rude and childishly he had behaved on learning she intended to return home. He'd be lucky now if she gave him the time of day.

But suddenly he knew he had to try and make things right between them again. From the moment he had stomped out of the Medfords' house, he had been miserable. He felt as if all the joy had gone from his life. He had to hope that it wasn't too late to repair the damage done and alter their present course. It was up to him.

Ali knew she was being pursued even before she felt the detaining hand on her shoulder.

"Ali—wait! Please," Adam demanded softly from close behind her.

Ali stopped and whirled around, determined not to let him see the damage his being with Molly had done to her already beleaguered emotions. She had to dig deep for the resources to clothe her features in a mask of cool indifference.

Evidently she had succeeded. So well in fact that it crossed her mind she should be nominated for an Academy Award for her acting ability. Adam recoiled from her as if he'd been struck.

"What do you want?" she asked, her words clipped and decisive when all she wanted to do was throw herself in his arms. But she didn't. She clamped her jaws together and waited.

It was on the tip of Adam's tongue to blurt out that all he wanted in the world was her, but something held him back. Gut instinct maybe. This wasn't the time nor the place, he thought, to get something started they wouldn't be able to finish, especially with people milling around them.

"We need to talk," he said, measuring his words, his eyes not releasing hers.

Every nerve in her body was drawn to the breaking point as she returned his stare. In the bright light of the open passageway she noted that he looked tired, as though he hadn't slept. A thin white line bordered his lips and a muscle twitched in his cheek. Serves him right, she thought.

"Why?" she said at last. "I thought you'd already had your say."

His slate-colored eyes impaled her. "Would it do any good if I said I was sorry, that I acted like an ass?"

"It—it might." Her head was spinning and her mouth was dry.

He expelled his breath slowly, heavily. "All right, then I'll say it, I'm sorry."

"What—what about Molly?" She hadn't intended to mention her, to even admit that she existed, but she couldn't help it, the words just tumbled from her lips.

A muttered expletive broke through his lips. "Forget about Molly," he said impatiently. "She means nothing to me, except as a friend."

"Oh?"

Dark color swept up to his hairline. "Dammit, Ali," he swore through rigid lips that barely moved. "Do you want me to get down on my knees and beg for your forgiveness?"

An answering color stained Ali's face. "No," she said bristling. How dare he try to place her in the wrong?

He was quiet for several seconds, his eyes steady on her flushed face. He was suddenly filled with self-loathing. "Oh, God, Ali, I'm—"

"Where do we go from here?" she interrupted softly, her eyes searching his face.

"That depends."

"On what?"

"Whether or not you're still holding that ticket to New York."

"I—I was planning to leave tomorrow."

"Could I by chance talk you out of it?"

"Yes, you could," she muttered indistinctly.

Suddenly Adam felt as if he would melt watching her. He longed to bury her in his heart and throw away the key. It nearly killed him to utter the next words.

"I—I can't see you until tomorrow morning, though."

"Why?" she asked, mistrust glazing her eyes with ice. Visions of him and Molly together for the rest of the day and evening skipped through her thoughts.

"Dammit, Ali," he demanded, "don't go cold on me now. I have to leave within the hour to deliver a colt. It's going to be a long, drawn-out affair." He paused, the lines deepening around his mouth. "I probably won't get back home until the wee hours of the morning."

Because she wanted so much to believe him, she did. "All right," she conceded softly.

"Will you be waiting? Tomorrow?"

A shudder shook her body. "Yes, I'll be waiting."

The moment the words escaped from her lips, she knew there was no turning back.

Chapter 11

It was noon the next day before a haggard-looking Adam arrived at Peaceful Valley. Ali had just come in from participating in a Ping-Pong contest and had stepped into the shower stall when she heard Cindy's knock, followed by her announcement of Adam's presence.

Mumbling to herself, Ali turned the water off and grabbed a towel. She quickly made her way to the door and poked her head around it.

"Oh, there you are," Cindy said as she crossed the room. "Did you hear me tell you Adam's here?"

"Yes, I heard," Ali responded breathlessly. Clearing her voice she went on before Cindy could say anything further. "Tell him I'll be there in a few minutes. Okay?"

Cindy smiled. "Okay." She paused a moment, running her swollen fingers through her hair. "By the way, I'm glad you decided not to go back to New York, at least not today anyway." She then placed her hand over her distended belly. "Something tells me Junior isn't going to wait his nine months before screaming his way into this old world." Although she still smiled, her eyes were troubled.

Ali didn't reply. Instead she threw Cindy a kiss and shut the bathroom door.

She was trembling as she jumped back into the shower and turned on the water, letting it penetrate her sensitive skin. Thoughts of Adam and the events of yesterday rose unbidden to her mind.

Somehow, after her turbulent encounter with Adam, she'd managed to make it back to the dining room and finish her cold meal. Keeping her eyes from straying to Adam's table had been one of the hardest things she'd ever done. She had briefly informed Cindy and Barry that she wouldn't be flying to New York tomorrow after all. Even though they figured Adam was behind her decision to stay, they had respected her privacy and hadn't bombarded her with questions.

The moment they had walked out of the restaurant an unexpected dizzy spell had hit Cindy sending them into a mild panic. They had scratched other planned activities for the afternoon, which had been just as well with Ali. Not only had it been imperative that Cindy get home and into bed, but Ali had that dreaded phone call to make to New York.

Even now as she lathered her hair, the conversation with her mother still rang loud and clear in her ears.

"What do you mean you're not coming back to New York?" Evelyn had mimicked Ali's exact words after Ali had been unsuccessful in tracking down Charles. In the end she'd had to call her mother.

"There are circumstances here that make it impossible for me to get away right now," she'd explained patiently.

"Ali, I'm not believing what I'm hearing." Evelyn paused significantly, the long-distance sounds crackling over the wire. "What, pray tell, could be more important than saving our business from ruin?" Evelyn's whining voice grated against Ali's nerves. "The stockholders are getting awfully edgy and I just might be tempted to—"

"Oh, spare me the martyrdom bit, Mother," Ali hissed through tight lips, patience having flown out the window. "I refuse to give in to this kind of blackmail. We both know you're not about to side with the board and agree to sell Cameron. You want to keep it in the family as much as I do, although for completely different reasons, I might add."

"Ali, you're being most unfair," Evelyn sniffed.

"Not unfair, Mother, just truthful," Ali corrected. "But all this is beside the point now. I want you to tell Charles that my plans for the new perfume will leave here by special delivery mail in the morning. If he'll casually mention it to a couple of the board members as I've asked him to, it should satisfy them that plans are definitely in the works to make Cameron a competitive company."

Still Evelyn was not quite ready to give up. "Don't you think you owe me and your uncle an explanation of why you are so adamant about not coming home?" she asked petulantly.

"Cindy's pregnant and not doing well at all," Ali conceded at last. "She became terribly upset when Charles called and demanded my appearance in New York." She hoped the good Lord would forgive her for not telling the whole truth. But she couldn't bring herself to mention Adam's name. She shuddered to think of how her mother would react to that kind of news. She would be mortified to think that her daughter would lower herself to fall in love with a veterinarian even if he could buy and sell Cameron Cosmetics twice over.

"Ali, are you still there?"

"Yes, Mother, I'm still here," Ali repeated with a sigh.

"When *may* we look forward to your returning home?"

"At the end of my allotted vacation time," Ali snapped defensively. "After all, Mother, I'm merely following Dr. Todd's orders. He'd have a fit if he knew I was even thinking about Cameron Cosmetics much less doing some actual work."

Suddenly the fight went out of Ali. Why was she bothering to explain anything to her mother? By doing so she was just wasting her time and effort. Her mother didn't care and nothing had changed. Her mother's selfishness used to hurt, but she had learned to accept it and live with it. Over the years, the shield around her heart had become thicker and no longer did Evelyn have the power to penetrate it.

"All right," Evelyn answered coolly when the silence became overpowering. "I'll give your message to Charles."

"Goodbye, Mother. I'll be in touch."

Now as she stood before her closet pondering what to wear, a towel wrapped around her, she felt liquid excitement wing its way through her body. She couldn't wait to see Adam, to have his arms around her. She felt like singing as she grabbed a pair of lavender Gloria Vanderbilt jeans off the hanger and a matching knit shirt with tiny pleats adorning the front.

Thrusting the towel aside, she stepped into a pair of lacy bikini panties and pulled on her jeans. Loving the freedom of going braless, she decided to do so again today as she lowered the top over her head and tucked it into her jeans. Then with as much adeptness as possible she made up her face and brushed her hair, leaving it bouncy and casual to caress her face. After slipping into a pair of thin-strapped sandals and spraying herself with perfume, she was ready.

Adam was chatting comfortably with Cindy when Ali waltzed into the kitchen. Although Adam didn't physically touch her when he rose to his feet, his eyes did. They exuded warmth and spoke volumes as they roamed leisurely over her, beginning with the honey-brown curls atop her head and going down to the dainty polished toes.

"What do you two have planned today?" Cindy asked, breaking through the tension that danced in the air.

Adam was the first to whisk his eyes away. He smiled at Cindy. "Nothing much, really." Then he shrugged, his gaze wandering back toward Ali who was now busily refilling Cindy's cup with hot chocolate. "I thought we'd just spend time around the ranch and clinic. There are several projects going on that require my supervision." His grin spread. "For one thing I'm supervising the breeding of two prize horses, plus I'm expecting a litter of puppies to be born any minute now."

Ali swung around to face him, her eyes wide with excitement. "Oh, can I watch—and help?" she asked eagerly.

Adam's eyes softened. "Wouldn't think of delivering them without you," he drawled intimately.

Again they were lost in each other, forgetting they were not alone until another voice interrupted. This time it was Barry.

For the next few minutes they visited over cups of hot chocolate and coffee and then Ali and Adam left.

There was a breathless silence between them as Adam nosed the Mercedes in the direction of his ranch. Ali was full of anticipation, for what she didn't know. But it was there, nevertheless, deep within her. *Did Adam feel it too?* she wondered. Maybe she just felt wonderful because she wasn't in New York but was instead with the man she adored.

"Wake up; we're here," Adam announced, jostling her out of her fanciful daydreaming.

She flashed him a warm smile. "What's first on the agenda?" she asked.

"This." His voice was deep and sensual as he scooted across the seat and fastened his lips on hers. It was a hot, soul-searching kiss. Then as abruptly as it began, it ended.

Adam leaned back and drew in a shaky breath. "I've been aching to do that since I saw you yesterday."

"Me, too," she whispered inanely, trying to regain her sense of balance.

His eyes darkened a moment, but then he reached for the door handle and pulled her across the seat to slide out on his side. Hand in hand they strolled up to the front door.

The following two hours were spent with Adam taking her on a tour of his clinic facilities. Ali found herself both impressed and fascinated by his operation. His clinic was outfitted with the best money could buy. She was introduced to the two women who helped him in the office and to the employee who cared for the sick animals as well as the ones that were boarded.

Although her mother never allowed her to have a pet of her own, she instinctively loved animals. She could remember visiting friends from school and spending half the time she was there playing with their dogs or cats.

As Adam had promised, the highlight of the early afternoon was the birth of seven collie puppies. Tears gathered on her eyelashes as she watched Adam's gentle, gloved hands coax and help the whimpering mother to birth one tiny puppy after another. Ali murmured words of comfort and patted the large dog on the head throughout the entire ordeal. When the collie began licking the afterbirth and cleaning the puppies, Ali looked on with awe, having never witnessed this act of nature before now.

Following the cleanup and seeing that the new mother was comfortable, Adam then took her on a tour of his ranch. He was like an eager boy as they meandered around the mowed pastureland that was close to the house. A special light sprang into his eyes when they came upon the acre of land that was his garden. He named every vegetable that he'd planted and nursed with his own bare hands, along with help from the latest in farm machinery, he added with a sheepish grin. So as not to miss one acre of his huge spread, they covered in the truck what they couldn't on foot.

During this time with Adam in such a relaxing atmosphere, Ali got another glimpse of the man behind the mask. When he walked his land, he was a different person. He laughed and was teasingly familiar. It seemed as though it gave him confidence, that somehow he knew it would never let him down. He truly loved and felt a reverence for every inch of the rich soil. Along with this insight also came the knowledge that Adam would never be happy away from the wide open spaces. She felt her heart die a little and the brightness of the day dim somewhat when she realized that never would she be able to lock Adam into any type of compromise. Even *if* he came to love her, she knew he would never be willing to leave his land.

Adam, however, refused to let her dark mood prevail for long. He teased and cajoled her until laughter shook her slender frame. Even though he hadn't made any further advances toward her, an electric tension hung between them like a keg of dynamite that needed only an errant spark to set it off.

Now, after having come back to the house and consumed a midafternoon snack, Adam pushed his plate away and smiled warmly at Ali. "While we can still move, we'd better wander down to the corral and check on the horses."

"That's a good idea." She grinned, and rubbed her still flat stomach. "I need to walk off some of this rich food. At this rate I won't be able to wear any of my clothes."

Now standing, his hooded eyes toured her body. "You're perfect the way you are." His gaze lingered for a long moment on the alluring swell of her breasts, causing her nipples to harden into twin peaks of desire and push against the soft fabric of her shirt.

"Let's go," he ordered abruptly, though it was obvious from the hoarseness of his voice that it took all his willpower to remove his eyes from her breasts.

Another silence fell heavily between them as they made their way toward the barn. The wide open pastureland was the only thing in front of her, the house having long since disappeared. Ali looked up, concern shadowing her eyes. In the short span of time it had taken them to eat and walk back outside, the sky had become overcast with dark, low-hanging clouds.

"Don't you think we'd better hurry? It looks like the bottom's going to fall out of the sky any minute now," she said.

Draping an arm casually around her shoulders, Adam pulled her close. "Don't worry. I think it'll hold off long enough for me to check on the horses, but if not, we can make a run for the barn."

"Good enough," she agreed, her mind preoccupied with being so close to him. She could smell his cologne and feel his hard muscles as she moved in perfect coordination against him.

After rounding another hill, a huge barn stood prominently before them. Moving closer, Ali could see the yellow hay that spilled from an open window. Catty-corner from the barn was a chestnut-colored mare watching them nervously.

"Isn't she a beauty?" Adam asked, his eyes shining. He removed his arm and moved closer to the fence.

"She certainly is," Ali declared, following his steps and moving closer.

"I've tried to buy her several times but my friend refuses to even talk to me about it."

"How long do you have to keep her?"

"Not much longer now," Adam said, turning his gaze on her.

"Why is that?"

"Because she's finally come into heat. And I have a stud locked up in the back part of the barn to breed her. Hopefully the breeding will take, and I'll get a colt out of the deal."

She smiled up at him sweetly. "I'll keep my fingers crossed."

"Come here," he demanded softly and reached for her, not giving her a chance to answer, not that she could have even if she had wanted to. She was too busy giving in to the liquid fire that had mysteriously replaced her blood. Adam held her tightly against him.

Then suddenly a weird sound filled the air.

Ali jerked her head up and around. "What—what was that?"

From the direction of the barn came the sounds of a horse whinnying. It sounded again momentarily, echoing through the still air, followed by another noise that sounded like the beat of a drum.

Ali had never heard anything like it before.

Adam released her, his gaze following hers. "That's my stallion. He's trying to kick the barn apart, wanting out."

Then their attention swung back around to the mare. She was putting on a show for them. First she lowered her head. Then she straightened and began to strut aimlessly around the pen. Suddenly she whinnied in return.

"Adam, what's going on?" Ali asked, feeling the ever-increasing tension about them, but unable to understand the reason for it.

Ignoring her question, he said to her instead, "I'm going to sit you up here for a minute." He then spanned his hands around her waist and lifted her onto the top rail of the fence.

"Adam—?"

"Just a minute. I'll explain," he assured her quietly and began peering at the mare closely. "Hallelujah! Just as I thought. She is in heat," he added jubilantly.

"What are you going to do?" Ali questioned anxiously.

Adam grinned. "Nothing at the moment. After I take you back to the house, I'll come back and let the stallion out of the barn."

"Are you sure he can't get out?"

"If you could see the stoutly fastened door, you wouldn't ask that. But the answer is no, he can't get out."

She stared toward the barn again. The pounding of the horse's hooves was louder.

"Come on," he said, "I'll walk you back." He put his arm around her to lift her off the fence. Behind them the mare bucked wild-eyed and whinnied loudly. Ali stiffened beneath Adam's hand. From the barn came the answering scream and clamor of the stallion.

Ali faced him, hypnotized. She moistened her suddenly dry lips.

"Adam," she whispered, her eyes wide and luminous, "I've—I've never seen..."

His eyes held hers motionless, breathless. Then slowly he unwound his gainly frame from the fence rail and strode jerkily toward the barn. Her heartbeat escalated as she heard the loud snap of the lock and the clanging release of the bar. He then raced around the corner and climbed back up on the fence to sit beside her.

For a moment all was quiet. The mare stood still, her neck arched, listening. Then she began to paw the ground nervously. Suddenly the huge stallion appeared. He whinnied and reared again, his front feet grappling with the air, before thundering toward the mare. Anticipating his presence, the mare screamed and reared, slashing down on his back with her front hooves. Simultaneously, the stallion reared, his front feet barreling down over her. She struggled to get up. She couldn't. He had her trapped, his teeth clamped to the back of her neck.

Ali's eyes were riveted on Adam's, terror in their depths, her face pale.

The mare lunged, frantic to escape. But her efforts were fruitless. Instantly the stallion reared, whinnying loud and long, and then he plummeted heavily on top of her back. His hips quivered convulsively. He stiffened and aimed, then drew back suddenly.

"Oh, God, Adam, he's hurting her," she cried. "Can't you stop him?"

Her hands grasped Adam's shoulders, digging her nails into him. She tried to look away, but she couldn't. As she watched the stallion take his last and final plunge, Ali trembled violently and fell against Adam.

Adam gripped her tighter as the stud screamed, shoving the mare's knees into the dirt. Then it was over.

Though neither moved, their eyes met and locked.

Ali reeled from the hot passion that burned from Adam's eyes.

"Adam—" she whispered.

Needing no further encouragement, he slipped from the fence, scooped her up into his arms and half ran with her into the dimly lit barn.

Chapter 12

In the corner was a pile of hay. Adam covered the distance from the door quickly and kneeling, set her down on the soft pile. Their eyes clung, their breathing heavy. Instantaneously they tore at their clothing.

He reached for her as a battle raged within him. He longed to love her tenderly but at the same time he wanted to grind her fragile bones to him, to take her savagely.

Ali read his message and answered him with one of her own. Wordlessly she extended a hand and closed it around him. He was thick and warm to her touch.

A guttural sound escaped his throat as he fell onto her. She tightened her hold on him as he crushed his lips to hers. His tongue ravaged her mouth before pulling it away only to latch onto a perfect, uptilted breast. He tried desperately to take the entire globe into his mouth, so greedy was his need for her. Failing at this, he was content to settle his attention on a nipple. He drew first one and then the other into the moist lining of his lips, feeling them expand into tiny hard knots.

Ali whimpered softly and thrashed about the bed of hay, oblivious to the pricks into her bare backside. She felt heat from his ardent adoration of her nipples expand and rush to her innermost being.

"Now—now!" she cried as his mouth moved to close again over the bruised softness of her.

His control snapped. He grabbed her hips. She helped him by arching to meet his bold thrust. She gasped as she gave herself up to the raw, primitive passion that ripped through her body as she welcomed his strength, giving as equally as she took.

She stiffened. She cried out suddenly.

He drove deeper. His cry echoed hers.

Then he moaned and was still.

"Is it raining?" she asked later, her voice soft and lazy. She snuggled against him, the prickly hay no longer a deterrent to her comfort.

"Pouring down." He lay quietly, not moving.

"I thought so."

He was silent.

"Adam—"

"Huh?"

Her mind was still reeling from the aftermath of their sweet, savage lovemaking. The erotic sensations had left her weak. He still lingered warmly in her flesh.

She rolled over onto her side and faced him.

"Hi," he whispered. He kissed her throat, the upper swells of her breasts.

"A penny for your thoughts," she said drowsily.

"I'm sorry," he countered, "they're worth much more than that."

"One dollar."

"You're not even close."

"One hundred dollars."

"You're still off the mark."

"I give up."

"That's not fair."

"Tell me."

Dare he tell her? *Yes, dammit, tell her! Tell her you love her. That you've loved her from the first moment you laid eyes on her.*

You're crazy, Forrest! Nobody falls in love at first sight. Still, he couldn't tell her. The words wouldn't come; they were frozen in his heart.

But maybe that was best for both of them, he thought, the pain inside now mushrooming into an endless, aching void. Love without sacrifice and commitment, he knew, would crumble and turn to dust. He had lived through the hell of that kind of love, and it had nearly destroyed him.

Yet, Ali was different, so wonderfully different from the other women he'd known, including Mary. Certainly Mary. He had never felt any of the emotions for Mary that he felt for this lovely woman in his arms.

But still, he kept his silence. Fear trapped the words in his throat. Fear that Ali could never love him and accept him for what he was. Especially when she learned the truth...

Suddenly he felt like crying.

Even though the light was dim in the musky barn, Ali could see the play of emotions that flickered across Adam's face. He looked lonely and pathetically unhappy. She couldn't bear it.

"If you won't share your million-dollar thoughts with me, then I'll share mine with you."

"Ali..."

The words spilled from her mouth, unedited, unrehearsed. She couldn't hold them back even if her life had depended on it. "I . . . I love you."

Tears danced on the tips of her eyelashes as she looked up at him, her heart in her eyes.

"Oh, God, Ali, I . . ." His voice throbbed with his own tears.

"Shh . . . it's all right," she whispered against his lips, cradling him in her arms, comforting him.

Adam, like a parasite, drew from her silent strength, feeling it purge the pain from his soul and melt the ice from his heart. She held him as if she'd never let him go. And in that beautiful moment, he knew that he had indeed found his Heaven on earth.

Like warm, sweet honey, the words flowed from his lips, "I love you," he said softly.

His quietly spoken utterance rivaled the tingling sound of the rain as it splattered down on the roof. But Ali heard it, heard it loud and clear. Her heart sang. Her pulse vibrated with a joy that she never thought would be hers. She wanted to shout her happiness aloud.

Then suddenly she sobered, feeling a chill tiptoe over her body. It took a moment to understand why. Adam's warm body no longer shielded her. He had turned on his side, facing the opposite direction. Something was wrong. Without having to search her heart, she knew it was his past. It forever haunted him. Somehow she had to get him to rid his soul of the poison that festered within. She was so close to catching her rainbow that she mustn't give up now.

Rolling over, she fitted herself into his back. She then began to brush tender kisses across his shoulders, down the middle of his back. She tasted on her lips the shiver that passed through him as she continued to nip him with tiny wet kisses.

"There's something you have to tell me, isn't there?"

"Yes," he confessed on a sigh. He rolled over on his back, raising his arms above his head and cushioning it in his hands. He stared at the lofty ceiling, listening to the raindrops.

Ali refused to give up. "Please . . . tell me."

"It's not a pretty story." His voice had grown cold, like chips of ice.

"I love you."

A shudder shook him. *Oh, God, please let her still love me after she hears what I have to say.* "All right," he said wearily, "I'll tell you."

She breathed a sigh of relief and laid her head on his chest and waited.

"I married my ex-wife, Mary," he began, "while I was studying to be a veterinarian. Having come from an upper-class, moneyed background in Boston, she was unhappy living on a struggling doctor's salary." He paused. "She also despised living in the 'sticks' of Arkansas, as she so aptly phrased it."

Ali listened for the pain in his voice but to her surprise, there was none. She detected only bitterness. Realizing there was nothing she could say, she comforted him the only way she knew how—she touched him. The ends of her fingers lightly pilfered the wiry cushion on his chest in a gentle soothing motion.

He stilled her hand and gazed at her naked limbs molded to his. "If you want me to continue talking, I suggest you stop what you are doing," he murmured, the tone of his voice low and unsteady.

"I'm—I'm sorry."

"I tried. God knows how hard I tried to appease her, to make up for the lack of material things. Of course, we weren't paupers in any sense of the word, but neither were we well off." He sighed. "I guess what I'm trying to say is that we were living like the average American married couple and that just wasn't enough for her."

"Did you—you love her, terribly?"

He thought for a moment. "Yes, I loved her or thought I did." His face was grim. "But it wasn't long until I realized that I'd made the same mistake so many other poor fools make; I confused physical attraction with love. She was beautiful, and with her alluring beauty, she led me on a merry chase. When I learned there was nothing beneath that facial beauty but selfishness, greed, and a will to control and manipulate everyone in her path my love died, never to be rekindled."

"She had qualities reminiscent of my mother," Ali interjected quietly.

"Oh, believe me, there's more," he droned sarcastically. "I've only touched the tip of the iceberg."

Ali sighed and burrowed closer.

"We had been married a year, a year filled with bitterness and unhappiness for both of us, when the blow fell that finally ended it all."

There was another prolonged silence.

Ali felt every muscle in his body stiffen.

"What happened?" she asked.

"She apparently forgot to take her birth control pills, or so she told me, and got pregnant...."

For reasons Ali didn't wish to pursue, this announcement knocked the props out from under her. "And that made you unhappy?"

"No, fool that I was, I was delighted." His laugh was harsh. "I thought maybe a child might serve as a stepping stone toward piecing together the torn remnants of our marriage.''

"Knowing that you no longer loved her, why didn't you just leave? Get a divorce?''

He sighed deeply. ''I guess I hated to admit that I had failed. Failed at what I hoped to be a lifetime affair.''

"The baby. What about the baby?''

The pulse at the base of his throat was beating overtime. ''She came in one afternoon and calmly informed me that—that she'd just had the child she was carrying—aborted.'' His voice was riddled with emotion.

She held him tighter, trying desperately to absorb some of the pain that raked his body. ''Oh, my love, I'm sorry, so sorry.''

He cleared his throat. ''I'm convinced till this day that if I hadn't been so stunned, I would have strangled her with my bare hands.''

"But...but why did she do such a thing?'' Ali was horrified.

"Because Mary couldn't stand the thought of it having a father who was illegitimate—a bastard, to put it crudely.''

There was another moment of dangerous silence.

Then his voice rose perceptibly. ''She went on to tell me that she couldn't allow a child of *hers* to bear the stigma of its father's background. You see, my mother died immediately after I was born. From all accounts, my father was a one-night stand.'' He paused significantly. ''She didn't even know his name.'' There was another pause. ''End of story.''

"Didn't Mary know all this when she married you?''

"Of course she knew. Even though she assured me at the time it didn't matter, it did. It was a bitter pill she never learned to swallow.''

Ali knew the next few seconds were crucial. She couldn't pretend she wasn't shocked by his admission. She was. His words had struck her like a thunderbolt. But she could never let him know this. To her, his past was just that—the past. Illegitimacy was no longer the stigma it used to be. She loved him for the man he was today, this moment. His family lineage or the lack of it had no bearing on her feelings for him. If only she could make him understand that she truly loved him, then their love would stand a chance.

"Adam, please listen to me," she pleaded softly, feeling his body tense up once again. "I couldn't care less what your past is. I love you." She paused, searching for the right words to act as a balm to his battered soul. "Granted, Mary and I came from the same background, but I'm not like her." Again she repeated the obvious. "I love you. You've got to believe me." *And I'd follow you to the ends of the earth if only you'd ask me to,* she added silently.

"Oh, darling," he groaned, turning and gathering her into his arms. He buried his face in her scented curls clinging to the side of her neck and kissed her through them, tiny, nibbling kisses. "I wish I'd met you a long time ago. How much different my life would have been."

Ali didn't trust herself to speak as unbelievable waves of excitement leapt through her. She gave herself up to his lips that blazed a path across her cheek to the velvet rim of her ear and then back to her mouth, sinking into it with a hungering intensity.

She melted into him, his fiery touch sending tingles of anticipation and shock down her spine.

Then he drew back. His eyes were slits of darkness. "Oh, God, Ali, please," he cried, his voice thick and warm like honeyed brandy. "Don't let this all be a dream."

Giving her no chance to speak, his lips burned into hers again. Tongues met, warred, devoured until they were both gasping for breath.

"Oh, Adam—oh, darling," she cried wildly as he suddenly but gently rolled her over on her side and pulled her back against him. She felt his vibrant hardness rest between her soft cheeks before sliding lower to pause at the gate of her silken valley. He began to caress her there, parting her ever so effectively.

She stiffened. Although swept away by the erotic pleasure he was bringing to her, she nevertheless couldn't help but be frightened by this experience that was totally beyond her comprehension.

"Relax, my darling, and trust me," he breathed close to her ear.

She did.

As he instructed and encouraged her with sweet loving words, he felt her yielding. His fingers that were roaming with tender eagerness over her thigh now ventured down to the tuft of curly hair that veiled her womanhood. There his fingers worked their magic, delving, probing until Ali thought she would scream aloud from pure pleasure.

He moved ever so slightly, easing his bold passion into her, stroking deeper as he felt her moistness yield to him. He began moving while a hand kneaded the ripe fullness of her breasts, tantalizing first one and then the other.

"Oh, yes—yes," Ali moaned as she writhed and pushed harder against him. He saturated her shoulders and neck with hot moist kisses as his hand anchored her thigh. Clutching it for support, his plunges became faster and harder and more powerful.

His tongue licked wildly at her ear and again at her bare shoulders as he poured into her, bringing them to a shattering and piercing climax.

"Ali...Ali...Ali," he moaned and slumped against her, locking his arms around her smooth scented flesh, knowing that he could never let her go.

They slept.

Ali was the first to awaken. She noted immediately that it was no longer raining and that it was late. Remaining within the confines of Adam's warm embrace, she shifted to a more comfortable position relieving the arm that had fallen asleep. No longer feeling the prickly sensations, she turned her attention back to Adam.

Tears flooded her eyes as she took in his sleeping form. His face was no longer strained, but totally relaxed and at peace. She loved him more than she ever thought possible to love another human being.

Tomorrow shone bright, full of promise. Somehow, someway they would be together. She would see to it. He had told her he loved her. That was enough for now.

They were making their way at a leisurely pace toward the house, arms entwined, when they heard the loud pounding of a horse's hooves.

"What the hell," Adam muttered as horse and rider came into view.

It was Matt. Adam grabbed the horse's mane as Matt brought him to an abrupt stop in front of him and Ali. The horse's nostrils flared wildly as he seemingly fought for his next breath. He pawed the ground vigorously.

Ali's eyes were wide and anxious as she peered up into the foreman's dark countenance. For an unknown reason fear curled at the base of her stomach, making her feel suddenly nauseous.

"Dammit," Adam was saying, "whatever you have to tell me had better be important." Adam scowled as he waited for an explanation. He resented this untimely intrusion, thinking it had to do with the clinic.

But the next words banished that thought from his mind. Matt's gaze swept past his and settled on Ali's. He removed his hat in a sweeping gesture. "Sorry, ma'am," he panted, "but you're to meet Mr. Medford at the hospital immediately." He licked his lips. "Mrs. Cindy's real bad sick."

They made it just as Cindy, with a frantic-looking Barry by her side, was being wheeled out of the elevator and down the long corridor.

Trying to keep the tears at bay, Ali grabbed Cindy's hand, forcing the attendant to momentarily halt the stretcher.

Cindy moved her head. "Ali . . . ?"

"Yes . . . it's me."

"I'm—I'm glad." A solitary tear dropped from the corner of her right eye and disappeared into her hair. "I'm—I'm so scared . . . the baby." Her breath was coming in short, raspy spurts.

"Shh, the baby will be fine; you wait and see," Ali whispered, continuing to cup Cindy's palm against her cheek. She felt her heart turn over as she noticed Cindy's other arm lying on the sheet. It was connected by a long tube to a glass bottle suspended upside down from a hooked stand attached to rollers.

Her face, which was always pale of late, was now drained of color to the bone. Her eyelids fluttered until her eyelashes yielded a screen for the dark circles beneath her eyes. She had fallen asleep.

Ali refused to let go of Cindy's limp hand as she raised frantic eyes to Barry. "What happened?"

Barry's Adam's apple jumped convulsively. "She—she fainted and I couldn't get her to come to." His eyes were dull with unsuppressed pain. "It began as a dizzy spell, but as you can see—" He broke off, obviously too upset to continue. He turned aside in hopes of masking the tears that glistened in his eyes.

Quickly and silently, Adam moved to Barry's side and placed a comforting hand on his shoulder. "Take it easy. Everything will be fine."

"Where—where are they taking her?" Adam asked, looking down again at Cindy's still, white form.

"To a room and then eventually to surgery," Barry said brokenly.

It was a subdued and silent trio who accompanied Cindy's stretcher, attended by two nurse's aides, to a sparsely furnished room on the first floor. Shadows clung to the wall and the furniture. After switching on the lamp above the bed, an aide asked them to wait outside for a moment.

"What exactly did the doctor tell you?" Adam asked Barry as they stood near the closed door to Cindy's room. His arm was draped casually around Ali's shoulders.

Ali stood stiff and straight, fighting back the tears that were hovering near the surface. She couldn't have made it this far without Adam and his comforting nearness. He was her wall of strength and she had to fight the urge to lean against him now and cry her heart out, letting him absorb the fear that numbed her body. But she couldn't do that. Not now. Barry needed her too much for her to crumble.

The trip from Adam's ranch to the hospital was still somewhat hazy in her mind. She remembered vividly, though, Adam's taking over. While he'd driven like a careful maniac from the ranch through the streets of Fayetteville, fear rode her like a master. Fear for Cindy, her unborn child, and for Barry.

Thoughts of her unsettled future with Adam had been shoved to the back of her mind. She had emptied her mind of everything except Cindy. And yet she had been aware of Adam's enfolding love. It had surrounded her like a warm cloak, easing the terror that had her in its grip. As the Mercedes devoured the miles, she couldn't help but think about the bleakness of Cindy and Barry's future compared with the brightness of hers.

Now as Adam's tender touch nudged her back to the moment at hand, she looked up at him. His brows were furrowed together, and his eyes were shadowed with concern. He was hanging on to Barry's every word.

Intertwining her clammy hands, she turned her attention to Barry.

"The doctor didn't promise he could save the baby," he was saying, "but he said there was a good chance that he could." There was a quiver in his voice that he made no effort to hide. He had the appearance of an old and broken man.

Adam had no chance to reply. Suddenly the heavy door swung open and both aides exited quietly. Following Barry into the dimly lit room, Ali and Adam waited at the foot of the bed and watched as Barry lowered his head very slowly to Cindy's hair.

"Darling," he breathed.

"Barry...?" Her voice was tense.

"Yes, love, I'm here."

"I...dreamed you had left...me."

Barry sat down on the side of the bed close to her and kissed her mouth. Her eyes were rounded, but vacant as though she was somewhere far away.

"I—I'll never leave you, you know that," he whispered.

"Our—our baby."

"What about it?"

"Is—is it all right?" Her finely boned fingers on her free hand began wandering over her swollen stomach. She reached for Barry's hand and placed it on her stomach. He roamed it lovingly, gently.

"Of course, it's all right," he murmured hoarsely. "Junior is going to be fine and so are you."

"I'm . . . so tired."

"Sleep, my darling, sleep."

Her hand clutched at his arm. "You—you won't leave?"

He held her hand tightly. "I'm not . . . going anywhere."

Suddenly Ali couldn't take any more. Tears were streaming down her face as she stumbled to the door and pulled it open. She barely made it to the waiting room before the sobs racked her body.

She was powerless to help ease the suffering of two of the dearest people in the world to her. Gut-wrenching worry for both Cindy and her unborn child made her mouth dry and her stomach heave. She tried to choke down the sobs, to get hold of her emotions.

Tenderly Adam circled his arms around her from behind and held her tightly against his chest.

"Honey, don't," he said, "you're going to make yourself sick."

"I'm—I'm already sick," she wailed, digging her nails into his arms that were like velvet chains around her body.

"I know, I know." He talked to her almost as if she were a small child. "I'm worried and hurting too. For both of them."

Realizing how selfish she must sound, she made an effort to get control of herself. Taking long deep breaths, she turned in his arms, laying her head against his broad chest.

"I'm—I'm sorry," she apologized. "It's—it's just that I feel so helpless."

Gentle hands were smoothing her tumbled curls. "I know how you feel," he responded with a sigh. "I'm not one to play a waiting game either."

It proved to be a long vigil. Several hours later Cindy finally was prepped and wheeled into surgery. The doctor had informed Barry that he was going to take the baby by cesarean section. He had gone on to tell him that by doing so now, the baby had a good chance of survival.

The minutes stretched into an hour. Then two hours. Still they waited. By the ungodly hour of twelve o'clock midnight they had the surgical waiting room to themselves.

Barry prowled the area like a caged lion, his shoulders hunched over, his face tear-stained and lined. Adam, though outwardly calm, looked worn out and haggard. Ali sat hunched over in the corner on the couch, her stocking feet tucked under her, and stared at her watch. None could bring comfort to the other as they waited, hoped, and prayed.

It was two o'clock when the doctor came slowly through the swinging double doors of surgery.

Ali's eyes flew to Barry as he stopped his pacing and whirled around to face the doctor. With Adam's assistance she got up from the couch and together they moved to stand beside Barry.

Ali watched as the doctor removed the green surgical cap from his head. His eyes looked like a road map, but he hesitated to look at Barry. She had to strain to hear his softly spoken words above the loud pounding of her heart.

"Barry." He spoke gently. "You have been blessed with a three and a half pound baby girl."

"Cindy?" Fear surrounded every syllable of her name. *"What about Cindy!"* he cried.

"I'm sorry," he said, "we were unable to save her." His frame sagged wearily. "She never regained consciousness."

"No!" He fell to his knees and gave a pitiful, angry cry. "Cindy!"

Then he bent over double and wept silently.

Chapter 13

Sorrow.

It saturated her heart and her mind until at times she felt she couldn't bear it. But she never allowed herself the luxury of giving in to this despair in public. It was a private matter. Outwardly she put on a brave front for Barry. If it had not been for Adam, though, she couldn't have done it. He was her mainstay and Rock of Gibraltar. As for Barry, he was both mentally and physically crippled. Nothing or no one could ease his inconsolable grief.

Adam took charge. He made all the funeral arrangements while Ali kept things together around the ranch. They both made sure Barry was not left by himself for long. Even the tiny baby girl who lay in the hospital fighting for her life failed to penetrate the sorrow that squeezed his heart and threatened his sanity.

The funeral was one of the saddest days of Ali's life. Tears flowed unchecked down her face and she was positive her heart would break as she saw Barry cling to his wife's lifeless body before Adam bore him away to allow the attendants to close the coffin.

Much of Ali's time was spent traveling back and forth from the ranch to the hospital. The baby, christened Cindy Marie, remained on the critical list since she was three months premature. It would be weeks, maybe months, before she would be able to come home. With Barry in the state that he was in, the responsibility for Cindy Marie rested squarely on Ali's shoulders.

And today, three weeks after Cindy's death, was no different, except for one thing: It would be her last trip to the hospital for a while. Tomorrow morning she would be on her way to New York.

She dreaded this day and the evening ahead of her. She had yet to tell Adam of her plans. Just the thought of it made her stomach lurch and her hands tremble as she tried to put the finishing touches on her makeup. Adam was due any minute to drive her to the hospital.

Suddenly a soft tap on her bedroom door claimed her attention. Adam? No. It couldn't be. He wouldn't just barge in. Anyway the front door was locked.

Frowning she glided across the room and opened the door. Barry stood there, looking lost and vulnerable.

She smiled sweetly and stepped aside. "Hi, come on in. I had no idea you were still here."

"I didn't interrupt anything, did I?" he asked, a hesitant smile crossing his lips, though his eyes remained listless, dull. She was worried about Barry and hated to leave him even for a few days. But after the phone call last night, she had no choice.

"I just wanted to remind you to tell the nurses that I'll be coming to the hospital every day from now on to check on—" He broke off and swallowed convulsively. "To check on Cindy Marie."

Ali emitted a sigh of relief. "You'll be surprised when you see her," she said softly. "She's improving more and more every day." She paused. "She's a living doll."

Barry turned his head and pawed the carpet uneasily with his boot. "I'm—I'm glad," he finally said, but Ali wasn't fooled. She could read the intense pain laced with disinterest in his voice.

For a moment Ali was tempted to scream at him, to tell him how lucky he was to still have a part of Cindy in flesh and blood to love and to cherish. After the numbness and shock had worn off and the feeling had returned to his dead body, he seemed to resent the child. Ali kept telling herself that this was a normal feeling, especially after the trauma Barry had been through and the responsibility that faced him. But she still longed to shake him for his sudden indifference toward his own child.

The tiny bundle of joy who had clung so tenaciously to life and was not out of danger as yet had soaked up much of her own grief. The baby could do the same for Barry if only he'd let her.

Ali sighed as she looked at his haggard, thin face, the deep lines pronounced around his mouth. At least she should be thankful that he would be going to the hospital in her absence. That in itself was a miracle.

"Adam's on his way now to pick me up to go to the hospital." She paused holding his gaze. "Now that you're still here would—would you care to go with us?"

He made a weary gesture and shifted his eyes. "No—no, there's several business matters that I have to attend to." He paused heavily. "It—it's time I went back to work."

A heavy weight descended upon her. "I—I understand." And she did, but it nevertheless tore her heart to ribbons to see him like this.

Barry turned as if to leave and then whirled back around, his eyes suddenly filled with tears. "Ali, do you have to go back to New York?" His plea was filled with anguish as the tears trickled down his cheeks. "Can't you wait until later?"

Ali had seen Barry cry many times during the past few weeks, but each time he did so, it increased her own pain. Now was no exception, especially since she was the cause of those tears.

"Barry, please—" she began, only to have her own voice falter. Finally, when she had gained control of her emotions, she went on, "You know I can't put off going home any longer. You heard my conversation with Charles and my mother last night." She paused, stifling her own tears. "Without harping on the gory details, the bottom line is that if I don't go back, I'm going to be an absentee witness to the demise of Cameron Cosmetics," she finished dully.

"I know I'm a selfish bastard," he declared harshly. "It's just that I've come to depend on you to take care of— Cindy Marie."

And that's another reason why I need to go away, she thought sadly. "You and Cindy Marie will do just fine, you'll see." She smiled. "But I'll be back as soon as I can. Before you bring the baby home, for sure."

His answer was to lean over and give her a peck on the cheek. He then turned and left the room.

His suffering pulled at her heartstrings, but Barry was depending on her to take care of *his* baby and as much as she loved them both, she couldn't accept that responsibility. She had the loose threads of her own life to tie up and secure.

Adam. Just thinking about him made her pulse quicken. He had been so gentle, so kind, so loving, and so dependable during this long period of sadness. But not once had she been with him alone. She had been deprived of the feel of his lips and his touch for such a long time that her body ached.

Out of respect for Cindy, coupled with the hectic pace they had been forced to keep following the funeral, she and Adam had kept their distance. But nothing had kept her from thinking about him and the warm promise of their future hovering at the edge of her heart. She knew Adam shared her feelings. She had seen it in his eyes, making words between them unnecessary.

Suddenly the musical chime of the doorbell snapped her back to the present. A thrill darted through her. *A whole day in Adam's company,* she thought. She could hardly wait.

Then she remembered. Before the day was over she had to tell Adam she was leaving. But this time when she told him, she vowed, there would be no misunderstanding, no harsh words. He would know that nothing short of death itself would prevent her from returning to Arkansas—to him.

The moment she flung open the door, they walked into each other's arms.

"I've been aching to hold you like this for the last three weeks," Adam said, molding her close against him and kissing her deeply. Then he drew back, a shudder escaping his lips. "As you can see or feel, I should say, I'm in intense pain." His eyes held a dancing gleam, but Ali knew he wasn't altogether teasing her.

She acted without thinking. Her eyes flew to his midsection where they centered with awed scrutiny on his taut thigh muscles that emphasized his steely hardness.

To her dismay her face turned a fiery shade of red. She stood motionless, her tongue clinging to the dry roof of her mouth.

"Come here," he commanded quietly, the teasing light gone from his eyes. "Oh, God, I need you so," he added in an urgent whisper.

An answering pulse in her own body sent her rushing back into the close confines of his arms. She melted next to him, feeling the strain and stress of the past weeks drain from her body. Contentment and love flowed through her, making her feel dizzy, yet acutely awake.

"I suggest we leave *now* or not at all."

They left immediately.

Adam drove straight to the hospital where they remained with Cindy Marie until lunchtime. They stopped for a quick bite of lunch, and then Ali rode with him to make several house calls. She looked on as he set a horse's leg and vaccinated cattle.

It had been a wonderful day, made even more precious to Ali because it was to be their last one together for a while. The evening shadows had cooled the day by the time Adam called it quits and drove them back to his ranch.

Now as Ali sat comfortably in Adam's den with her feet curled under her, she watched as he came toward her with a tray of drinks.

"I thought this might help you relax," he said.

"Mmmm, that looks good."

He sat beside her and handed her a glass of chilled white wine.

"Here's to us, my darling," he whispered, holding his glass up to click with hers.

"To us," she echoed thickly. *Now,* her heart prompted. *Tell him now.* But suddenly her tongue felt like it had been dipped in concrete. She told herself it was because she didn't want to shatter this wonderful moment between them. But actually, she feared his reaction. She couldn't help but remember the last time she had mentioned returning to New York. She shivered.

Adam's eyes darkened. "What's wrong, darling?" He set his glass down on the coffee table and drew her into his arms. "Ah, this is more like it." He sighed into the fragrant swirls of her hair. "We can take up where we left off this morning."

"Oh, Adam, I love you," she cried. The words tumbled from her lips as she locked her arms around his neck.

His hold tightened. Mouths locked. Suddenly Adam scooped her up into his arms and strode with her to the bedroom. His insides were on fire. He could wait no longer. What he aimed to do was make love to her until she couldn't breathe anymore.

He kissed her neck and her shoulders as he fell with her onto the bed and groaned with rising passion.

"Oh, Ali, can you feel how desperately I want you, how desperately I need you, love you?"

She moaned with pleasure at the sound and meaning of his words. Then his hands were everywhere. Naked, they blended together as one, mouth to mouth, breasts to breasts. Every nerve, every cell in her body was electrified as she felt his throbbing arousal rub against the sensitive place that guarded the threshold of her womanhood.

Only when her cries filled his mouth did he relent. He then lavished his attention on her breasts where he wooed each one with languishing deliberation.

His name, over and over, was a pitiful whimper on her lips as he continued his sweet assault on her body.

His love filled every pore on every inch of her skin. And he left no portion unattended or untouched. A hand began caressing the right side of her body greedily before stroking the honey-gold triangle between her legs.

She received his fingers as a bud opening to the summer sun. There he paid his homage until he had reached his own limit. He then lifted her hips and forcefully penetrated her, delving deeper and deeper until he was cocooned by her sweet softness.

They moved together as one until Ali reached her last and final pinnacle of bliss.

He moaned simultaneously, and she felt him quiver and shudder.

"How about something to eat?" Adam asked later as Ali wandered into the kitchen looking like a bemused teenager sporting his terry cloth lounging robe.

"Nothing for me, thanks," she said, walking lightly in her bare feet to the table and sitting down. She propped her chin in her hands and studied him.

"Mmmm, you smell good." He wrinkled his nose. "Good enough to eat in fact. Much more tempting than this salad I'm preparing," he teased.

The tip of her pink tongue appeared and circled her lips. "You won't hear any objections from this corner," she teased back.

Dark passion leapt into his eyes. "Don't tempt me," he cautioned softly.

Ali lowered her gaze, stunned that even after hours of lovemaking, she still wanted more of him.

He smiled suddenly, and with it, the tension eased. Sitting down in front of her with a bowl heaped full of salad, he said, "Well, if you won't eat, then you'll have to keep me company while I do."

It didn't take him long to consume his meal. Shortly Ali found herself once again lounging comfortably on the couch, the strains of a Bach piece floating softly from the stereo.

She watched the play of muscles in his shoulders as he fiddled with the stereo speakers. She had to tell him now, she thought. Time was running out.

Before she could change her mind, his name bounced off her lips, "Adam—"

"Yeah, hon," he replied absently, continuing with his busy work.

She hesitated. "I—I need to talk to you."

"So talk. I'm listening."

She toyed with the tie on the robe. "I'm—I'm flying to New York in the morning. But I'll be back in less than a week," she added hastily before he had a chance to counterattack.

She saw his back muscles tense. The haunting sounds of Bach came to a screeching halt. Silence. It was as scorching as the sand on a barren desert.

He stood up slowly and turned around. His eyes glittered dangerously. "What did you say?"

Knowing that he'd heard her, she didn't bother to repeat the statement. Instead she said, "Please, Adam, try to understand." She grappled for the right words that would erase that black look from his face and eyes. "Mother and Charles phoned again last night." She swallowed. "The board was thrilled with my ideas for the new perfume line. So now I have no choice but to go to New York and see that they become a reality." She paused, clutching her trembling hands together. "If I—I don't go back, they're going to sell Cameron." Those words broke through her lips with an agonizing whisper.

"Don't go." His words were clipped and final.

Her heart slammed painfully against her ribs. "Adam, you're being unreasonable. I have to go!" She retched the words out.

"No!" he grated harshly.

"No, what?" she countered, wetting fear-dried lips and trying to hold onto her temper.

"No, I'm not being unreasonable and *no* you don't have to go."

Ali stared at him wild-eyed. "Yes, I do! Didn't you hear what I just said? They're threatening to sell Cameron."

"Let 'em."

"No!" she shouted.

"How can you think about leaving now?" he demanded savagely. "Even if you don't care about my feelings, you know that Barry's counting on you to help him with Cindy Marie, especially when he brings her home from the hospital." He heard the thread of panic that ran through his voice, but could do nothing to squelch it. And he knew he was being unreasonable, but he could do nothing about that either.

Ali prayed silently for patience. "I know that, Adam," she said with as much calm as the volatile situation would allow. "You know the minute I get things squared away in New York, I'll be on the next plane." She blinked. "And you don't have to remind me of my obligation to Barry. I'm well aware of it."

"What about me?" He turned his back on her.

She struggled to hold back the tears. "Adam..." *Oh, God, how could she make him understand?*

The silence was deafening.

Then suddenly he whirled around. His eyes blazed with fire. "Was the romp in the sheets for the sole purpose of softening me up, getting me ready for the kill?"

Ali's head snapped back, his words a stinging slap in the face. She stared at him dumbfounded. When she finally collected her scattered senses, cold fury raced through her bloodstream. She jumped up, her fingers clenched to her sides tightly, her jutting breasts the result of a pounding heart. "How dare you insinuate..." She could not go on. What he'd said was so ludicrous and so grossly untrue that she would not lower herself to acknowledge it.

"Easily!" he hissed, his own voice cold as steel.

Then just as quickly as her anger rose, it subsided. What was she doing? she berated herself silently. A shouting match was not the way to settle their differences.

She tried another approach. "What I feel for you has nothing to do with my returning to New York." Her soft lips suddenly began to waver. "I love you. That will never change. But I do have a responsibility that I have to fulfill. There are loose ends that have to be tied up before I can come to you a free woman."

Another uneasy silence followed her words, his eyes never relinquishing hers.

Then he spoke, "Do you remember shortly after I met you, saying these words to me? And I quote: 'If you're going to wade, you might as well go knee-deep.'" He paused and waited for her response. Remembering the statement clearly, Ali nodded, though she frowned in puzzlement.

"If you'll also remember," he continued, "I told you I'd remind you of that statement later. Well, I'm reminding you now. I'm asking you not only to plunge knee-deep but all the way." He paused and moved closer to her, so close that she could smell his warm breath. She couldn't tear her eyes away from his mouth. "Marry me. Now. Tomorrow. And then tell your family to take that business and do anything they damn well please with it!" His last words were ground out on a desperate note.

Ali's senses reeled. Marry! He was asking her to marry him! A surge of happiness invaded her heart and threatened to overwhelm her. But then she remembered the words that followed. Suddenly she saw her future go up in flames, leaving nothing in its wake but a pile of ashes at her feet.

Seeing the excited gleam in her eyes turn to dark despair, Adam felt his own heart plummet to his toes. "Ali—"

She turned away. "I want to marry you more than you'll ever know. I've dreamed of hearing those words from you, even though I didn't know how we could build a life together being from two different worlds." Her eyes closed briefly. "But I knew down deep that if our love was strong enough and enduring enough, we could work it out—compromise our two lifestyles into one that we both could live with."

She turned back to face him, defeat masking her delicate features. "But I can see I was wrong."

She watched as a mask of defeat and pain settled over his visage. It was almost as if he knew what her next words would be and he wanted to shield himself from them.

"If there's no trust between us," she said, "then we're doomed before we ever get started."

"Trust has nothing to do with it." He spoke quietly. "My gut instinct tells me that you haven't completely gotten your work out of your system, that the challenge of launching this new perfume line is more important to you than our life together." He cleared his throat. "I can see that so clearly, even if you can't," he finished sadly.

Ali opened her mouth to deny this accusation, but her jaws locked before the words could pass through her lips. *Oh, God,* she thought, her stomach beginning to jump, *could there be any truth to what he said? Of course there wasn't,* she vowed defiantly. She *was* willing to give up everything for him. But still she had this unfinished business in New York to attend to. A deep sigh shook her body. Maybe Adam was right in one respect. Maybe she was obsessed with proving to her mother as well as her constituents in the glamor business that she could claw herself from the bottom back up to the top. She would never admit, though, that this was more important to her than Adam. It wasn't. It was just something that she *had* to do.

Adam saw the conflicting emotions that warred in her face. He knew then what it must be like to face a firing squad. He stood dying inside, knowing she was leaving him and there was nothing he could do about it.

"Adam, please . . ."

"Do you intend to be on that plane in the morning?" he asked, without hope.

She could only nod, her throat suddenly constricted.

Adam's eyes were dark and unreadable. "Then I guess there's nothing left to be said."

For a moment their eyes locked in silent combat.

"I'll get the car while you dress," he told her formally, his tone that of a stranger. "Then I'll take you home." Those last and final words followed him out the door.

Ali stood paralyzed in the middle of the room frantically clutching at the lapels on the robe. Tears engulfed her as she saw the rainbow that had shone so vividly a while ago fade from her life with the same swiftness as sand slipping through her fingers.

New York. The moment she arrived she plunged headlong into her work. Not a day passed, however, that she didn't relive the scene in Adam's house. And each time it made her depression deeper, her unhappiness stronger, and the emptiness more complete.

Her mother and Charles were deliriously happy that she was back in the fold. Work became her only friend, her ally. She left no stone unturned in transferring her ideas on paper into reality.

She pushed herself. She spent days solidly researching the fashion and perfume industry. She had to come up with a designer to underwrite the line and a sponsor. But that was easier said than done with Cameron fighting for its life. Finally, through hours of behind-the-scenes negotiating, she managed to obtain Lauren Lucas, a new but top-notch designer of women's clothing.

She also spent many long, tiring hours at the library learning the chemistry of perfume, different in many ways from that of cosmetics, and what went into making a fragrance spicy, floral, or woodsy.

In the end, however, she scratched many of her original ideas because of the time element. The board was pushing her to launch this new line as soon as possible. She didn't argue, knowing herself that time was critical. Cameron Cosmetics had been out of the competitive market far too long as it was. So instead of taking eight months to manufacture a completely new fragrance, she settled for a variation on an older but exciting perfume. It was a long way from fulfilling her dream of a new and exotic scent, but still, with her chemical expertise to guide her, she knew she would not be ashamed of the finished product. And Lauren Lucas hadn't withdrawn her support, which was another point in her favor.

During these long, gruelling days, she talked to Barry often. For him her hasty exit had been the best thing. He had managed to pull himself together and take sole responsibility for Cindy Marie. Although still in the hospital, the baby, Barry had assured her, was doing fine. He never asked her when she was coming back to Arkansas. He seemed to know that she wasn't. He took great care not to mention Adam, and she never asked. But each time Ali hung up the phone, she cried until her body ached with fatigue.

Now, a month later, Ali made her way hurriedly into the Cameron Building. The lobby was cool, spacious, and impersonal. But none of this registered on Ali's cluttered mind as she stepped into the proper elevator and rode to the top floor.

A tailored three-piece Dior suit hugged her lissome figure with a stunning impact. She looked every inch the responsible executive as she entered her office.

Today was important. In twenty minutes she was to have her first meeting with the board. Outwardly she appeared calm, but inwardly she was a mass of nerves. She had worked hard and given up so much for this chance to prove herself. As she stood at the window and stared out on the misty day, waiting for the board to summon her, thoughts of Adam overtook her. An ache passed through her.

The buzz of the intercom suddenly hurled her out of the past.

Shaking her head to clear it, she crossed to the desk and punched the button. "Yes, Sara," she said.

"Mr. Sullivan called, and they're ready for you."

"Thank you."

"Yes, ma'am."

All eyes were on Ali as she squared her shoulders and marched into the room. They would like to have her head on a silver platter, she thought, taking in the skeptical countenances. Even her mother was here, she noticed, for the kill. Well, she would show them—knock those smug looks off their faces. They would be eating out of her hand before this was all over.

"Gentlemen—and Evelyn," she began, "I would like to introduce you to Cameron Cosmetics' newest and only perfume, Rare Essence. Barring no complications, it will be on the market one month from today."

There were several under-the-breath murmurs, but she ignored them and continued, "Acting as a consultant to this wonderful scent is top-notch designer Lauren Lucas."

Again there were more low-key mumbles.

"Gentlemen, I predict that after we've laid out costs for the bottle and outer packaging, shipping, advertising, and overhead, adding to this the cost of the fragrance itself, we will clear anywhere from four to eight dollars on every ounce sold."

There were more guttural sounds, but this time their faces held respect while hearty applause shook the room.

"Rare Essence will be a heady mixture of floral scents with sandalwood, amber, and patchouli. I wanted something which represented what I want to feel when I dab or spray on perfume, something seductive. After all," she added with a smile, "a bottle of perfume is a dream, a hope."

And so it went. The meeting lasted another hour. Ali answered questions in detail and ended the session with the board behind her a hundred percent, giving her carte blanche to do as she pleased.

Walking back into her office, she paused at Sara's desk. "Get me Lauren Lucas on the phone, please, and then come into my office. We have our work cut out for us. Let's get to it."

Today was the day. Ali had accomplished what she had set out to do. She had worked a miracle. Right now, this minute, thousands of bottles of Rare Essence were being delivered to fine department stores throughout the United States.

She had just come down from the celebration party in the boardroom where she and her immediate staff had been congratulated, kissed, and pawed until a blinding headache had sent her scurrying to her office.

Now as she sat at her desk, she kept waiting for the excitement and exhilaration to lift her tired body. But none was forthcoming. Instead she felt like crying. She was bone weary, her doctor was threatening to put her in the hospital, and her mother harped at her relentlessly about what happened in Arkansas. Evelyn seemed to sense she was unhappy and restless. But Ali kept her silence and buried her pain deeper each time it surfaced.

What now? she asked herself as she lowered her head on her desk and let the tears flow.

She must have fallen asleep, because she remembered nothing until she felt a firm, but gentle hand on her arm.

Ali sat up with a start. Sara stood beside her desk, a frown on her face. "I'm—I'm sorry to disturb you, but there's a man on the phone insisting that he talk to you."

Adam! Ali's breath quickened. Oh, God, please let it be Adam. "Thank you, Sara." She smiled weakly. "I'll take it now."

When the door had closed behind her secretary, Ali lifted the phone with quivering fingers.

"Hello," she said hesitantly.

"Ali—"

"Yes," she replied dully. It was Barry. Then she felt both heartbreak and shame course through her, the latter because she knew Barry could sense that she was obviously disappointed.

"Ali, are you all right?" His voice held concern.

"Yes, I'm fine," she lied. "Just tired. How about you?"

"Fine. Just fine," he replied. Then a muffled curse reached her ears. "Dammit, that's not true."

Fear made Ali hold the phone in a death grip. "Cindy Marie. Is there something wrong with her?"

"No, she's fine. Growing like a weed. I'm going to bring her home next week."

"Oh, Barry, that's wonderful news." She paused to lick the tears from her lips. "I would love to see her."

"Ali, come back." There was almost a pleading note in his voice.

"Oh, God, you know I can't," she whispered.

"It's Adam," he intoned softly. "I'm worried about him. He needs you, Ali, desperately."

She bit down on her lip so hard, she felt the taste of blood on her tongue. "Did—did he—tell you that?"

There was a moment of silence.

"No—no, he didn't in so many words. But I know him, Ali, and he's hurting, hurting bad. Hell, I don't know who's the biggest fool. You or Adam."

There was another pause. Ali couldn't get past the lump lodged in her throat.

"You—you neither one realize how damn lucky you are to have each other. If only..." His voice trailed off on a sob.

Ali was sobbing openly now.

"Forgive me, Ali, for upsetting you. I'll—I'll talk to you later."

Ali dropped the phone in its cradle only after the dial tone bruised her ear.

Then something clicked in her head. Suddenly everything fell into place, like the pieces of an ancient puzzle. She knew now why none of her recent success meant anything to her. It couldn't take the place of Adam. Simple as that. Adam was what she wanted out of life, nothing more. *Thank you, Barry,* she whispered silently, *for helping me to realize just how precious time is.* If something were to happen to Adam she didn't think she would want to live.

She no longer needed glamor and excitement to make her life complete. Love was the essence that life was made of—not *success,* not *things.* She understood now what Adam had tried to tell her: She must be willing to put love before anything else—pride, parents, career. If not, it would count for naught. Well, through stupidity and blindness, she had almost thrown her one chance away.

She would go to Adam, beg him to take her back if she had to, but if Barry was right she wouldn't have to beg. He would welcome her with open arms.

But first there was something of vital importance she must do. She had one last cord to sever, then she would be truly free. Jumping up, she moved to a safe camou-flaged behind the coffee bar and opened it. Clutching a plain manila envelope close to her chest, she grabbed her purse and practically ran from the room without so much as a backward glance.

A short time later Ali found herself vacating a taxi in front of her mother's house. Still clutching the envelope against her, she paid the driver and marched up the front steps.

Dory, the housekeeper, met her at the door. "Why, Miss Ali, this is a pleasant surprise."

"Thanks, Dory," Ali said, leaning over and kissing her round cheek. "Where's Mother?"

"In the den, waiting for her bridge party to show up."

Without announcing her presence, Ali barged into the room.

"Ali, what brings you here this time of day?" Evelyn Cameron asked.

Ali's eyes took a complete inventory of her mother's features. She was a tall, regal woman in her sixties. At-tractive, but her dominating and overbearing nature had chipped away at this attractiveness until one had to search deeply to find it.

Suddenly Ali wondered if it would ever be possible for her and Evelyn to make peace with one another. Now that her own priorities were straight, she promised herself that sometime in the not too distant future she would work on that. Maybe what she was about to do would be a step in that direction.

"Mother," Ali said at last, "I want you to have this." She handed Evelyn the envelope.

Evelyn made a face. "What's in it? Why the cloak and dagger bit?"

"Open it," Ali insisted.

Evelyn slowly unwound the string from around the tab and then reached in and pulled out several papers stapled together. Evelyn recognized them immediately. She raised shocked eyes to her daughter's face.

"I don't understand. Why are you giving me your shares in Cameron?"

"I no longer want them, that's why."

"But—"

"I'm on my way to Arkansas to marry the man I love, that's why." A smile added to her already glowing features. She leaned over and kissed her mother on the cheek. "Take care," she whispered. "I'll be in touch."

Then she turned and walked out of the house, slamming the door softly behind her.

Chapter 14

As Ali steered the rental car down the long driveway toward Adam's house, she was besieged by butterflies. He just had to be home, she kept telling herself over and over. When she saw both the car and truck, she breathed her first sigh of relief since leaving New York. Braking the car to a halt at the edge of the circular drive, she remained behind the wheel for a moment in order to gather enough courage to make it to the front door.

She had told no one her plans, not even Barry. After leaving her mother's house, she had gone straight to the airport and caught the first available plane out of Kennedy. Barry's words that Adam needed her had been the lifeline to which she had clung during the entire trip. She hadn't even considered going to Barry's first, subconsciously placing him at the hospital. Besides, she had been desperate to get to Adam. It had been so long....

Now as she made an effort to get out of the car, the butterflies in her stomach were replaced by sheer panic. It invaded her limbs like poison. Nonetheless, she forced her legs to move in the direction of the house.

The closer she came, the more her legs seemed to regain their strength, and before she knew it, she was running toward the front door—and Adam.

Not bothering to knock, Ali pushed the door open and all but tumbled inside, her heart pounding in her chest.

Adam was sitting in his lounge chair, holding a young boy on his lap. At first Ali was puzzled, then blind pain rendered her speechless. It was Molly's son, Chad, who occupied the coveted position.

"What the hell—?" Adam swore as he raised startled eyes toward the door. When he saw Ali standing there, a horrified expression on her face, every ounce of color drained from his face.

Then in slow motion, never taking his eyes off her, thinking all the while that she was a mirage, a figment of his imagination, he gentle scooted the child from his lap and stood up.

"Ali!" he gasped.

Ali, like a frightened doe, whirled and flew through the door and down the steps to the car. Although tears blinded her vision, she managed to fling herself inside and crank the engine. She jerked the gear into drive and ground her foot down on the gas pedal. She left a cloud of white dust behind her as she spun on the gravel in her efforts to get away.

With no place else to go, she drove at high speed toward Barry's ranch. Molly and Adam. Molly and Adam and Chad. Their names, their images, kept pounding her brain. A family. Oh, God, no! She couldn't, wouldn't accept that. But it was the truth. If Chad was there with Adam, then Ali was certain Molly wasn't far behind. Probably in the bedroom, she thought bitterly and with a degradation so intense, she was afraid it would eventually kill her.

How could Barry have done this to her? *No!* she screamed silently. It wasn't Barry's fault. She should have known better than to think Adam would still want her, especially after she had so foolishly put her career before him.

She slammed on the brakes, this time in Barry's drive. There were no lights shining through the windows. Thank goodness, she would have the house to herself, she thought. All she could think about now was finding a safe place to nurse her near fatal wounds in private.

How long Ali paced the floor and cried, she didn't know. She wallowed in her own self-pity, anger, and heartbreak. *What now?* she asked herself when there were no more tears left to cry. Without Adam, her life loomed in front of her as nothing but an empty shell.

"Ali—is it really you?"

Thinking that she was alone, Ali's stomach jumped into her throat at the sound of the deep, raspy voice.

Ali spun around to see Adam standing behind her looking lost and uncertain. Her heart swelled with love as she dashed away the rivulets of tears that clung to her thick eyelashes.

He looked awful. Or was old and haggard a better description? How could she have failed to notice the change in him? His clothes hung loosely on his tall frame. His eyes were sunk far back into his head and the lines around both his mouth and eyes had deepened considerably. He, too, appeared a mere shell of his former, vibrant self.

Ali stood and gawked at him, her throat too paralyzed to speak.

Adam blinked and then blinked again. "I—I was sure my eyes were playing tricks on me." His voice was uneven, coarse. "Are . . . you for real, Ali?"

Her tongue, her legs refused to obey the signals from her brain. She remained motionless, numb. *Dare she hope that he still loved her?* In spite of Molly? In spite of everything? Was it possible?

Choking down the huge knot in her throat she finally stammered, "Yes—yes, I'm real."

Still neither moved.

"Why? Oh, God, why did you come back?"

She heard a clock ticking somewhere in the distance, lending to the tense moment a sense of reality. "Why— why do you think I came back?" she fenced, wanting to prolong this moment. She was starved for the sight of him.

"Was it to see Barry and the baby?" His voice was low, terse.

Ali closed her eyes for a moment. "You don't understand, do you?" she said heavily.

"Understand!" His mouth curved scornfully. "What's there to understand? You made your position clear two months ago."

"Oh, Adam!" Ali shook her head helplessly, her surging hopes of a moment ago dying a slow death. She had thought his following her had been a good sign. Despair wrapped its tentacles around her.

Yet she knew she couldn't leave without revealing her heart to him one last time. "I—I came to tell you that— that I love you." She vented air through her lungs. "Don't—don't you want me anymore?" she cried. *Of course he doesn't, he has Molly.*

Adam's hand fell from the doorknob. "Damn you, Ali," he muttered violently. "Yes, I want you." He clenched his hands at his sides. "God help me, I've never stopped wanting you. But, damn you, your terms weren't acceptable!"

Ali flinched inwardly. "And Molly's were!" she spat back at him heatedly.

He looked genuinely puzzled, caught off guard. "Molly? What the hell does Molly have to do with this? With us?"

Ali floundered. "Well—I—er—I saw Chad and—and assumed that you and Molly—" Her voice cracked and faded.

Adam's eyes fluttered shut now against the unconscious appeal of her dark brown eyes and tear-stained cheeks. "If I remember correctly, *you* were the one who spoke of trust." His expression was bleak. "Well, just to set the record straight, I've never breached that trust. Molly was my past. You *were* my present. And Chad. Well, he's just an innocent child who came to visit and ended up getting dumped on my housekeeper. End of story."

Then his face turned to stone. "Please, Ali, just go back to New York where you belong," he ordered harshly, "or I won't be responsible for my actions."

"Oh, Adam—don't do this. Don't send me away." She swished the liquid pain from her eyes with the back of her hand. *"I love you!"*

"Ali—"

Adam's groan of anguish stirred her. They met halfway. His muffled oath of defeat was music to her ears as he bent his head to hers.

Lips joined and clung violently, an outlet for the starved emotions they had both suppressed for so long.

When he finally released her mouth, she was trembling uncontrollably. He tightened his hold and rocked her against him. "Oh, Ali, Ali, I love you so much," he whispered into the velvet rim of her ear. "I'll never let you leave me again."

"I'm where I want to be forever," she muttered tremulously into his chest. "I was so afraid I'd lost you."

He drew a long shuddering breath. "We were both fools, weren't we—to risk throwing away something so valuable as our love. When I think of Barry's loss—"

Ali quivered and dug her nails deep into his back. "Me too. It—it was Barry who made me realize what I was throwing away."

"We'll have to show our appreciation to him somehow."

Ali drew back slightly and tipped her face up to his. "Speaking of Barry, where is he?"

"You don't know?"

Ali shook her head.

"He's gone to Hot Springs to get his aunt. She's a widow with no family and was absolutely thrilled when Barry asked her to come and live with him and look after Cindy Marie." He bent down and kissed her red nose. "By the way, he brings Cindy Marie home tomorrow afternoon."

Ali squealed delightfully. "Oh, Adam, I'm so happy, I could shout it for the world to hear."

He grinned. "Well, don't let me stop you."

She pinched his cheek. "Well, on second thought, I think I'd rather kiss you instead."

His eyes skipped over her. "Now that, my darling, is the best idea yet. But I know a much more promising place to scal that agreement." His voice was a throaty caress.

With anxious hands, he swept her up in his arms and carried her to the bedroom she had used while staying in the house.

"Carrying you to bed in my arms is getting to be a habit," he teased as he laid her tenderly on the soft spread. He began to remove his clothing.

"I think it's fitting," she responded softly. "After all, you're my knight in shining armor, aren't you?"

There were warm lights glimmering in his eyes as he stared down at her. "I wouldn't have it any other way," he murmured urgently before lowering his naked body onto the soft mattress.

Eager hands wasted no time in stripping the clothes from Ali's body. His hand snaked out to cover a breast, nurturing it to swelling hardness before moving to the other one. He handled them as if they were fragile objects.

"You're a sexual pervert," she whispered, laughing.

"You're one to be talking," he countered, a leering grin softening his mouth.

"I'll be the first to admit it. There's something about your touch that makes my blood run hot."

"You can't imagine how often I've had to drown my sorrows in a cold shower when I'd dream about how it felt to be inside your warm sweetness. I—"

She aborted his sentence by placing her fingers to the corners of his mouth and pressing them back. Exposing her tongue, delicate and pink, she licked daintily at his teeth, including the inner lining of his lips in the assault.

"Good Lord," he moaned, hugging her close.

Her tongue nudged his teeth apart and slipped into his mouth, roaming at leisure, searching out the crevices in his soft cavity that she might have missed the countless other times she had kissed him this way.

She loved him so much she was frantic to touch him everywhere—at once. She felt a fiery ache in her stomach that spread to her womb. She nibbled at his neck and shoulders. "Adam...Adam...Adam" filled the cool night air.

"God, Ali, I can't stand any more."

"Take me now!" she cried.

Moving like lightning, Adam closed his hands around her buttocks and hauled her atop him. Entering her swiftly, accurately, totally, they began to move in perfect harmony.

Ali's back and neck were arched as she strove to reach the stars, her pleasure mounting with each stroke.

The end was equally as complete as the beginning. Reaching a shattering peak of no return, their cries intermingled as they plummeted back to earth.

"Mmmm, you smell delicious," Adam murmured later, after having awakened from a short nap. His face was buried in the silky skein of her hair.

"What time is it?" she asked, burrowing closer to him.

"Does it matter?" he drawled lazily.

"No—I guess not." She then stretched like a contented kitten.

Adam began to caress the thigh closest to him. "Ali, we need to talk."

Instantly she became alert. "What—what about?"

"Us. Our future. Your job."

She stiffened. "I—I thought that was all settled."

He laughed and slapped her bare bottom playfully. "Don't go cold on me, my darling." Then his voice became serious again. "Would you like to get married tomorrow?"

"That goes without saying," she said, happiness bubbling inside her.

"Now about your work."

"Adam—"

"Shh, let me finish. If you don't think you will be totally happy without your work, I'd be willing for you to spend part of each month in New York or whatever it takes."

Ali pulled back and looked at him. The moonlight shimmering through the open curtains allowed her to see his face. His eyes were pools of pain, but his voice was unwavering. She knew what it must have cost him to say those words, but there was no doubt in her mind that he meant them.

Another warm surge of happiness pierced her heart, spreading throughout her entire body.

"Thank you, my love, but no thanks."

"What's that supposed to mean?" he inquired softly.

"I no longer own any part of Cameron Cosmetics." She ignored his sharp intake of breath. "I gave my shares to Mother the day I left New York to come to you. So you see, I've closed that chapter of my life, and now I'm waiting anxiously to begin a new one with you here in Arkansas, hoping for children as strong and beautiful as the mountains that surround us."

Tears suddenly fringed his lashes as he leaned down and kissed her tenderly.

"I've never known this kind of love," he whispered brokenly.

"Nor have I," she responded. "I wasn't aware that it existed except in fairy tales."

"Believe me, my darling, our love is more than a fairy tale. It's the stuff that dreams are made of."